Praise for Buried In The House

"Once you pick up *Buried In The House* you won't be able to put it down. You never know what treasures, trash, or trouble you'll find under a hoarder's accumulation, but with Sergeant Corrine Aleckson wading through the labyrinthine, twisty paths, it's sure to prompt a careful investigation. Only upon reading the final word will you know everything comes together in the end."
~ Mary Seifert, author of the Katie and Maverick Cozy Mysteries.

"*Buried In The House* is a captivating tale from start to finish. Sergeant Corinne 'Corky' Aleckson responds to a welfare check request regarding a man in a house she thought had been abandoned years ago. From there things become much more intense and the story develops into two captivating tales, each one heart breaking. You will become immediately hooked as Aleckson and Detective Elton 'Smoke' Dawes work their way through an incredibly complex case and an absolutely wonderful read."
~ Mike Faricy, author of 70+ entertaining crime fiction books.

"From the first radio call "Winnebago County. Six 0 eight. I'm Ten-eight." to the last "Six 0 eight, Ten-seven," you'll be right there with Sergeant Corinne Aleckson through every head-scratching, heart-breaking minute. *Buried in the House* uncovers the sad story of a hoarder and the grim secrets he was keeping buried - literally. Husom skillfully organizes the chaos into answers in this fast-paced, complex novel you'll find hard to put down."
~ Karen Engstrom, author of *The Fox*.

"Christine Husom handles the sensitive subject matter with delicacy and respect. Sergeant Corinne Aleckson, her main character, continues to evolve professionally and personally, providing detailed and realistic insight into the many aspects of a rural enforcement officer's life. A definite Must Read for those who enjoy small town crime."~ Amy Pendino, award winning author of The Witness Tree series.

"I love both the pace of this book and its most unusual topic."~ Rhonda Gilliland, author and editor, the Cooked To Death Series.

"Sgt. Corky Aleckson is called to a potential murder/suicide. Corky and the rest of her department get a handle on one death when things get a little crazy and a lot more interesting. Corky's able to keep on her toes and determine who killed, shot at, or stole from whom. From cover-ups to questionable ethics, *Buried in the House* will keep you guessing until the very end."~ Tes Sparks, writer and author of *Details* in Cooked To Death.

"Sergeant Corky Aleckson is back with one of the most baffling, multi-layered mysteries she's ever faced. Christine Husom's newest Winnebago County Mystery, *Buried In The House*, is everything you could want in a police procedural. Expect late nights - you won't want to put this one down until the last page is turned."~ Timya Owen, author/editor, *Dark Side of the Loon, Minnesota Not So Nice, It Was A Dark And Stormy Night Dontcha Know.*

"Christine Husom paints a riveting scene of a hoarder found dead surrounded by his hoard. A sad end to a man's life who had parted with his wife after the death of their son, and who turned to possessions to soothe his grief.

"The hoarder's family was distant and not fully aware of the man's circumstances. It fell to them to eliminate the hoard via a specialty company. The shocker is when the skeletal remains of a couple are found in the process. Deputy Corky Aleckson and her fiancé, Detective Elton (Smoke) Dawes, bounce solutions off each other, giving a glimpse into their relationship while they navigate the investigation

"There are tidbits of investigative techniques sprinkled through the novel. A dash of nervous humor, "the room's creep factor was off the charts" keep the novel from being too dark. Author Husom deals with the topic of hoarding disorder in a compassionate and thoughtful manner. The web of what happened, who did it, and why, will keep the reader awake late into the night. A must read, with a solid plot, and a satisfying conclusion for crime fiction readers." ~ M.E, Bakos, author of the Home Renovator Mystery Cozies.

Titles by Christine Husom

BURIED IN THE HOUSE

Eleventh in the Winnebago County Mystery Series

Christine Husom

The wRight Press

12-21-24

The wRight Press edition published
November, 2024

Cover photo by Rodney Harvey
Cover design by Precision Prints,
Buffalo, Minnesota.

The wRight Press
46 Aladdin Circle NW
Buffalo, Minnesota, 55313

Printed in the United States of America

ISBN: 978-1-948068-25-3
ISBN: 978-1-948068-26-0

Dedication

To mental health professionals who do all they can to help people with a variety of issues. And to law enforcement officers who respond to difficult and often complex calls. To protect and serve is a noble calling. In addition to enforcing the law, they help people in ways that lead to positive and impactful results. I thank each of you for your service.

Acknowledgments

My humble thanks to my faithful beta/proofreaders and editors who gave their time, careful reading, and sound advice: Arlene Asfeld, Judy Bergquist, Barbara DeVries, Rhonda Gilliland, Ken Hausladen, Elizabeth Husom, Chris Marcotte, Chad Mead, and Edie Peterson. Also, thank you to all the respected authors who read the manuscript and wrote reviews. I greatly appreciate each one of you and your talents.

Once again, deep gratitude to my husband and the rest of my family for your patience and understanding when I was stowed away for hours on end, researching and writing.

And to all my faithful readers. I couldn't do this without your support!

Thank you all from the bottom of my heart.

1

I pulled my squad car onto County Road 35's shoulder by Whitetail Lake to review a deputy's report. It was a favorite spot for me to sit on or off duty. The side benefit: it alerted drivers to pay attention to their speed and other behind-the-wheel careless behaviors.

I took a moment to appreciate the scene. A dozen fish houses sat on the frozen lake. A truck was parked next to one large enough to sleep at least six people, and likely doubled as a camper. Smoke billowed from its chimney, so the owner had a toasty fire to keep warm while he angled for fish. Many houses on area lakes were equipped with beds, kitchenettes, small bathrooms, television sets, and other amenities.

A Minnesota January cold snap with temperatures below zero for ten days had come to a welcome end. The morning's thirty-degree Fahrenheit temp felt balmy in comparison. More people would no doubt head out to their houses after work.

The warmer temperatures also expanded the opportunity for people without fish houses—portable canvas, or permanent wooden or steel—to protect them from the elements. Many stood, or sat in chairs on the ice, and dangled their lines in the drilled holes. Groups gathered in a particular spot provided a strong hint where fish were biting.

The sun glistened off snow crystals on the hills that surrounded three sides of the lake. On the southeast side, with no shore to speak of, the land climbed up at least fifty feet until it reached level ground above. The steep slope down to Whitetail did not lend itself to a safe toboggan ride to the bottom. I wouldn't chance it. Even with a helmet and a padded body suit on.

Three houses sat atop the area where an old farmstead had once stood, a property where heinous actions ended two young lives. The crime was buried for decades and finally brought to light a few years back. Over the course of the involved cold case investigation, long-held secrets were revealed and included one that tipped my family's world on its side.

My brother John Carl and I learned we had an older sister named Taylor, our father Carl's daughter. Taylor's mother never named the baby's father—not to Carl, not to her parents, or anyone else—before or after she put Taylor up for adoption.

Carl died when John Carl was a baby, months before I was born. I mourned for a father I'd only heard about, and after we met Taylor, it took my sorrow to another level. Carl had fathered two daughters he'd never known, never held in his arms, never made silly faces or cooing noises to coax smiles from.

With Taylor, life as we'd known it for thirty years changed in a heartbeat. Neither our mother nor father had siblings so

John Carl and I had no aunts, uncles, or first cousins. We two made up that entire family generation. Until Taylor.

We gained a sister and brother-in-law and their children—two nieces and a nephew—who upgraded our status to uncle and aunt, brother-in-law and sister-in-law. Taylor and family were unexpected and treasured gifts. It filled Grandma and Grandpa Aleckson with immense joy to have another granddaughter and three great- grandchildren.

My personal cellphone rang from its holder on the dashboard. *Taylor* appeared on the screen as though my thoughts had prompted the call. I smiled and pushed the accept button. "Hey."

"Oh Corky, thanks for answering. I don't know what to do, who else to turn to. Are you on duty?" Her words were stilted, her voice tense.

My heart picked up speed. Had something happened to one of her children? "Yes, but on a little break. What's wrong?"

"It's Silas." Her husband. "He's been different for weeks now. Secluded. Secretive."

Secretive brought a recent major criminal case to mind. Dr. Blake Watts's wife had kept her addiction hidden from her husband for months, until her death brought the sad truth to light. "Secretive?"

"I feel like he either doesn't love me anymore, or he's hiding something."

"You're saying his behavior has changed?"

"Yes."

"How?"

Taylor sniffed. "I've told you before how he's always worked long hours at the investment company. But it's gotten much worse. He's late every night, like he's staying away on purpose."

A red flag that meant something was awry. "You've asked him about it, right?"

"I've tried, but he says with all his demands at work when he gets home he doesn't want to get harassed with questions," she said.

Harassed? "Oh."

Her voice cracked. "Something is wrong, and he won't tell me what it is."

"Taylor—"

Communications Officer Randy's voice on the radio interrupted. "Winnebago County, Six o eight."

"Taylor, sorry, gotta go," I said.

"Sure, later then."

I disconnected and pressed the radio button. "Go ahead, County."

"Sergeant Aleckson, we have a welfare check request on a Brett Winston at Four-one-six Davidson Avenue. His brother is on the scene but is unable to enter the house. I'll send the details to your screen."

"Ten-four." I shook my head. If that was the house with a long driveway—a good tenth of a mile on a dead-end road—it piqued my curiosity. I thought that property had been abandoned years ago.

Randy's message appeared on the screen. *Shane Winston reports his brother is a hoarder, confined to an upstairs bedroom. Shane climbed the ladder to deliver supplies and saw Brett slumped over on the couch. Knocking on the window didn't rouse him. Brother thinks he may be unconscious. I contacted EMS. They're tied up at Oak Lea Hospital for some minutes and will head out there ASAP. I'll send you their ETA when I have it.*

I replied, *Thanks,* and I clicked the radio button. "Six o eight, Winnebago County, I'm en route to the Emerald Lake Township address."

"Copy that Six o eight, at ten eleven," Randy responded.

Winston's brother climbed a ladder to deliver supplies to an upstairs bedroom where his brother was confined? The situation sounded suspicious, ominous. Shane said Brett was a hoarder. Was he confined to an upstairs bedroom because the rest of his house was filled with stuff, or did he have a form of agoraphobia where he couldn't make himself leave the room?

I had taken hoarder-house calls over the years when concerned family members broke their silence and reported on loved ones who were unable to part with things, oftentimes junk or trash. The sad part: when a hoarder's house or apartment or designated area was cleaned out by others, it took their behavior up a notch or ten, and compounded the problem. Hoarding was a defined mental health condition most often brought on by traumatic events in one's life. Accumulating stuff—the more the merrier—was a coping mechanism.

Brett Winston. I didn't recognize his name, had never gotten a call from or about him, if memory served. I drove four miles west past Brandt Avenue, the road I lived on, and turned left on

Davidson. Winston's place was a mile south of County Road 35. On patrol, I had driven to the property several times over the years—as to similar homesteads—to check for broken windows or other acts of vandalism.

I'd had no official reason to be on the property, so I would drive in and take a look from my car. It was a decades old, two-story white house in need of paint. Curtains had been drawn across the windows, in the same way, each time. I'd never detected activity around the place, or an indication it was occupied, given the unmowed grass, no vehicles in the yard, no dogs or cats, no lights on in the house, and no mailbox at the end of the driveway to show someone received mail there. Classic indications it was unoccupied, abandoned.

It surprised me to find the driveway had been plowed since the past week's snowfall. I pulled to a stop behind a white SUV with Wisconsin license plates. A man in his mid-forties clad in an army green fleece jacket and camo stocking cap stood beside it, his phone to his ear. When he noticed me he dropped it into his pocket and rushed to my car before I'd come to a complete stop. I held up my hand in a "whoa" sign and radioed the county I had arrived at the scene.

I pulled on gloves and a wool cap. As I climbed from the car, Winston's intense brown-eyed stare bore through me, but he didn't utter a word.

"Shane Winston?"

"Yeah." It came out as an exhale.

"I'm Sergeant Corinne Aleckson."

Shane swiped his hand across his face. "Oh Sergeant, what a relief you're here. I don't know if my brother's unconscious, or worse. His face looks flushed. The window's locked and I pounded on it a bunch of times, yelled as loud as I could, but it didn't rouse him." He whistled his s's.

"All right. I'll take a look, and EMS should be here shortly."

Shane puffed out another breath. "Ahhh. Thank God."

"Communications said you had to climb a ladder to bring him supplies?"

"Right. Long story. Come, it's on the other side of the house," he said.

Shane took off at a brisk pace through the snow-covered ground with me a half step behind. I spotted a single set of tracks going there and back: Shane's last trek. When we rounded the corner, the heavy-duty aluminum ladder in question was propped against the house, its bottom two rungs covered by inches of packed-down snow. The ladder extended to a window twelve or so feet above. Two plastic shopping bags of groceries/supplies lay on the snowy ground near its base.

"I brushed the snow off as I went up," he said.

I nodded. My boots had good traction soles, yet I couldn't recall a time I'd climbed twelve feet to an upstairs bedroom window in the winter. Or any other season. Rubber mat pads were attached to the center of each rung, so they weren't slippery.

I reached the top step and peered into the window. The amount of clutter in the space overwhelmed me. My imagination had underestimated it by a long shot. A paisley-patterned brown couch sat in the middle of the room, about eight feet back. A small area, perhaps four feet by five feet in front of the couch, was clear of debris for the most part and provided a clear view of Brett Winston.

Winston's stockinged feet rested on the floor. His upper torso was tipped to the left, his head on the armrest. His skin tone was a cherry red, and his tongue hung out the side of his mouth, pointed down toward the couch, and his slack jaw rested on his left shoulder. I concentrated on Brett's chest and noted it didn't rise and fall. No inhales or exhales.

It appeared his gaze was directed at papers stacked on the floor in front of him. I realized it was an illusion because his lids were fixed in place. He didn't blink, and his eyes showed no sign of life. Brett Winston had passed on. His spirit had left his body sometime after he'd talked to his brother the previous day.

On the opposite end of the couch I spotted a thermal sleeping bag and a stack of comforters piled next to it. A small heater sat on the floor near the bedding. I put my ear against the window but didn't hear it running.

I felt drawn to stay put, to keep my focus on Brett's body in the bedroom. Instead, I descended the ladder, drew in a slow breath, and locked eyes with Shane's.

"Yes?" The wary look on his face told me he suspected the news I was about to deliver.

"Shane, there's no easy way to tell you this. I can confirm what you feared; your brother has passed, and I am truly sorry."

His eyebrows shot up and he shook his head back and forth. His loud cry of "No!" was muffled by nearby trees and the snow-covered earth.

"We'll need access into the house. Do you have a key to the entry doors?" I asked.

"To the front one, but not the kitchen side door. After I called nine-one-one, I used the key and opened the front door. There's a small entry area that doesn't have a lot in it for a few feet. Then stuff is piled up high and blocks the entrance, so you can't get inside."

"How about the other door?"

"I tried it, but it's locked. And all I could see in there was piles of junk. It might take a bulldozer to get in either way." Shane clamped his hands over his eyes a moment, cried out, "no!" again, and took off around the corner without another word.

I clicked the call button on my radio. "Six o eight, Winnebago County, on channel three."

"Go ahead, Sergeant."

"Randy, we can cancel EMS. I can't access the room without breaking the window, but I can tell the victim is deceased. We'll need the medical examiner and Oak Lea Fire's platform truck. His brother said both entries into the house are blocked."

"Copy that, Sergeant. I'll contact EMS, the ME, and Oak Lea Fire."

"Ten-four. Thanks."

"Do you need assistance?" Officer Randy asked.

Detective Dawes would be tied up on a burglary investigation in the southern part of the county for some time.

"When one of the area deputies clears, they can report here," I said.

"Ten-four."

I sensed Shane Winston needed time to process what he'd seen and heard. I climbed the ladder again and returned my focus to Brett Winston and the cluttered room that cocooned him. From floor to ceiling little wall space was visible, but I spotted a small patch of beige wallpaper curled down from the ceiling in a corner.

The heater by the bedding didn't appear to be on, but I detected a faint kerosene odor I hadn't noticed before. Stacks of clothes, stuffed animals, large plastic Christmas, Halloween, and Easter lawn figurines, board games, books, newspapers, more papers, and other items were in the first rows and covered whatever was between them and the walls several feet away.

An open narrow path led to a window on the south side and provided Brett solar heat on sunny days. Another six-foot-long and two-foot-wide passage led to what I guessed was a bathroom. The back wall was stacked to the ceiling.

2

Randy in Communications came back on channel three. "Winnebago County, Six o eight."

"Go ahead, County."

"The ME's ETA is forty to forty-five. They'll let Oak Lea Fire know when they're a few miles out."

"Copy." Hurry up and wait. Under the circumstances, forty minutes started to feel like hours away.

Shane Winston hadn't returned to the backyard, so I took a last look at his brother and descended the ladder rungs. I stepped around the shopping bags and found Shane on his phone next to his vehicle. When he noticed me, he nodded and disconnected. The poor guy looked like he'd aged a decade since I'd arrived minutes before.

"My wife," he explained. "She just told me she wished she'd come with me today. Truth is, she's had trouble dealing with Brett's condition for years." Shane shook his head. "Sergeant, I really had *no* idea it had come to this. That my brother was confined to our parent's bedroom."

I pulled out my memo pad and pen and nodded. "It's a difficult situation for your family. For my report I'll need your full name, date of birth, address, and phone number."

I recorded the information as he rattled it off. Shane Mitchell Winston, age 46, Stephens Point, Wisconsin.

"Shane, when was the last time you talked to your brother?"

He glanced up at the sky a second. "Brett called me yesterday morning around ten, said he was in a bad way, that he needed some groceries but was too afraid to leave the house. I was at work. Plus I live over four hours away. I work ten-hour days and have Fridays off, so I told him I could come today. Brett said that was fine. And then he said, when I got here I should go around to the back of the house, that he'd open the window for me.

"I didn't understand what he meant and asked him to explain. All he'd say was, 'call me when you get here.' Then he told me the driveway was probably snowed over, and gave me the number of a guy who had plowed it in the past. I didn't question why he wanted me to call, just figured he wasn't able to for some reason. Like maybe why he couldn't leave the house either."

"You got a hold of the plow guy?" I asked.

"Yeah, and he'd cleared the driveway before I got here today." Shane paused and dug his heel back and forth in the snowy gravel. "Of course Brett didn't answer his phone. I can't tell you how dumbfounded I felt when I went around back like he'd told me to do and saw the ladder propped up on the house, extended to the upstairs window. *What in the hell!* was all I could think. Why would he do that?"

"That would be a shocker all right. Shane, your brother gave you the snow plow driver's number. So he had some outside contacts?"

"Yeah, but no one he socialized with. When we talked yesterday, it didn't occur to me to ask when he had last left the house. Was it days, weeks? I don't know. Now that I see how horrendous it is here, I know he must've felt really desperate to reach out to me. He hasn't let me inside the house for a couple years now."

"He may have wanted to keep the extent of his accumulations secret, didn't want you to see them," I said.

"I know he didn't. Even though I knew the reason, no way could I have guessed it would ever have gotten to this level. Why didn't I leave work right then and there when Brett called, come straight here? He'd probably still be alive. I hope in his bad state of mind he didn't hurt himself, like drink some poison, or something."

Suicide? "We'll find out, get that answer for you. If we can go back to Brett's fears. Did he say why he was afraid, what he was afraid of?"

Shane shook his head. "No, just that he couldn't step outside."

"You think he was paranoid or had agoraphobia?" I asked.

"Maybe both. But not that I knew about, not before he called yesterday. The way he talked sounded like he was paranoid *and* agoraphobic. And it's obvious he had a hoarder disorder."

"Anxiety can cause all three disorders," I said.

He stared at the ground. "I guess."

"Was your brother on any prescription medications for his mental health issues?"

"No. Doctors ordered some for him, tried different ones, but Brett didn't like the way they made him feel, so he wouldn't take them," Shane said.

I jotted a note on my memo pad. "Shane, how long has your brother been hoarding?"

"It started after his son was killed in a car crash. Horrible tragedy. Brett was driving when a guy ran a red light and T-boned their car. Aiden was in the back seat, on the passenger side." Shane teared up. "The little guy was only nine."

"I'm so sorry. When did it happen, how long has it been?"

He used a thumb to brush at his tears. "It's been five years ago now. Poor Brett. He was always on the sensitive side, and liked to collect things back when. You know, like baseball cards, model cars. Like a lotta guys.

"But after Aiden died, it was like a switch flipped in his brain. He started bringing home all sorts of odds and ends. Giveaway stuff people left by the road. Even old mattresses and couches thrown into ditches. Junk. His wife tried to get him help. She suffered from awful grief herself—of course—didn't know what to do. She hired a team to clean out the junk in their Minneapolis place. Brett came home and went into a rant, threw a tantrum like he was two years old, according to Deena. That's Brett's wife. Ex-wife."

Shane took a moment, and I waited for him to continue. "After that, Brett multiplied his collecting habits. He refused the counseling he desperately needed. Finally his wife gave up, served him divorce papers, told him he had to leave. He asked Tricia—that's our sister—and me if it'd be okay if he moved here. It's where the three of us grew up. Tricia's in Michigan now."

I made a note of that.

Shane went on, "We've talked about selling the farm off and on over the years—there's eighty acres here. Taxes are low enough and we didn't need to sell, so we held on to it. The barn and other old out buildings are gone, torn down long ago." He pointed at a big steel building with double doors about thirty feet from the house. "Except for that pole building shed my dad put up about seven years ago, just before he passed. Mom died a year later. And then of course, we lost Aiden the next year."

"That's a lot for any family to go through. Brett and his wife, in particular."

Shane lifted a shoulder and nodded. "After the divorce, Brett's life fell apart big time. No wife, no son, and being a bit of a loner besides. Distanced himself from friends. Tricia and I thought it'd be good for him to be home again. So he could both heal and keep an eye on the place for the time being.

"Deena had stopped talking to Tricia and me. She dealt with her sorrow by partying. Another sad story. Anyway, Brett rented a moving van, packed it full, and brought his accumulations here. We didn't realize that his condition would get worse, go down as far as it did. Seems like it didn't take him long to fill up the shed—

I found that out when I was here last summer. I sneaked a peek when he went into the house to get us a beverage.

"Tricia and I did *not* want to enable him, but that's what we did. We should've arranged some kind of intervention, but after the way he freaked out when Deena stepped in, we decided if collecting stuff helped him cope, maybe it wasn't the worst thing in the world. Well, turns out it was. Worse than worst. Like I said, I figured it was bad, but it's a god-awful disaster. And now he's gone, and we didn't get him the help he needed."

I touched Shane's hand. "If I can ask, how has Brett managed financially, to live here and accumulate everything he has?"

He turned his hands palms up. "He's been on Social Security Disability for over four years. After he moved here, he had his checks sent to my house at first. Now they're deposited automatically into his account. My name's on the account too. I paid the property taxes and utility costs, like fuel for the furnace and electricity. Neither amounted to a lot. Not compared to what my wife and I pay. That said, Brett had money to buy what he needed. Which wasn't much, if you don't count all the stuff he felt compelled to collect, that is," he said.

"When we deputies are on patrol, we check on abandoned properties from time to time, ones we believe are deserted. I ran a check, a year or so ago, to see who owned this property. It came back as Winston family trust and I had no idea anyone lived here."

"I think Brett must've made it look like no one did so it didn't open up an investigation."

"An investigation?"

"So no one would take away his things," Shane said.

A vehicle's tires crunching the gravel caught our attention as it approached. Deputy Amanda Zubinski's squad car. I'd heard her clear a loose dog complaint minutes before. She parked behind my car and climbed out. Her eyes traveled from me to Shane.

"Shane Winston, this is Deputy Zubinski," I said.

Each one nodded at the other.

"Mister Winston, I heard the call, and you have my condolences about your brother," Mandy offered.

"Thanks," he said.

Mandy turned to me. "Sergeant, anything I can do?"

"We're waiting for the ME and Oak Lea Fire for next steps."

Mandy glanced at the house then back to me. "The victim is upstairs?"

"Around back. Come with me."

"Okay."

"I'll wait here," Shane said.

Mandy followed me to the ladder propped against the house and glanced upward. She kept her voice low when she said, "What in the world is this all about? When the call went out, I figured I'd heard the address wrong. I thought this place was vacant."

"Same here. We probably all did. And it sounds like it was for some time, until brother Brett moved in three years ago. Shane said Brett wanted it to look that way, to hide the fact he was a hoarder, so no one would check him out and take away his stuff," I said.

"Man alive. I guess we've been through other situations with hoarders."

"Yes we have. Mandy, go up and take a look. Brett's body is on the couch."

She didn't hesitate and scooted up the ladder until she was near the top. I heard her suck in a breath before she climbed the last two rungs. Mandy shook her head as she took in the scene: Brett's body surrounded by the hundreds of items he'd collected.

She had to wonder as I did, how much more was packed in the rest of the house that had confined him to a second-story room and left him with only one exit route?

When Mandy was back on the ground she moved near me and said, "Mister Winston's face is flushed. I saw the kerosene heater and caught the odor up there. He shouldn't have used it in small spaces without good ventilation. It's risky, given possible, or probable, carbon monoxide poisoning."

"No question. I smelled kerosene too. The heater's not running, but it could've been on and then run out of fuel, either before, or after Brett was overcome by the CO. He told his brother Shane he was in a bad way. If his brain was deprived of oxygen, that could've made him feel worse."

"Sad." Mandy shook her head. "Man, his room is even more cluttered than I'd pictured. Makes you wonder what the rest of the house looks like."

"I know, my thoughts exactly. When you hear about hoarders and their accumulations, it's something you can't imagine. And after you see it, it's something you can't forget."

"A good way to put it. Like a hundred other things with this job. His brother delivered supplies to him via the ladder?" Mandy asked.

I ran her through the known details then added, "So until Shane got the call about how he should deliver the groceries, he didn't know how bad things had gotten for his brother. We know Brett was alive when Shane talked to him yesterday morning and died before he got here today. Now it's up to the ME's office to determine the approximate time and cause of his death."

"What time will they get here?" she asked.

I looked at my watch. "About twenty minutes. Along with Oak Lea Fire and Rescue."

"Or recovery, in this case." Mandy looked up and lifted her hand. "At least there's no snow predicted until later tonight. That helps."

We returned to the front of the house. Shane stood by the shed with the door open as he peered inside.

"I feel really bad for him," Mandy said.

"For sure." We walked over to Shane.

He glanced at us and scrunched up his face in an expression somewhere between a scowl and a grimace. Disgust or pained. Maybe both. He pulled the door open wider so we could get a glimpse inside. It was packed to the hilt, full of machinery and things heaped on top of it. It appeared there were three narrow access paths, maybe more I couldn't see.

I wanted to shout out, "Ahh!" but held my tongue.

Shane cleared his throat and waved his hand at the shed. "What is all this stuff for? It's not like he could ever use most of it, or any of it. Even if he could access it. I just don't get it. Where and how did he find this junk?" He pointed to the right. "I can see how packed his truck is so he couldn't have used it again until he emptied it. And that seems like an impossible dream."

Mandy and I looked that way and we both nodded.

"Looks like there are other vehicles besides, covered with tarps. Brett has gotten *way* worse in the last year, and it makes me wonder why. What could be more traumatic than losing his son, the tragedy that started his hoarding in the first place?" Shane said.

"It's a difficult disorder to understand. We can't know what goes on in anyone's mind unless they tell us." I gave him a moment then asked, "How often did you talk to your brother?"

"Most every week, but we didn't have long conversations. Brett never had much to say, so it was mostly up to me to think of things. My two boys are grown and I'd give him some updates, like if they moved or got a different job. It seemed to hurt his heart if I said much more. You know, because I had a family and he didn't," he said.

My eyebrows drew together. "Brett didn't mention anything that bothered him in particular, nothing that had made him feel worse lately?"

Shane shook his head and his shoulders lifted a tad.

"We wondered about the kerosene heater, why he used it?" Mandy said.

"What kerosene heater?" Shane asked.

"The one in his room. It's close to the couch," I said.

He shook his head again. "I didn't see it."

"I'm sure your focus was on your brother," I said.

"Yeah, it was. Even him sitting there on the couch was a little fuzzy. I guess because what I saw didn't seem real. I don't get it, about the kerosene heater, I mean. Unless it was something else he'd collected. In case."

Shane pointed at a tank on the south side of the house, kiddy corner from the shed doors. "We have a furnace—fuel oil, like I mentioned earlier. We make sure the tank is filled so the heat stays on, at least forty degrees, or the pipes might freeze and break. I guess you'd know that."

We nodded. Cold weather people had to know that.

Shane's shoulders lifted. "All I can think is he didn't want to keep the whole house warm when he lived in one room, and that's why he had a kerosene heater. I feel terrible the way I let my brother down, that I didn't know how much he needed help, how we should've stepped in."

3

Randy's voice came over the radio on channel three. "Winnebago County, Six o eight."

"Go ahead, County."

"The ME will arrive at your location in about ten, and Oak Lea Fire any minute."

"Copy that. Thanks." Part of the weight I felt lifted, and I could only guess the range of emotions Shane experienced.

He looked down, dug the toe of his boot into the snow, and moved it back and forth like he'd done with his heel earlier. To relieve some stress it seemed. His brother Brett was gone, and the body he'd left behind needed to be removed from a room packed full around it.

We all turned at the sound of a heavy vehicle on Brett's driveway as it made its way toward us. An Oak Lea Fire truck came into view a moment later, and pulled to a stop in front of the house. Fire Chief Corey Evans climbed down from the driver's seat, and Fireman Jack got out the passenger's side. Both wore turnout pants, jackets, gloves, and boots.

"Morning, Sergeant, Deputy," Corey addressed Mandy and me then locked eyes with Shane. "Sorry about your brother, sir."

Shane gave a slight nod. "Thanks."

"Wyman and Matty will be out here shortly." Evans said. Two other firefighters. Oak Lea Fire was an all-volunteer department, except for Chief Corey Evans. The city determined they needed a full-time chief to oversee operations, manage details, and staff an office at the station. The city offered Evans the position and he'd accepted. He was no question the right man for the job.

Evans had as many years with his department as I had with mine. Ten. Of all the times we'd been at the same scene, this particular body recovery operation was a first for me, and I guessed it was for him too.

"Chief, let's assess and figure out how to proceed," I said.

Corey, Jack, Mandy, and I trooped to the back of the house. Shane stayed put. We gazed up at the second story window. "When Officer Randy called and explained the situation, I asked him to repeat it so I could wrap my head around it, what the recovery would entail," Corey said.

"Seeing is believing. Sort of. You shouldn't have any trouble getting your rig in here, at least. The trees are back far enough from the house," I said.

"Agreed. As far as getting into the room, we have a drill we can use to open the window latch when the ME gets here. I don't know who's coming, but Doctor Patrick might have trouble with that ladder."

Bridey Patrick, middle-aged and on the round side, was the chief medical examiner at the Midwest Medical Examiner's Office. The entry challenges this case presented would be better suited for her second in command Calvin Helsing, accompanied by a death investigator.

"I'll go up and check things out," Corey said.

"I'll do the same after you come down, given it's a one-person-at-a-time ladder," Jack said.

After they'd both gone up and down again, Corey said, "This will not be the easiest removal we've done, but it's not as heart-wrenching as burned bodies we've had to recover."

"Yeah," Jack agreed.

I shook my head. Heart-wrenching was right.

Mandy and I went back to join Shane by his SUV. "We're going to move our cars to make room for the other firefighters, and the medical examiner's van," I said.

"Okay. I can do that too," Shane said.

We pulled our vehicles close to the shed's doors and parked. It left adequate room for more vehicles in the driveway.

"What does the fire chief think about . . . everything?" Shane asked.

I didn't give him a direct answer. "He's experienced in different kinds of rescue and recovery efforts, and will do a fine job with your brother."

The Midwest Medical Examiner's van arrived and rolled to a stop by the fire rig. Chief Corey and Jack came around the corner of the house. Corey went to the driver's side window. "If you want to move ahead a bit, we'll be driving the rig around the house when you're ready to proceed."

I heard a man say, "Okay," before he pulled the van to a stop. Mandy and I stood by. Shane edged even closer to the shed.

Doctor Calvin Helsing, dark, striking, and almost as tall as his partner, death investigator Roy Swanson, climbed from the van. Helsing was Doctor Patrick's assistant, and on more calls of late. Swanson, a former Carver County deputy with chiseled features resembled Skeletor of Mattel and *He-Man and Masters of the Universe* fame.

Both sets of eyes darted around the property.

"Hello," I greeted them.

"Sergeant," they said in near unison.

Wyman and Matty arrived in a white pickup truck a moment later. Corey waved for them to park next to our squad cars, then our group gathered by the ME's van.

I lifted my hand, homed in on Helsing and Swanson, and kept my voice quiet. "That's the victim's brother Shane Winston by the shed, the one who found the body. More about that later. It'd be good for you to meet him before we proceed. It'll give him some assurance when he sees you're nice guys."

Swanson cracked a small smile. "I guess if we've got you fooled, he might think so too."

Helsing was the more serious one and nodded. "Sure."

When we started toward Shane, he met us halfway. After introductions, Helsing extended his hand to Shane. As they shook, Helsing said, "This must be very difficult for you. Please accept our sympathies. We'll take your brother back to our office and find out what caused his death, get the answers you need."

Shane nodded as tears gathered in his eyes. "I didn't know how bad it was here." A sentiment he would likely share over and over again.

Without another word, our group, minus Shane, headed to the ladder. I summarized the situation for them and added, "The window is locked from the inside. Shane Winston said both the front and side entries are blocked. The victim's face is quite red. Deputy Zubinski and I both detected a kerosene odor coming from the bedroom."

Corey went into more detail about the recovery plan. "We'll drill through the wood frame to unlatch the lock and open the window. And use our bucket to help recover the body."

"Sounds like a solid plan. We'll don our protective gear before we enter the room, but first I want to go up and take a look. Roy, you will too," Helsing said.

"Yes. Good to get the lay of the land before we set foot on it." Roy replied.

Each climbed the ladder, took a moment to study the scene, then joined us on the ground.

Helsing narrowed his eyes on me. "Sergeant, it's going to be a tight fit in there, so I suggest the two of us—you and I—go in first. Take photos. I'll do an external exam of the body and check his temperature while you take a look around the room for possible evidence."

I nodded. "I have a protective suit, but yours might be better. You have an extra one?"

"Sure, even in your small size. And for anyone else who will be going in," Helsing said.

It took but a few seconds to decide Helsing, Swanson, Evans, and I would help recover Winston's body.

Detective Elton Dawes phoned as I was putting my jacket in my vehicle. "Hi, Smoke."

"I understand you've got quite the deal going on at your location."

"Quite the deal."

"I cleared the burglary and am headed your way. It'll be a half hour or so," he said.

Thank you, Lord. "Good. The ME and I are about to enter the second-floor room via a ladder, check things out, and then they'll remove the body."

"Randy in Communication filled me in. See you then."

I closed my car door, and Swanson handed me a suit. "Detective Dawes will be here in a bit, maybe in the middle of our operation," I announced to the group.

Mandy raised her eyebrows and nodded.

The team had suits on in a minute. We'd put on vinyl gloves and boot covers before we stepped into the room.

Helsing slung his bag of equipment over his shoulder. "Roy, make sure we have a bag with the gurney."

"Yes, we do," Swanson said.

"I'm the one appointed to open the window," Jack said. He was a wood worker by trade and remodeled older homes on the side.

Jack made quick work of the job. He drilled, managed to unlatch the lock, and lifted the lower pane. He climbed down and told Helsing to and me, "All set."

"It's been a while since I've climbed through a window, if you want to go first," Helsing said.

"Sure." It'd been a while for me too, but we'd trained for different entries, and I had determined from the start of the operation I would not be diving head first into Winston's room. The panes, upper and lower, were about three feet wide by three feet tall. Adequate for us to gain access to the room.

I climbed up, pulled on gloves, slid one leg onto the sill then the other, and gripped the sides of the windows as I slipped in, taking care not to bonk my head. My smaller frame made it easier for me than it would be for the other three.

The kerosene heater had likely run out of fuel, and caused it to shut off. The odor dissipated as cold, fresh air filled the room. I stood about seven feet from the body. A sense of sadness washed over me for the way his life had ended in a house surrounded by collections of items, not used for anything. They just occupied space.

I pulled on boot covers then turned my attention to Dr. Helsing who'd reached the top of the ladder. He pulled on gloves, and passed his equipment bag through the window to me. Helsing used a different entry technique. He was over six feet and slid one leg in until his foot hit the ground, then bent over, backed his upper body through it, then pulled in his other leg. He closed the window and balanced on one foot then the other as he slipped on the covers.

To give him space, I backed up into a pile of brown garbage bags filled with unknown items. It felt soft. I cringed and convinced myself more stuffed animals or blankets were inside them. The room's creep factor was off the charts.

"I knocked off most of the snow, but there was still a little on my boots," he said.

"Yeah." I handed Helsing his bag, and we did our best to not bump elbows, or other body parts, as we moved forward to conduct our business.

Brett's long grayish brown hair was pulled into a ponytail. A full beard the same color touched the top of his chest. His prominent cheekbones were made more so with next to no muscle on his face. He wore gray sweat pants and shirt, neither with pockets. A one-inch-length cross with a small diamond in its middle hung from a gold chain, and rested below his neck. The top of a navy crewneck was visible under his sweatshirt.

I scanned the area by his body and around the couch. A Bible rested on the end table. "He called his brother, but I don't see his phone. We'll want to check it."

"He may have set it somewhere else before he sat down on the couch," Helsing said.

"We'll do a search of the room later," I said.

"The other thing to look for is medications. There are none on the end table or in the vicinity around him that I can see." Helsing studied Brett's body. "My my my. Mister Winston's cherry red coloring indicates he did indeed die from carbon monoxide poisoning. It's caused when CO binds to the iron in hemoglobin, or Hb. Oxygenated blood in the arteries is normally rich in Hb-O2.

"But with CO toxicity, the Hb-O2 in blood is depleted and replaced by the Hb-CO that continues to circulate in the blood. The blue color of the veins changes to red as blue Hb is replaced by red Hb-CO. It shows up as a red color in the epidermal veins of the skin."

I sensed Helsing needed to verbalize the process as he thought his way through it.

He took a whiff of air. "Kerosene odor is present in the room, but it's faint. Those heaters consume oxygen as they burn. Without good ventilation when oxygen is reduced, often to a dangerous level, it produces carbon monoxide. However we won't be able to determine his actual cause of death until autopsy. No obvious trauma to his body in any area I'm able to see without moving him."

Helsing studied Brett's body another moment. "He is very thin, perhaps ill or malnourished."

"He likely was not eating regularly, depending on how long he had to use that ladder to get supplies. I think I mentioned that Shane figured Brett must've been desperate when he called him and asked for help," I said.

Helsing did a quick glance around the room. "And how might he have prepared food in here?"

"When we do our search, we'll see what we uncover."

"In this case, uncover means literally." He held up his room thermometer. "Only fifty-four degrees in here. Looks like he relied on that heater to warm the place up."

"Shane said they have a furnace, but Brett probably didn't want to heat the whole house and kept the thermostat low, just high enough so the pipes didn't freeze."

"Ah. A body cools about one-point-five degrees Fahrenheit per hour for the first twelve hours. Then it's about half that rate over the next hours. Cool ambient temperatures, like in here, speed up the rate of cooling," he said.

Helsing touched Brett's forehead and the inside of his wrist then gently laid hands on his arms and legs. "His body is stiff and cold. Given when he talked to his brother, he could have died between then and within the last ten to twelve hours. We'll narrow the time down more closely at autopsy to get a fairly accurate date and time of death." He pulled out his camera and snapped photos of the deceased and his surroundings. I followed suit with my phone camera.

"He who dies with the most toys wins, as they say," Helsing said.

"That's what they say, but I've wondered if a posthumous win even counts."

"Good point. And in this case, you could substitute 'things' for 'toys'. Let's get Roy and Chief Evans up here with the gurney, and get the basket into position."

"Sure." I opened the window, saw the ladder had been moved away, and called to the two men. "There's room in there for both you and the gurney, right?"

"No problem," Corey said.

Jack crawled into the tower truck and lowered the basket. Corey and Roy crawled in then Wyman and Matty lifted the gurney up for them. The two pulled it in between them.

"All set," Chief Corey yelled, and it lifted at a slow pace until it was level with the bottom of the window. "That's good!" Corey yelled, and it came to a halt. Helsing leaned out to receive the gurney as Corey and Roy rolled it in the window. I moved to one side, and Helsing to the other, as we brought the gurney inside. We rolled it close to the couch so the other two could enter.

Helsing removed the body bag from its cover and laid it on the gurney. I helped him spread it out, then stepped into the narrow path that led to the south window, and prayed no piles would topple down on top of me.

4

Corey and Roy climbed into the room, pulled on boot covers, and took a moment to look around. Roy visibly twitched. "Sorry, I'm a little claustrophobic."

I nodded. "Me too. Take a slow breath, then we'll focus on the task at hand." A few years back, I'd been knocked out and locked in a killer's trunk. I'd avoided small spaces whenever possible since. The room wasn't small, but all the collections made it seem so.

"I don't need to tell you there's not a lot of room in here to work, but we've made do in tight spaces before," Helsing said.

"Yeah. Brett is tall, but he's also very lean. Given the circumstances, it'd be tough for three of us to get into an ideal position to move him." Roy waved his hand toward Brett's head. "How about I squeeze in at that end of the couch and get my arms under his upper body."

"That'll work. I'll take his lower body and legs. One arm under his hips, the other under his knees," Corey said.

"We have a plan. All right then, I'll move to the other side of the gurney and help position him," Helsing said.

When they were in place, I stepped in ready to assist if the need arose.

"On three," Helsing said. "One, two, and lift."

It was a smooth transfer, and I helped position Brett's legs inside the bag.

"We'll zip it up just to his neck; in case Shane Winston is there waiting when we bring Brett's body down. In any case, Shane should say goodbye to his brother before we take him to our office," Helsing said.

After Brett's body had been strapped to the gurney, Corey and Roy climbed out the window and into the basket. Helsing and I rolled the gurney over, bottom end first. The two got ready and pulled it when we lifted. Corey and Roy lowered the bottom of the gurney so the top was elevated and fit inside better.

"We'll send it back up for you," Corey told us then hollered, "All right, Jack, we're ready to descend."

I saw Shane standing a ways back from the rig and felt relieved he'd see Brett's body before the ME left with it. Matty and Wyman helped remove the gurney, then Swanson and Chief got out. Seconds later the basket lifted for Helsing and me. We climbed in, and I pulled the window down behind me.

"Okay, Jack!" Helsing called, and we were on the ground seconds later. "Easier than the ladder," he told me.

"And faster," I said as I climbed out. Mandy caught my eyes and blew out a relieved breath. I gave her a quick nod back.

Shane moved in next to the gurney and rested his gloved hand on his brother's shoulder then touched his cross. "I see he still wore it. A Christmas gift from our parents. I got one too."

Tears formed in my eyes. I blinked and willed them not to escape.

"We'll have the cross cleaned and returned to you," Helsing said.

Shane nodded then lightly brushed Brett's cheek. "Why is his face so red?"

Helsing moved in closer. "That's a sign of possible carbon monoxide poisoning."

Shane's eyes squeezed together. "How, what from?"

"The kerosene heater is the suspected culprit," Helsing said.

Shane shook his head a few times. "Dear God. Rest in peace, Bro." He gave Brett's shoulder a final squeeze and walked away.

I did a double take when a tall man, his dark hair streaked with gray, his eyes bluer than the sky, came around the back corner. Detective Smoke Dawes. We locked eyes a second, then he scanned the scene and the people gathered there. Smoke focused on Brett Winston's body as they prepared to close the body bag.

Dr. Helsing paused when he spotted him. "Detective Dawes."

"Doctor." Smoke stepped up to the gurney. "CO?"

Helsing nodded. "That's what we presume at this point. We'll be able to do the autopsy this afternoon, unless something more urgent comes up."

"It'll be good for the family to get answers. And for our investigation too." Smoke pointed at the rig's basket. "The recovery operation went okay?"

"It did. We had a good team here. Sergeant Aleckson can fill you in on the details," Helsing said.

Smoke threw me a glance and blinked.

Chief Corey Evans and his crew checked their equipment, bid their goodbyes, climbed in their vehicles, and headed back to their jobs.

Mandy and I stayed near Shane while Dr. Helsing, Roy Swanson, and Smoke lifted the gurney into the ME's van. After they got into their vehicle and drove away, Smoke joined our group.

"This is so unreal. What do we do next? Here, I mean," Shane asked.

"The sheriff's office will check the room your brother occupied first, see if the evidence agrees with the ME's findings. Then your family will need to decide next steps," Smoke said.

"I know there are crews we can hire to clean out his stuff," Shane said.

"Shane, there are likely items of value and hidden treasures among his accumulations. Along with his personal things," I said.

Shane reached up and squeezed the back of his neck. "I suppose. It's about impossible to know where to start."

"As you mentioned, there are companies that specialize in those details," Smoke said.

"Yeah. I don't remember who my sister-in-law hired, and that was in Minneapolis. We've lost touch with her. Last time we heard from Deena she said she was moving away."

"Deena hired a cleaning crew?" Smoke said.

Shane nodded and filled Smoke in about Brett's son's death, his hoarding, his reaction when his wife tried to get rid of some stuff, and how their marriage had ended.

"Sorry to hear that. Sounds like your brother had some sad and difficult years." Smoke said.

"Very much so."

"As the sergeant said, there are likely things of value on the property. Something to think about is, get both a dumpster and a portable storage unit. As you go through things, you can decide what to toss and what to save, or maybe donate," Smoke said.

"I'll talk to my sister about that. From what I've told her so far, she's pretty freaked out, with Brett dying and everything."

"Of course."

Mandy got called to a disturbance complaint, gave Shane her sympathies once again, and hustled to her car.

Shane zeroed in on me. "What should I do? Should I stick around here, or go home, or get a room in town? What?"

Grief often blocked a person's decision-making ability.

"You live four hours away, and your sister's in Michigan. Why don't you talk to her, see if you can form a game plan," I said.

Smoke added, "Sergeant, you got Shane's contact information?"

"Yes, but I didn't give him mine." I pulled a business card from my pocket and handed it to him.

"For our records, we'll need your sister's information also. We're authorized to search the room your brother was in. If you'll sign a form that gives us permission to search other parts of the house—if need be—that would help expedite the process," Smoke said.

"Okay, I can do that," Shane agreed.

"When you decide to start the property cleaning process, we can provide a list of companies that specialize in that type of work. So you know, hoarding—in different degrees—is more common than you might think," Smoke said.

"I read house inspectors and fire departments estimate ten to fifteen percent of people here in Minnesota hoard. The last seminar we had about it, the presenter said it's as high as twenty-five percent of our population in some areas of the state. Much higher numbers reported than twenty or thirty years ago," I said.

"Hmm, I had no idea." Shane studied the ground a moment. "Detective, back to the property cleaners. Any idea how much they charge?"

"Could be several thousand dollars, depending on the time it takes," Smoke said.

Shane nodded a few times. "Seems well worth it. I wouldn't know where to even start something like that."

Smoke withdrew a business card from his jacket pocket, gave it to Shane, and pulled out a memo book. "What's your sister's name, address, and phone number?"

Shane provided the information while Smoke and I each jotted it down. "Thanks—" Smoke was interrupted when Shane's phone jingled.

Shane held it up. "It's my wife." He walked away to answer the call.

Smoke looked at me, and I hoped he read in my expression how grateful I felt he was there, both on a personal, and a professional level. His instincts, expertise, and people skills were valuable assets in our office. And his presence lightened whatever load I carried in almost every circumstance. We did our best to keep our work life separate from our personal relationship, but my abiding love for him was always in my heart.

"This is one for the books, huh?" Smoke asked.

I came out of my reverie. "Ah, *yeah.*"

"We'll see what we can uncover in Brett Winston's room and take it from there."

"I'll grab the release form for Shane to sign." I retrieved it from the briefcase in the front seat of my car and attached it to a clipboard.

Shane returned with a brighter expression. "My wife's on her way here. Well, to Oak Lea anyway. We'll get a hotel room. She told me my sister Tricia is making arrangements too, checking on flights. So like you said Detective, we can sit down, hash it out, and come up with a game plan."

"Good to hear. The shock about your brother—his sudden death and having his many possessions to deal with—I know it must feel overwhelming. But like everything else in life, you need to take the process one step at a time."

Shane half-smiled. "One step at a time will be good to remember as we figure things out." He rubbed his arms. "I'm starting to get a chill, maybe from being out in the cold, but mostly I think the emotional overload caught up with me. I'm going to head into town, get a room, take a hot shower, and wait for my wife."

I passed the clipboard to Shane, along with a pen. "This release form gives us permission to search areas of the house necessary in our investigation."

He scanned the paper, signed and dated it, and handed it back to me.

"Thank you," I said.

"Okay. I'm going to ask for the next week off work, at least. We'll need to make arrangements for Brett. And get some of this stuff taken care of. The sooner the better." Shane waved his hand from the house to the shed. "The longer it hangs over us, I think the worse it will be."

"I can get you a list of companies and their contact info later today, if you'd like," I offered.

"Thanks." Shane rubbed his arms again.

"You should go get warmed up," Smoke said,

"Yeah. We'll be in touch. And thank you for what you do. Something like this can't be easy for you, either."

"We protect and serve. That covers a lot of territory," Smoke said.

Shane lifted his hand in a wave, climbed in his SUV, and headed down the driveway.

Smoke nudged my arm. "Ready, Sergeant?"

"As I'll ever be. As soon as I change into clean coveralls. In case."

"Sounds like a plan."

We kept sets in our trunks along with other gear and equipment. I secured the release form in my briefcase then stripped off the suit the ME gave me, inside out, and put it in my trunk. Smoke and I removed our jackets and threw them in our front seats.

We found the protective coveralls that covered us from head to toe, pulled them on, and stuffed vinyl gloves in our pockets. I left the radio mic attached to my collar and could unzip the top inches if need be, and dropped my cellphone in the coveralls pocket. Smoke withdrew a case with supplies that held a 35 mm camera, evidence bags, markers, and a flashlight.

"We'll brush the snow off our feet before we climb in the window," Smoke said.

We made our way around the house. The ladder had been placed into position against the house before the firemen left.

I pointed at it. "Me first?"

"Sure. You can show me how it's done. It's been a while since my last window entry."

"Doctor Helsing said the same thing. Like you'd forget."

"More like I'd rather forget and not do it at all," he said.

I smiled as I shook my head and counted each rung as I climbed. On the fourteenth step I pushed the window open and climbed inside.

Smoke was close behind me. He handed me the case and stuck his head in the window. "You made it look easier than I have a feeling it's gonna be for me."

"I've had practice today. It's my third—and hopefully last—time using that entry method here."

Smoke used the same technique Helsing had. He slid one leg in until his foot hit the floor then bent over, backed his upper body through, then pulled in his other leg.

"Piece of cake," I said.

"Yeah, except for the cramp in my back." He closed the window and did a slow visual sweep of the room. He reached in the case for the 35 mm camera and snapped photos of the room, section by section, then zeroed in on the kerosene heater. "The probable killer culprit." He took shots at different angles then turned toward the couch. "Brett Winston's death bed?"

"Yes. We got photos of his body on it."

Smoke set the camera back in the case, made his way to the heater, and checked it. "It has a safety valve that shuts off when it runs out of fuel. We have no definitive way to determine the time that might have happened, when it shut down."

"No. When we entered the first time, the smell was there, but we let in a lot of cold air that helped dissipate it."

5

An older model television set and a radio sat on a table several feet back from the couch. It butted up to more piles. I waved that direction. "He had those to give him company anyway. They must be connected by a long extension cord."

Smoke shook his head, walked a few steps to the couch, and picked up a Bible from the end table. "What have we here?"

"What?"

An inch of yellow notebook paper was sticking out the top. He pulled it out. "It's a handwritten note."

I moved in next to him. "I saw the Bible but didn't notice that. What does it say?"

"The writing is messy, like his hand was shaking." Smoke read it out loud. "'To whoever finds this. I never meant for it to happen. I tried to stop it. Afterwards I didn't know what to do and decided to let it go. I'm feeling really sick now and if I die I want you all to know how sorry I am about the crime that happened last year.'" Smoke raised his eyebrows.

"What crime? Is that some kind of riddle?" I reached for the note and Smoke passed it to me.

"Kinda sounds like it. Riddles have answers and you posed the obvious question, what crime? We can presume Brett wrote the note, but we'll need to confirm it. Ask his brother if this looks like his handwriting."

"True. Let's go on the assumption Brett wrote this. Look how his sentences slope downward. It's a sign he felt pessimistic. That, and the words in the note itself suggest he was depressed."

"Say Brett did write it, who wouldn't feel down, given how he was living in these circumstances?" Smoke took the note from me and studied it again. "Did he mean he tried to stop himself or someone else from committing the crime? It would've been helpful if he'd included a detail or two. The crime. The date."

"Ah, yeah."

"The fact that Brett has been gathering things from parts unknown for years is a given. With all the holiday figurines stacked over there, maybe he scouted some out and stole them in the dark of night. People report their decorations disappear around holidays every year," Smoke said.

"That's true. But would Brett be driven to steal? Shane told me his brother was always on the sensitive side. I'm trying to think of unsolved crimes from last year. We've had burglaries, thefts, gas drive-offs. Ones that we haven't yet tracked down the offenders. If Brett didn't commit the crime himself, that means he was with someone who did. Someone he couldn't stop. He said he didn't know what to do. If he was too fearful to report it, you have to wonder why."

Smoke pulled an evidence bag from his pocket, slid the note in, carried it to the case, and secured it inside. "If he'd said what the crime was we could start an investigation. Was there one—or more than one—perpetrator involved?"

"That in itself is curious because according to Shane, Brett didn't really associate with other people anymore. I think it's safe to say he didn't entertain people here. He wouldn't even let his own brother inside. So where was he when the crime occurred? He could have been scavenging anywhere. It may have happened in another county, or in downtown Minneapolis for all we know."

"You're right. We'll need to look at his contacts and calls." Smoke glanced around. "Where is his phone, by the way?"

"It wasn't on his person, and I asked that same question when we didn't spot it earlier, before we removed his body. Helsing said he could've set it somewhere before he sat down on the couch."

"You didn't check the couch cushions?"

"No. After we moved Brett to the gurney, I forgot about the phone," I said.

Smoke wrestled out a couch cushion. Nothing. When he pulled out the next, it was behind it, and dropped onto the base below. An old flip phone. Smoke held it up for me to see. "We wouldn't need a passcode to access his information, but we'd need permission. Or a warrant. Shane should be willing to help us get names and numbers from his brother's phone."

"Man, getting back to that strange note. It presents another shocker for the family to grapple with, wonder about."

"A big one at that. It also begs the question I need to ask, did Brett use the kerosene heater to bring on his own death?" Smoke said.

"That question has crossed my mind more than once in the last hour. Was he depressed because he felt sick, or had he decided he was ready to end it all? The thing that keeps coming back to me that contradicts that is he reached out to his brother for help."

"That he did." Smoke retrieved another evidence bag from his pocket, dropped the phone inside, and put it in the case with the note. "Well Sergeant, we've got some exploration ahead of us. There might be some other mysterious notes among his things, or in those stacks of papers."

"First let's take a look in the bathroom. Doctor Helsing wondered about medications, and we didn't see any bottles near his body. Then we'll see if we can access the flight of stairs. Maybe he wasn't trapped up here after all." I said.

I made my way via a path to the bathroom with Smoke close behind. The door stood open. Boxes of supplies—rags, bathroom cleaners, and brushes—blocked it from closing. A white tub by the west wall was filled almost to the ceiling with random items; towels, shaving kits, plastic containers with bars of soap and hygiene items, along with an estimated fifteen 12-packs of toilet paper.

I opened the old metal medicine cabinet that hung above the sink. A few bottles: ibuprofen, antacids, and vitamins sat on the bottom shelf. The second shelf had a box of bandages, antibiotic ointment, and iodine. The top shelf was bare. "Neat and organized. And has an empty shelf. You'd think Brett would've found something to put on it."

Smoke looked over my shoulder. "No prescription medications or illicit drugs here."

"Unless he kept them somewhere else."

"Unless." Smoke pointed at the tub. "He couldn't bathe or shower there, so you gotta wonder, did he just sponge bathe from the sink?"

"Probably." I glanced at the toilet. "Surprisingly clean, like the sink. So he used his cleaning supplies. But what about his clothes? Is there a washing machine hidden around here somewhere?"

"It'd have to be connected to a water source with a drain. In this old house it's either buried in the basement, or it could be on the main level," he said.

Smoke turned and headed down a narrow path, out the bedroom's open door into a short hallway. I followed. Two doors, one on the left and one on the right, would be inaccessible until the stacks against them were cleared away. A long table with a mini-refrigerator, microwave, and hotplate stood at the end, in front of the stairs. They were plugged into a multi-plug surge protector outlet. Shelves of cooking supplies and boxed food stuffs lined the walls several feet on either side.

"That's an odd spot for these appliances, blocking the stairway like that." Smoke moved the table enough to get around it and peered down. "Lots of filled garbage bags thrown down the steps."

"Must not have any rotting food in them. Not that I smell anyway. Still, I'm surprised it doesn't stink anywhere in the area—except for a musty smell—given all the stuff Brett has picked up from who knows where."

"The lower fifty-degree temperature probably helps reduce any potentially bad odors," he said.

We made our way back to Brett's den of sorts. "This was the master bedroom, so that meant the kids would have to go into their parents' bedroom to get to the bathroom."

"A lot of houses built back then did not waste space on hallways. In some, you had to go through one bedroom to get to the one behind it."

"Yeah, I took a call in a house like that. My first thought was, whoever had the pass-through bedroom didn't have much privacy," I said.

"My brothers and I would've fought over the back room."

"Like about everything else when you were kids, from what you've told me."

Smoke chuckled. "We did have a few teenage tussles."

I scanned the room and its endless contents of items. "So how many days would it take the two of us to go through all the piles, if we had to?"

"Too many. To narrow it down, given Winston's confession to a crime, either as an accomplice or an observer, we'll need to take a look through his papers. If not today, then at some point. See if he's had incriminating correspondence with someone. Or wrote another curious note about it," he said.

"Hmm."

"That said, given the large stack there—and we can only guess at how many more there are—the best course of action is to wait until the cleaning company is able to gain entry to the main level and starts removing items. In addition to interrogating his phone, the sheriff's office should have the first look through his papers before we hand them over to the family. But there could be any number of personal records, life insurance or other legal documents they might need."

"Unless they come across a file cabinet with all those things in them," I said.

"Unless. But the chances of that are slim to none. A sad thing with hoarders is they have trouble organizing. When they attempt to do so, they end up moving things from one pile and start another pile."

"I've heard that. Although there does seem to be some order to Brett's piles. Stuffed animals, holiday decorations, books, newspapers."

"But then you have the other random item piles and garbage bags full of who knows what," he said.

"I hate to say this, but I'm hoping there's actually garbage in them. When I backed into a couple I wondered. One positive thing though, whatever is inside them, it makes it easier for the crew to remove a bag instead of individual items."

"Yep."

The stack of papers was about five feet high and a messy four feet square. Numbers of envelopes and other papers had slid down the sides. "We'll see if we discover anything useful in the next hour or so. If not, we'll call it a wrap. We can assemble a team, hopefully in the not-too-distant future, to have at it." Smoke said.

He picked up a stack of envelopes from the top and fingered through them. "Shane didn't know the last time Brett had left his house, but it looks like the most recent postage stamp was eleven days ago. That tells us it's probably been eight or nine days since he collected his mail."

We scoured through papers in hopes of uncovering an answer, or at least a clue, to his mystifying death bed note. Instead, we found probably every piece of junk and other mail he'd gotten in the last year or more, along with a tall stack of advertising flyers from a lengthy list of companies.

I held up a flyer. "Look how some of these have pin holes in the corners, like he confiscated them from the bulletin boards some stores have by their exits. Unless he found them in their trash containers. It seems the poor guy couldn't help himself."

"Seems that way all right," Smoke said.

"We don't know how long it's been since he trapped himself in this room, but he sure did a good job filling it."

"He must've stowed most of it in here when he could still use the stairs."

"All the big items for sure," I said.

Smoke brushed his forehead with the back of his gloved hand. "I gotta say a thing that's gnawing at me is why would he block his way down the stairs?"

"It's like he made this small area his prison, and like you said, why? At least he set up an escape route to get supplies or in case of fire," I said.

"As long as the ladder didn't go down in a strong wind."

"If he'd thought about that, he would've needed a Plan B. Brett must have a long rope in here somewhere."

"He no doubt does. If Brett could've navigated a maneuver like that. I haven't climbed down a rope in ages, and it's not the easiest training procedure we've had to do. Worse than climbing through a window," Smoke said.

"I agree that's a tougher maneuver. Even with gloves on."

Over the next hour we did not come across anything that referred to a crime or suspicious activities, so we called it a wrap. Smoke picked up the case, scanned the room one last time, and made his way to the escape window.

"I'll hand that to you when you're on the ladder," I said.

He passed it over and climbed out. After I gave him the case, I climbed onto the ladder and pulled the window closed. On the ground, we made our way to our vehicles. After we'd secured the evidence in Smoke's car, we removed our protective wear and put it in his trunk.

"All right then," Smoke said. "See you back at the ranch. Let's stop by the sheriff's office first, fill him in, and show him the note. We'll make copies before we enter it into evidence. A handwriting expert should analyze it. And the family needs to see it to confirm whether or not it is Brett's handwriting. Plus, they may have an inkling what it means."

I nodded. "Let's hope. See you there."

6

Smoke knocked on Sheriff Mike Kenner's doorframe. Kenner's eyebrows lifted as he waved us in. "Sergeant, you had an interesting call this morning. Different."

One way to classify it. "Among the most different I've ever had, that's for sure."

"I was tied up with meetings until a few minutes ago or I would've stopped out there," Sheriff said.

"It was a relief when Smoke reported to the scene and took the lead on the investigation. Also a relief he was there when we searched Winston's quarters."

"All I can say is, seeing is believing," Smoke said.

"A sad way to live, and a sadder way to die," I added.

I shared details of the scene, how distraught his brother Shane Winston was, the blocked entries, the packed shed, and how Brett had confined himself to a small area on the second floor. I showed the sheriff photos of the deceased and his surroundings.

Kenner shook his head as he viewed the photos. "Unbelievable. And the ME suspects CO poisoning was the cause of death?"

"Yes. We hope to get the initial autopsy report later today. There's something else. Smoke found a note that has us wondering if the victim died accidentally, or if he committed suicide. If it turns out he's the one who wrote it," I said.

Smoke passed the bagged note to the sheriff. He read it out loud, as Smoke had earlier. "Well that adds a wrinkle, all right. A crime last year he couldn't stop. Huh. Two mysteries, huh? How he died, and whatever it was he referred to in his note."

Smoke and I summarized our discussions and suppositions for Kenner as he jotted notes on his desk pad.

"We'll connect with Shane Winston this afternoon, give him a copy of the note, and his brother Brett's phone. See what he can come up with for contacts," Smoke said.

"We also need to give him names of some companies," I added.

"From the sound of it, in addition to the dumpster and portable storage unit you mentioned, the family might want to contact an auction house about the vehicles and equipment in the shed," Kenner said.

It took me almost thirty minutes to finish my report. I printed the photos from my work cellphone and attached them to the typed narrative. It would go up the chain of command and land on the sheriff's desk before the end of day.

After I dropped it in Lieutenant Randolph's box, I headed to Smoke's cubicle and found him typing away on his keyboard. "Just about wrapping up here. I'll give Shane Winston a call next, see if we can swing by his hotel, or ask if he'd rather meet us here."

As I waited, I checked my work cellphone for text messages. One from Amanda Zubinski. *I heard you cleared the scene and hope it went okay after I left.*

I responded, *I'll bring you up to speed when I see you. How's Vince doing?*

Still down for the count. Hasn't even shaved his head for days.

He normally ran the electric razor over it daily. I sent her a sad face emoji back. Deputy Vincent Weber, one of my best friends and Mandy's love, was rarely sick, but had caught a bad cold.

Taylor was in my list of calls and reminded me I hadn't gotten back to her. I sent her a text, *Sorry, I've been tied up since we talked. I'll call you after work.*

Her response was immediate. *No worries. Whenever you have time. Thanks.*

I sent her a thumbs up. Taylor. What in the world was going on with her husband Silas?

Smoke finished his report and said, "Here goes." He picked up his phone, punched in Shane's number, and was connected a moment later. "Hello, Shane, Detective Dawes. Did you get checked into a hotel? . . . Good. Sergeant Aleckson and I wondered if this would be an okay time to stop by. . . . Sure, that works for us. See you then." They disconnected and Smoke said, "He's at the Country Inn and is expecting us in about ten minutes. I feel bad his life is about to get a whole lot more complicated."

"I wonder how many times I've thought 'poor guy' since I met him this morning?"

Smoke put Brett's note and phone in his briefcase. I added the list I'd printed of companies that specialized in hoarder house cleaning.

Smoke and I drove our squad cars to the Country Inn on Highway 55. Shane was in the small lobby. He had showered, evidenced by his damp hair. It was brownish gray, wavy, and neatly trimmed around his ears and neck. We nodded our greetings.

The young female hotel clerk eyed us, no doubt curious. Perhaps she wondered if Shane Winston was in trouble. I smiled to assure her. "Hello."

She smiled in return. "Good afternoon."

"My wife packed some things for the two of us and got on the road about an hour ago. My sister is catching a flight tonight," Shane said.

"It'll be a relief to have them here with you," I said.

"You have no idea. Well, maybe you do."

"Shane, we have a couple of things to go over with you," Smoke said and walked to the pool room window. "Let's head in there. No one to hear our conversation."

Shane's shoulders jerked up and down a few times as he glanced at the briefcase in Smoke's hand. Smoke opened the door for Shane and me, and we filed in. A few tables and chairs were placed around the pool's and hot tub's perimeter. Smoke led us to one on the opposite wall, furthest from the lobby entry.

When we'd settled on mesh-seated metal chairs, Smoke had the briefcase on his lap, opened it, and withdrew the copy of Brett's note. "Shane, we found this in your brother's Bible on the table by the couch. First of all, can you confirm that this is your brother's handwriting?" He kept his voice low, but it still echoed in the high-ceilinged room.

Shane took the paper, and his hands shook as he studied it. "What in the hell," he mumbled. He looked from me to Smoke. "It's Brett's writing, but it's like his hand was shaking, or something, when he wrote it. And what a weird message." his brows furrowed as he inspected it.

"Do you have any clue what it refers to, what Brett meant about a crime?" Smoke asked as he set the briefcase on the floor.

"Not even an inkling. Wait. Sergeant, remember how I told you that Brett seemed to get worse last year? Maybe it had something to do with that. But Brett was *not* a criminal. I can't imagine where he'd be, or who he'd be with. Someone that committed a crime Brett witnessed and couldn't stop?"

Smoke reached down and pulled Brett's phone from the briefcase. "We'd be obliged if you'd take a look at your brother's list of contacts for us. See if there are any names you don't recognize."

Shane scrolled through Brett's phone, his contacts and calls. "Not many contacts listed. Me, my wife, our sister, her husband, the plow driver, Brett's ex-wife Deena. But she must've changed her number since then, because it's not the same one she used when she contacted us last time. Unless she has two phones.

"A few others I don't know. I'll look through his calls." He scrolled for a while. "Most are either to me, or from me. Ah, this is interesting. He got a call from Deena last summer. A short call, only two minutes. Must've been about the same time she sent us a text to let us know she was moving out of state."

Shane shook his head and handed the phone back to Smoke.

"Since Brett referred to a crime, the sheriff's office will want to interrogate his phone." Smoke withdrew a release form and pen from the briefcase. "If you give us written permission to search it, we can cut through the red tape."

"I can do that." Shane picked up the pen and signed the form.

I raised my hand a bit. "One thing we need to ask, and it may sound insensitive. Brett sounded pretty down in his note. Did he mention that he'd thought about self-harm?" I asked.

Shane's eyebrows shot up. "No, never. But with his different mental health issues, I guess it's possible Brett had reached the end of his rope." He rested his elbows on the table and leaned his head in his hands. "When he finally did reach out for my help, I got there too late to save him."

As information was brought to light, and things unfolded, Brett's family would have more traumatic things to deal with than his untimely death.

I gave Shane a moment then said, "We brought the list of cleaning companies for you."

He lifted his head. "Okay."

Smoke reached in the briefcase for the list and handed it to Shane. "You have unexpected decisions you'll need to make. We mentioned a couple options at your brother's house. And another resource for your family to consider is an auction house. We have several companies in the county you could talk to about vehicles and equipment in the shed you don't want to keep. That goes for contents in the house too. Furniture, or other hidden treasures."

Hidden was an apt term. *Treasures* were to be decided.

Shane nodded and read over the list of cleaners. "Who would you recommend? Who have you heard the most good things about?"

"They're all reputable. You can check out the posted reviews. I know the one used most often around here is Metro Area Cleanup, from Plymouth. After they remove the clutter, they clean and sanitize walls, floors, the bathroom, kitchen appliances," I said.

"Now that you mention it, I don't know the last time the house was even cleaned. Brett got to be a hoarder, but he liked things clean, believe it or not. We sort of left him to his own devices when he moved back to the home place," Shane said.

Maybe that accounted for the fact Brett's house didn't smell like garbage, and his bathroom was sanitary.

"Shane, back to Brett's ex-wife. Someone should contact her, let her know what happened. You have no idea where she moved?" Smoke said.

"Not a clue. I think she blamed us, at least a little, for not doing more to help her with Brett. She started drinking a lot and running around with different guys. The worse she got, the worse Brett got. And vice versa. If we'd been closer, maybe we could've helped somehow. But it's hard to step in and do that if they don't want you to."

"That's a given. And it doesn't always turn out the way you would hope. We'll do a search on Deena. What's her middle and maiden names, and date of birth?" Smoke asked.

"Deena Rae Holden Winston. Her birthday's April twentieth." Shane thought a second. She'll turn forty-two this year."

"All right. We've got her phone number in Brett's phone, if she still has the same one. She's out there somewhere, and we'll do all we can to track her down," Smoke said.

"Thank you. Tomorrow, after my sister is here, we'll do our best to figure things out. The medical examiner's got my number too. Between the arrangements for Brett, and deciding on a cleaning company and all that, we'll do what you said, Detective. Take things one step at a time," Shane said.

I'd clocked ninety minutes of overtime after we finished at the Country Inn. Smoke glanced at his watch. "Go ahead and take off, Corinne. I'll catch up with you later."

"Sounds good." I climbed into my squad car, let it warm for a minute, then clicked on my radio. "Six o eight, Winnebago County, I'm clear the last address."

"Copy, Sergeant. You're clear at sixteen thirty-three."

Now to clear my racing mind. I drove down County Road 35, and as I passed Whitetail Lake, I thought about Taylor's call a minute before I'd been dispatched to the Winston home. What was Silas up to, and what could I do to help Taylor and her family find a positive resolution? She was struggling, as was the Winston family. For polar opposite reasons. The Winstons had a long road ahead to clear their property of Brett's numerous accumulations. I hoped and prayed Taylor and Silas's issues could be resolved in a fraction of the time it would take the Winstons.

I pulled into my driveway, let Communications know I was 10-7—off duty—picked my briefcase from the passenger seat, climbed out, and locked the door. I'd finished my six-day work stint with the next three days off. Another sergeant on the night shift would pick up our shared squad car for his rotation later that evening.

I pressed in the garage door code on the side panel, and as the door lifted my English setter, Queenie, barked and wagged her tail from her kennel in the back of the garage. I stepped inside and pushed the door close button. "Hey, Girl. Glad to see you too."

My classic GTO was in its usual spot. I kept the other side open for Smoke's vehicle for whenever. We hadn't had a chance to discuss tonight. In any case, he'd need to go home first, take care of his yellow lab Rex, and check on things.

Queenie excited to get released from her kennel. She had a doggie door inside for outside access and went out whenever she needed to. I bent over and rested my forehead on the top of her head. She sniffed at my uniform, and I wondered what her sensitive smeller detected from things inside Winston's house.

"All right, inside. Time for me to shower, and de-germ."

She let out a small "yip" like she agreed. I made my way into the laundry/bathroom area off the kitchen, removed my duty belt, and hung it on its designated hook. My uniform shirt and pants went on another hook until I could empty my pockets and remove my badge. My Kevlar vest on a third hook to air out until my next day on duty.

Queenie headed to her water dish, and I climbed into the shower. It always felt good to cleanse my body after work. Sometimes in a hot scented bath, other times in a shower where I shampooed and soaped and scrubbed, rinsed then soaped and rinsed again, as much to dilute my emotional responses, what I'd experienced on the job, as to clean my body.

Water pounded on my neck and shoulders and eased some tension. I did my best to clear my mind, relax, and release part of the burden I felt for what victims had been through, what their families had to cope with, and endure going forward.

I would never forget many criminal cases I'd responded to. Ones where a person had been victimized, or had lost their life, or suffered great trauma. They bubbled to the surface of my consciousness from time to time. Some more often than others.

I towel dried and shuffled through the pile of clean clothes on top of the dryer that hadn't yet made it into drawers. I selected underwear, sweats, and wool socks. I needed a little down time with Queenie before I spoke with Taylor.

We settled on the living room couch. Queenie rested her head on my lap. I stared out the window and watched the eastern sky grow darker as the sun descended beneath the western horizon. The winter solstice—and shortest day of the year in Minnesota—was a few weeks behind us so we gained about a minute of light every evening. In five months we'd have the longest day of the year.

I didn't suffer from seasonal affective disorder—SAD—caused by lack of sunlight, but I felt peppier when the sun shone, more than on cloudy or snowy days. I thought of Brett Winston's condition and the mental health issues he battled. Trapped in his crowded room with the shorter days and longer nights of winter no doubt had a negative impact on his mental state.

My personal cellphone chimed and gave me a start. My best girlfriend, and my brother's fiancée, Sara. "Hey," I answered.

"Hey. So it's Friday night and you actually have tomorrow off, right?"

"Yep. For the next three."

"You got big plans?" she said.

"It's been an unreal kind of day, and I hadn't thought that far."

"Unreal, huh. In what way?"

Sara, a Winnebago County probation officer, often heard about calls the sheriff's office took. I gave her a brief overview of the hoarder house call, and how we'd recovered a body from the scene, via the fire department's bucket truck.

"Oh my gosh, Corky. I *cannot* even imagine that whole scenario. I'm surprised word about it didn't travel to our office. Although it was crazy busy today. We were scrambling to wrap things up before the weekend."

"I'm sure most county employees will know about it come Monday," I said.

"I'm sure."

"You and John Carl doing anything fun?"

"It's takeout and movie night. That's what I was going to ask you, if you and Smoke wanted to join us," she said.

"I appreciate that, but after six days in the saddle that ended with a really difficult case, an evening on the couch sounds really appealing."

Sara let out a "hah!" then said, "We used to look forward to weekends and adventures. Now look at us, it's all about non-exciting activities instead."

"You think all the exciting things we deal with at work has anything to do with that?" I said.

"You make a strong point. Cork, why don't you try some of those relaxation techniques your therapist gave you? Calm your mind."

"Good idea, thanks for the reminder."

Sara ended with, "Sure thing. Take care, my friend."

I felt better after we talked. Since we each had gotten engaged, we had fewer girls' nights together. We used to enjoy takeout meals and a movie, or a board game. Not what you'd call wild, but things we enjoyed.

7

I glanced at the time: 5:30. "Queenie, I need to check in with Taylor, see what's going on."

Taylor answered on the second ring. "Oh Corky, thanks for calling."

"Is this a good time to chat?"

"It is, but let me head into the bedroom first." She talked as she walked. When I heard the door close she said, "Silas is out somewhere. The girls each have a friend over, and Charles is at his friend's house."

"Okay. Tell me more about the problem you're having with Silas," I said.

"It's major. I feel like I don't even know him anymore."

An affair was the first suspicious activity that came to mind, but it was a sensitive subject to broach with my sister. I'd let Taylor bring it up first. "You said earlier that he stays out late, won't say where he's been, what he's up to?"

Taylor sniffed four or five times. "Yes."

"All right. How long has this been going on?"

"About six weeks. It started maybe two weeks before Christmas," she said.

"Do you have access to his emails, his text messages?"

"Not his work cell. He used to leave both his cellphones on the kitchen counter half the time, and now I never see the work cell at all. Same with his laptop."

"Do you have a family plan for your phones, so you can track where he goes without him knowing about it?" I said.

"I didn't even think about that. He probably figured it out, and it seems even worse if he did. He keeps his personal phone at home when he leaves and takes his work phone with him. I've even thought about following him when he goes out at night. Katie's twelve now, so she can babysit. But I don't want to lie to the kids about where I'm going, and why."

"Have they said anything, wondered what their father is up to?"

"Silas tells them he has to work late to finish things. Like I said before, he's always worked long hours, so they're used to him leaving before they get up in the morning, and eating supper before he gets home at night sometimes. But this is different. The way he avoids me, and doesn't touch me. Since he won't tell me what's wrong or let me help, I thought maybe if I gave him a wide berth he'd be able to resolve whatever it is," Taylor said.

Optimistic, but it often didn't work out that way. "All right. Taylor, there are a couple things you could check. You know how far it is to his office, right?"

"Yes. it's about three miles. I can gauge it to be sure."

"Okay. Does he meet with clients at work or off-site?" I asked.

"Mostly at the office, I think. Before he stopped talking to me, he'd mention meeting one of his bigger clients for lunch. I think most of his business is done over the phone. He watches the stock market and advises his clients."

"He parks his car in your garage?"

"Yes," she said.

"I'd suggest you keep a mileage log of his vehicle. Sometime after he gets home for the night, or before he leaves in the morning, look at his odometer. Then check it the next day, and the next."

"Because?"

"You'll find out if he's going unexplained distances," I said.

"I wouldn't have thought of that. Thank you."

"Also, look for any unusual expenses. You have joint accounts, like checking and savings?"

"Yes, checking, and a small savings for emergencies. Silas moved all our automatic and utility payments and such to a separate account in his name. He also has a business account that's not included with our personal ones. My name's not on that one either. We have other investments he takes care of," she said.

Hmm, a joint personal, a separate personal, and a business. Three separate accounts. "You could check his expenses in your personal account, at least. Like if he's doing more gas tank fills. Withdrawing cash for things you aren't aware of."

"You think he's having an affair," she said.

"Taylor, I have no idea. There are other possibilities."

"Okay, I didn't want to say this out loud, but what if he gave some bad financial advice and is in trouble that way? So he's working extra hours to recoup it."

"That is a possibility."

"Corky, this is a lot to ask of you, but I'm desperate and don't want to hire a private detective to follow him. When you have a day off, could you come down here, check things out?"

What to say, what to say? "Taylor, Silas knows me. If he spots me sitting in a car spying on him, he'll know you asked me to do that."

"I suppose. Can you disguise yourself, or know someone we can ask? I can hire them," she said.

"Let me think about it, see what I can come up with. I just finished my six-day rotation and have the next three off, with nothing special planned."

"That's good, but you'll need some time to unwind."

"I'll be sure to do that, and I'll be happy to help you in whatever ways I can," I said.

"Thank you, thank you, thank you. You know I'll always be in debt to you for finding out who my birth parents were, who my grandparents are, and about you and John Carl, the brother and sister I didn't know I had."

"Taylor, that was a win-win for all of us. And there is no debt for you to pay. Remember that."

The overhead garage door opened. Queenie recognized the sound of Smoke's vehicle and ran to the kitchen door to greet him. I fell in behind her to open the door. Rex was with Smoke and ran in ahead of him. The dogs barked their greetings and sniffed each other's snouts.

"Okay, settle down you two." Smoke stepped into the kitchen behind Rex. I caught his clean, fresh showered scent as he took me into his arms. I nestled my head into the crook of his shoulder and we held on tight a long moment.

"Challenging case today, to say the least," Smoke said.

I pushed out a breath. "Yeah. And how many times have we said, 'Now I've seen it all, or heard it all,' and then we get called to a scene like Brett Winston's."

"Pretty often, seems like."

When we dealt with difficult scenes or interviewed people in any number of compromised states, we kept any negative emotions we felt in check as best we could, to maintain professionalism. But after work, we could let it all hang out. Do an informal debrief.

Smoke's work cellphone dinged. He stepped back, pulled it from his jogger pants pocket, and looked at its face. "ME's office." He pressed the accept button. "Detective Dawes. . . . Yes, Doctor. Sergeant Aleckson's here. I'll put you on speaker phone so she can hear your report too." He pressed that button.

Calvin Helsing said, "Hello, Sergeant. We've completed the autopsy and found something unexpected during the examination."

My heart rate picked up speed as we waited.

"And that was?" Smoke said.

"It appears Brett Winston was wounded by a small caliber bullet through the muscle above his left clavicle."

"*What?*" I said.

"Yes. The bullet missed the carotid, or he wouldn't have survived of course. The wound left an irregular oval-shaped depression, and the scar tissue is rigid around the edges. Our measurements show it was a twenty-two or a twenty-five caliber, shot at fairly close range. The bullet didn't strike bone or travel around inside—as they might do—and exited his back.

"The exit wound was almost level with the entry wound. That suggests that had the shooter been standing, he was not much taller or much shorter than the victim. Or the shooter was Winston himself."

Smoke sounded more collected than I felt when he asked, "Any guesstimates of when that may have happened?"

"It's healed over, but hasn't darkened much, like they do as years pass by. That said, it's not very recent either. You asked for a guesstimate, so I'd say six months to two years ago, given how people heal at different rates," Helsing said.

"If Winston shot himself, makes you wonder why he didn't put the gun to his heart or his temple?" Smoke said.

"You raise a valid point, Detective. The copy of Winston's note you sent to our office was curious to say the least. Naturally, it made us wonder if Winston was shot during the course of the crime, because he tried to stop it. I'll read it again. 'I never meant for it to happen. I tried to stop it. Afterwards I didn't know what to do and decided to let it go. I'm feeling really sick now and if I

70

die I want you all to know how sorry I am about the crime that happened last year,'" Helsing said.

"Winston didn't report the crime, and didn't get treated for his gunshot wound—in Winnebago County anyway—or we would have gotten the report. Did his words, what he wrote, factor into your findings at all?" Smoke asked.

"No, not per se. Even if he was shot during the commission of a crime, he didn't die from it, or from any complications of it. Winston did sound despondent in his note, however. He had no fat and little muscle, with a body mass index of sixteen, so he was severely malnourished. Depression may have hampered his desire to eat."

Smoke cleared his throat. "What did you determine as his official cause of death?"

"CO poisoning, as we'd suspected. Brett Winston did not specifically say he planned to commit suicide so we'll classify the manner of death accidental. And likely, it was."

"Doesn't seem like he would've asked his brother to bring him food if he planned to kill himself," I said.

"No. We're running a tox screen to see if any drugs were present in his system. Since no meds or other drugs were found at his house, I think it's safe to say we can rule that out. But we need to verify, and should have the results in a week or two. By the way, I'll speak with Shane Winston myself, fill him in on everything we know about his brother's death," Helsing said.

"Thank you. It's best coming from you. You'll fax your findings to the sheriff's office then?" Smoke said.

"Yes, we'll take care of that shortly, and send you the toxicology report as soon as we receive it."

"Good, thank you. And Doctor, we're grateful you performed Brett Winston's exam today," Smoke said.

"Yes, I'm glad it worked out. What started as an unusual case, became even more so at autopsy. Most important, in my opinion, is we have some answers for the family. It may not give them the assurance they hoped for, but Brett Winston basically went to sleep and didn't wake up. That knowledge should help provide some closure," Helsing said.

"It should, yes. Later then, Doc."

After Smoke disconnected, we settled on bar stools by the kitchen island.

"I'm glad Doctor Helsing will contact Shane Winston and give him the findings," I said.

Smoke nodded. "The medical examiner is the one best equipped to answer any questions he might have. It's hard to imagine the range of emotions Brett's family is coping with, and all they'll go through as they deal with how he died. The gunshot wound adds another mystery, no doubt about that. But in time, they'll come out on the other side."

"One step at a time," I added with a smile.

He smiled back. "I'll have to remember to use that line more often."

Smoke and I were lost in our thoughts until my stomach let out a growl so loud it sounded like a bear was inside me. It reminded me I hadn't eaten since a granola bar and yogurt breakfast about twelve hours before.

"How can a little stomach like yours make that much noise?" Smoke asked.

I rubbed my middle. "If it had cried out, 'feed me' at some point today I didn't hear it. I guess it needed to be sure it was heard this time."

He reached over and squeezed my shoulder. "When was the last time you ate?"

"Breakfast."

"Why didn't you grab something at the office or a drive thru?"

"I had zero appetite until a minute ago." I slid off my stool, opened the refrigerator door, and peered inside. "Anyway, we may have to settle for peanut butter and honey sandwiches."

"That's not the worst option."

I pulled the freezer section door open. "Ah, disregard. I forgot about the chicken and broccoli casserole from Mother I'd stuck in there. Yay," I said.

Smoke grinned as his fingers drummed his stomach. "Thank you, Kristen. That will, without question, hit the spot."

My mother was a topnotch cook. She worried about my nutritional intake and often left meals in my crockpot, or put a dish in the refrigerator to be heated, or delivered something for meals. It had been a sensitive subject at times, after Smoke and I got engaged. We decided—me in my thirties, him in his fifties— we should cook for ourselves.

I'd told Mother over and over she didn't have to provide meals for us, that I'd gotten better at cooking. It was mostly true. However, I was still more reactive than proactive when it came

73

to eating in general, and meal preparation in particular. I rarely planned in advance, and deep down knew I should make grocery lists and have items on hand. Or at least strive to get into the habit.

8

I set the casserole in the microwave, hit the defrost button, and turned to Smoke.

He took a couple steps toward me. "You look a little perplexed. Something else on your mind?"

I nodded. "With all we had going on in the Winston case, I waited to tell you. It's Taylor. She's concerned about Silas."

"Why's that?"

"Taylor said he hasn't been himself. He's staying out late and won't tell her why, won't tell her what's wrong. Basically, won't talk to her," I said.

"Questionable signs. I don't know him well, but the few times he visited us with his family, he seemed like a decent enough guy."

"I agree. But Taylor said his behavior has changed. A red flag that something is up with him."

"He still work at the same investment company?" Smoke asked.

"Yes."

"Things are a little unstable with the stock market, have been for a few months. It could be something like Silas is working to protect his clients' investments. Maybe he's under a lot of stress and can't bring himself to talk to Taylor about it."

"If that's what it is, he needs to find a different job. Actually, Taylor mentioned something along those lines. She didn't come right out and say it, but the way Silas is avoiding her, she's afraid he's having an affair," I said.

"I hope for the family's sake that isn't true. But other possibilities aren't that great either."

"No. Smoke, so you know, Taylor asked me to put a tail on Silas. I told her the obvious. He knows me, and if he spotted me spying on him, he'd know the reason. So then she asked me if I could find someone else to do it, or disguise myself."

He pinched the bridge of his nose as he digested my words. "You've done a great job of pulling off some different looks, undercover, or in costume. No doubt. I'm not going to advise you one way or the other on this, but remember what Alexander Pope said, 'Fools rush in where angels fear to tread.' You're no fool, but it's a great reminder."

"You and your Pope quotes," I said.

"He's a good one to quote because he was wise and his sayings are, well, quotable. He had common sense sentiments, not always common among the masses."

"True. So he's not the one who said, 'throw caution to the wind?'"

Smoke chuckled. "No. I doubt that would have been a Pope opinion."

I raised my hands. "Okay, okay, I have to confess that I like Pope too."

"I figured you did. I've noticed your subtle nods of agreement when I quote him."

"Seriously?"

He grinned. "Seriously. Back to Taylor and Silas. My advice is do what you think is best."

I pondered his words a moment. "All right. First off, I'll do some research on his company, get an overall picture of it and its ratings. This whole thing feels a little strange, checking on my brother-in-law for possible misconduct. I suggested Taylor look at his odometer readings for unexplained mileage. Also, any unusual expenses."

"Two good places to start," Smoke said.

"So what are your thoughts, if you had to hazard a guess what Silas might be involved in?"

"Sex, money, and power are three strong motivators for errant and criminal behaviors."

"Yeah. I'll need to keep an open mind, not make assumptions, be objective. Like we should do in any investigation," I said.

"That's a given."

After some thought, I said, "I may enlist help from George."

Smoke's brow creased into a slight frown. "The ex-con?"

"Turned private investigator. As a former financial wizard, George would be the right person to get in touch with Silas's company."

"And?"

"And talk to their head of HR or the company's top dog. Maybe tell them he's a recruiter or a headhunter who's interested in Silas and wondered if they'd give him a recommendation," I said.

"I don't think it's that simple."

"Just throwing darts at the wall here. George could work on it."

The microwave beeped. I pulled the casserole out, and Smoke got plates and flatware from the cupboard and drawer. As I dished up the food, Smoke said, "Wanna beer?"

"Sure."

He found two bottles in the fridge and popped off the caps. I carried the plates, and he brought the beverages to the dining area table. We took our seats, bowed our heads, and gave thanks for the food. Then he lifted his bottle and I followed suit. As we clinked the necks together, he said, "Here's to you, Corinne. Your Friday night falls on an actual Friday night."

I added, "Thanks. And here's to you, Elton Dawes. It's Friday night and you are not on call this weekend."

"Cheers. It's rare the stars and planets align so we both have the same weekend off." We clinked our bottles again.

"Sara asked if we wanted to join her and John Carl to watch a movie tonight. I hope you don't mind that I declined."

"Hah! Not at all. After the stressful day we—especially you—had at the Winstons' house, and then with Taylor's dilemma, I think a quiet evening in a warm house sounds like the best plan of all."

"Got any ideas?"

"I'll come up with something." He moved his eyebrows up and down a few times. I shook my head then gave him a wide grin.

The light of dawn woke me a little before eight o'clock Saturday morning. I rolled on to my back and glanced at the other side of the bed. No Smoke. Queenie's sleep sounds rose from the floor beside me. I thought about the depth of my love for Smoke, and the perfect night we'd spent together. My body tingled from head to toe when I was in his arms. Whether together or apart, I often ached for him.

I stared at the ceiling, and my mind switched to a replay of the calls I'd taken over the last week. A domestic assault that ended with the boyfriend's arrest; a disturbance at a fast-food restaurant that led to a man's trip to the hospital for an evaluation; and an impaired driver traffic stop and subsequent arrest, were the more notable calls. Until Brett Winston's. My mind ran through the details for the umpteenth time. Those details and unanswered questions were difficult to comprehend.

It would be easy to cast blame on Brett's siblings, given the way they had turned a blind eye to their brother's condition. Brett was debilitated to the point that, as he neared death, he required immediate hospitalization. Shane was right. Had he been there four or five hours after Brett called him, Brett might still be alive.

Brett's wife's purging attempt to clear Brett's things from their house had ended badly and caused him to intensify his hoarding efforts. What Brett needed instead was intensive help from a professional intervention team.

I thought of the other hoarders I'd dealt with for different reasons over the years. One husband told me, "My wife's eyes actually light up when she brings home stuff." Another family paid for a storage unit to keep grandpa's things that no longer fit in his house. At least they could navigate through pathways in his one-story. And he was able to access his shower, washer and dryer, and kitchen appliances. Plus enter and exit his house via his entry doors.

Some people lived in cluttered spaces with possessions scattered around, but it didn't disrupt their normal activities. They could part with stuff if need be. Others had collections they continued to add to. It wasn't a problem until they ran out of space. With hoarding, unorganized piles of clutter prevented normal activities in their living spaces, like Brett's did. His was the most extreme case I'd seen in my career.

One mental health professional shared that his client defended his disorder when he told him, "If it's between my things that won't leave me, and people that will, I'll stay with my stuff." I found it sad the way some people had a stronger emotional connection to stuff than to people.

I learned one challenge the disorder posed was to uncover the root cause. The sheriff's office held a class for deputies on hoarding. The presenter shared pertinent information and facts. He said hoarding had been classified as an obsessive-compulsive disorder until it was given its own designation. For hoarders who also had OCD, it was recognized as biological, genetic, and linked to chromosome 14 where Tourette syndrome, Alzheimer's, and other disorders were found. In those cases, their hoarding often began in childhood. Many could not recall how or why it started.

For people like Brett, it had manifested itself after a traumatic loss. For others, it started due to unresolved issues, like after an assault, or time spent in poverty, or negative feelings they harbored and couldn't express. The list of reasons and conditions was long and complex. One thing I'd learned years back: it was critical to enlist help from professionals, not only for the hoarders, but for their loved ones as well.

Most people without the disorder believed cleaning out the clutter would solve the problem. But it didn't work that way. Instead it made it worse, as it had for Brett Winston. Other mental health issues like anxiety, paranoia, and depression often compounded the problem, as it likely had for Brett.

I rubbed my face to help clear my mind. Instead my thoughts switched to Taylor and her situation. Time to call private investigator George, given his personal experience with financial institutions and his crimes.

When I climbed out of bed, Queenie jumped to her feet and wagged her tail. I leaned over and scratched her head. "Morning, Girl. Where's your buddy Rex? Smoke take him home?" She barked a reply. "That's why it's so quiet around here."

I made the bed then headed downstairs for the first order of business: let Queenie outside. My second order of business: make a cup of strong black coffee. I watched Queenie rub her snout in the snow before she started her exploration of the backyard. Smoke had left a note on the counter in front of the single-cup coffee maker.

My dearest Corinne, How do I love thee? Let me count the ways. Elizabeth Barrett Browning, not Alexander Pope 😊. *Hope you slept well after our bedtime adventures. I can promise you that I did. Rex and I have household chores to attend to. Later, Love.*

My heart pitter-pattered as I put a coffee pod in the machine and pressed the button. After the cup filled, I carried it to the living room where I found both my personal and work phones on the coffee table. I had a missed call from Mother, and a text message from Mandy.

Hey Corky, checking to see how the rest of yesterday went.

I phoned her. "Hey, Mandy, to answer your question, I don't even know where to begin. The whole thing was so unreal. And the ME did rule Brett Winston died of CO poisoning."

"That's what it looked like to me," she said.

"I think it did to all of us. But we found a strange note he'd written on his death bed."

"How strange?"

I found Brett's note on my work cellphone photos and read it to her.

"That is *bizarre*," she said.

"It made Smoke and me wonder if he died of CO poisoning on purpose. That he couldn't deal with the guilt anymore."

"It does make you wonder."

"Unless we find something else to confirm that, we'll never know. The ME listed the manner as accidental," I said.

"That's better for the family than to list it as undetermined."

"For sure. They have enough on their plates, between the guilt they feel and buildings full of a million things to deal with. Shane and his wife plan to stay in Oak Lea for a while, getting things arranged. And his sister must have arrived by now."

"Good. Try not to focus on the Winstons on your days off. I know you can't help yourself sometimes, but you need to go into a semi-vacation mode for a few days," Mandy said.

"I know you're right. So how's Vince?"

"Better. He wise-cracked that he'll probably be feeling good about the time he has to go back to work, after his scheduled days off."

"If he's more like his wisenheimer self, then he's better all right." Although after his near-death experience two months before, it was likely he'd never be like his *old* wisenheimer self again. "Tell him hi and maybe I'll see him before we go back to work Tuesday," I said.

"Will do. Later then."

"Later."

I wouldn't have much time to obsess about the Winston case, given how Taylor's family trouble moved to front and center in my mind. I couldn't fill Mandy in about Taylor, and hoped whatever it was would be resolved soon, so no one outside the family would need to be the wiser. Plus it was up to Taylor to decide what she wanted to disclose, and to whom.

9

I phoned Mother next. "Oh, Corinne. I'm just about to leave for the shop. I called earlier to see how you're doing."

"I'm well, thanks. We had a tough case yesterday, and I'll tell you all I can about it soon. And no, I was not in any danger." *Because nothing had fallen on me, and I'd safely navigated my trips up and down a high ladder.*

"That part is good anyway. I'm fine too. Sorry to cut this short, but I have to run."

"Bye, Mom. Love you."

"Oh! I love you too. Bye, dear."

It surprised us both that I was the first one to say the L word. It dawned on me why I had. I planned to help Taylor without Mother's knowledge, and it stirred a measure of guilt in me. Taylor was not my mother's daughter. When our family learned the truth about Taylor's father, it filled Mother with a sadness that cut deep into her psyche.

Her husband Carl had fathered a baby before they married. A child even Carl hadn't known about. Mother and Gramps Brandt were not part of Taylor's biological family. If my father were still alive, my mother would be Taylor's stepmother, a totally bizarre scenario when I had figured the whole thing out.

Mother fought against her negative attitude, but harbored some jealousy nonetheless. Everyone else in the Aleckson family—Grandpa, Grandma, Taylor and her children, John Carl, and I—were blood relatives. All, except Mother.

I was not at liberty to tell her about Taylor and Silas, so if she learned about it at some point, she'd feel left out—again—that I hadn't confided in her. It wasn't logical, but dynamics within a family often weren't.

I let Queenie in when she barked her "let me in" woof. I filled her food and water dishes, made myself a second cup of coffee, and returned to my spot on the couch. I found George's number in my contacts and brought his image to mind. He was in his mid-fifties, average in height, weight, and looks, with thinning gray hair. The way his eyes twinkled when he smiled disarmed a lot of people.

I pressed the call button, and George answered after the first ring. "Sergeant Aleckson, to what do I owe the pleasure?" His voice was upbeat. Yes, he was a bit of a schmoozer.

I smiled. "Hi, George. Good to hear your voice, it's been a while. Have you got a few minutes to chat?"

"Sure do. What can I do you for?" One of his quirky phrases.

I gave him an overview of Taylor's situation, how Silas's behavior and habits had changed, and that she'd asked me to follow him. "We both know it involves a lot more than just tailing him to see where he goes," I added.

"How right you are. So let's say he's having an affair. The big reveal is usually a pretty straightforward deal. You see X meet Z somewhere, take photos, and figure out who Z is. It often gets messy after that. You know I only take those kinds of cases on the rare occasion."

"Yes I do. That's why I have something else for you to check into. Silas Franson is a financial advisor. There are a few possibilities to look at. He might be in trouble with one or more clients. Like maybe he made some bad investments, and he's trying to recoup funds before he gets caught."

"If that's the case, unless he stays within the law, that would not end well. I don't have to tell you I learned that the hard way. You can't rob Peter to pay Paul and get away with it forever."

"That's the way those of us in law enforcement and the justice world hope will happen. And it's even better when the offender turns his life around, like you did."

"Yeah." He sucked in a loud breath. "Back to Franson. Does he have his own company?"

"No, he works for Your Investors, located in New Ulm."

"All right."

When he didn't say more, I added, "If you can help with the case, I'll be the one who works with you, and then keep my sister in the loop."

"Well, you are in luck. I'm between gigs at the moment. If you could get me Franson's date of birth, home address, vehicle make, and license plate, along with a photo, I'll get started."

"Sure. I'll need to get his plate number and verify his DOB— the year he was born—and will send everything to you pronto."

"Good. We'll be in touch then."

"Thank you, George."

I stared at my phone a moment after the call ended and prayed the investigation would be swift, and things would turn out well for Taylor, Silas, and their family. That whatever Silas was hiding from her would come to light, and they could weather the storm. If there was one.

I phoned Taylor and disconnected when it went to voicemail. As a busy mother of three children, ages seven through twelve, she could be anywhere on Saturday morning. I headed to the kitchen for my usual cup of yogurt—blueberry was the day's choice—and pulled an overripe banana from the bunch.

When I was about to throw some out a while back, my mother told me to peel them, put them in storage containers, and freeze them. I tried it, and was surprised how good they tasted. They took on an ice cream-like texture. My mother mashes her frozen ones and puts them in breads and muffins. If I ever developed an interest in baking, I might do the same.

I leaned against a cupboard, and as I spooned yogurt into my mouth, thought about next steps in Silas's case. My work cell rang out from the counter top, and broke my reverie. I read Shane Winston's name on its face and couldn't ignore his call, off duty, or not.

I swallowed and cleared my throat. "Sergeant Aleckson."

"Oh Sergeant, it's Shane. Thanks for taking my call. I wasn't sure about your schedule."

"It's fine. Call any time, and leave a message if I don't answer."

"Thanks."

When he didn't go on, I softened my voice and asked, "How are you and your family doing?"

He made a humph sound. "Good question, Sergeant. Doctor Helsing, you know the medical examiner, called last night and gave us the report. My wife's here, and my sister came in kinda late last night too. We feel shell shocked; I guess that's the best way to describe it. Between Brett dying in all that clutter, and then come to find out he'd been shot at some point besides. Dear God, what could he have gotten himself involved with?"

"I can tell you we ran a criminal history check in Minnesota, along with the other forty-nine states, and nothing popped up. If your brother went to the emergency room with a gunshot wound, hospital staff would've been required to report it to the local law enforcement. At least here in Minnesota, and all but a few other states as well."

"That means Brett didn't get treated. If someone else shot him, why in the hell didn't he report it?" Shane posed the question we all wondered about.

"That might bring us back to the curious note he left about the crime he witnessed that he couldn't stop," I said.

"It's has been driving us crazy. It's like a riddle, and I don't get why Brett didn't just come out and say what crime he referred to. I look at it this way: if he had lived he could have destroyed the note and we'd be none the wiser. Unless he told us sometime down the road. But since he died, we haven't got a single clue what happened."

"It's possible you'll learn more when you go through his things. Detective Dawes and I scanned over papers in the piles, but we didn't do a thorough search. That will happen as the house gets emptied."

"I hope we find out a lot more about him and his dealings. It does make sense that the crime Brett mentioned and him getting shot were related. He said he tried to stop it, but couldn't. Maybe that's why. He got injured, shot. The other thing we talked about is that he could've shot himself in the left shoulder, since he's right-handed. But why? He never owned a gun, not that I ever knew about anyway," Shane said.

"It's a big mystery at this point."

"Yeah. The medical examiner told us they'll release Brett's body to Anderson's Funeral Home today, so we can make those arrangements. If we knew where Deena disappeared to, we could let her know what happened. As much as we know so far, that is."

"Like Detective Dawes said, the sheriff's office can help with that. We've got her name, date of birth, and possible phone number. We'll do a search on her whereabouts," I said.

"That'd be good, thanks. It's like she fell off the face of the planet."

"A surprising number of people manage to disappear, even in this day and age."

"You gotta wonder how. Anyway, I wanted you to know we hammered things out, and were able to contact a cleaning service. They'll meet us at the house on Tuesday morning," Shane said.

"I'm glad to hear they can get there that soon."

"Yeah. The rep I talked to asked if we wanted to sort through some things between now and then. I told him we can't even get into the house to do that. Without the right equipment we might get buried alive. He said they've dealt with similar situations, believe it or not."

"Shane, your family is not the only one to go through something like this, that is for sure," I said.

He cleared his throat. "Anyway, Mick, that's his name, told me we should be there to give them directions of where to put stuff. They'll have a dumpster, and a storage unit, on site by nine o'clock Tuesday morning. All I had to do was give him a down payment."

"Nice. That saves you having to rent those things, makes it easier on your family."

"Yeah. Anyway, we talked to our sons and Tricia's son and daughter. We've got to figure out when they can all get here for the memorial service. But that's another deal. Tricia and I will probably head out to the farm later today. But it's not like the old days when my parents were alive and we got together for holidays and birthdays. Back when it was a well-kept place," Shane said.

"The cleaning company will help you eliminate the clutter, and then you'll all feel better."

If only it had turned out to be that simple.

I was throwing a load of laundry in the washer when my phone rang. I wiggled it out of my pajama pocket. Taylor.

"Hey, Taylor."

"Hi, Corky. Sorry I missed your call."

"No worries. I wanted to let you know I talked to a friend of mine who's a private investigator, and we're in luck. He's free to help us look into what's going on. He used to be in the investment business when he lived in Winnebago County. Now he's in Mankato, closer to you than I am."

"Oh. Okay."

"His name is George, and he needs some info I'm not able to ethically access at the sheriff's office, since it's not official business," I said.

"Oh. Okay. What do you need?"

"Silas's full name, date of birth, his vehicle make, model, and color, and the license plate number."

"Sure," she said.

I jotted the information on the kitchen counter memo pad as Taylor provided it. Silas Aaron Hall born December 1, 1984. White Jeep Cherokee, 314 CTX.

"Corky, I managed to look at Silas's odometer in the middle of the night. I wrote it down, so I can see how far he drives today."

"Good. Taylor, what are Silas's usual habits on any given Saturday or Sunday?" I asked.

"He just gets up and leaves. Not like before when we might've planned a family event, and we always went to church together on Sunday. That's another thing, people have asked me where he is. So some Sundays I've dropped the kids off for

Sunday School, and skip church myself so I don't have to make excuses."

The old cover for your errant spouse routine. "What time does he normally leave in the morning? Weekdays or weekend days, I mean."

"Weekends, usually around seven or eight. Six thirty, sometimes as early as six is normal during the week now," Taylor said.

"So if I sat somewhere close to your house on Monday morning about six, I'd likely be there before he left."

"Corky, I don't want you to do that. You must have other things to take care of."

"I have today and tomorrow off. Plus I don't plan to spend the whole day following him. But I'll see where he goes, and that will give us an idea, at least a hint of what he may be involved in," I said.

"If you're sure. He might go straight to the office, and then somewhere else after that."

"True. I'll borrow Gramps Brandt's Buick. Unless they're into older cars, people don't seem to pay much attention to it. Plus, it's still dark out that early. With my stocking cap on, Silas won't recognize me."

"Okay."

"Depending on things, we can enlist George's help after that."

"Thank you *very* much," Taylor said.

After we disconnected, I texted George the information he had requested. He sent me a thumbs up emoji back.

Smoke and Rex came back early afternoon. I turned off the vacuum, glad for a break. Smoke gathered me in his arms. "The way you were attacking that rug, it looked like you're working off some stress."

I tightened my hold and snickered. "I didn't realize I was 'attacking' the rug. However, I was working through things that could be classified as stressful."

"Hah!" He took my hand and led me to the couch. "Sit down with me and unload some of that stress."

I sat down cross-legged to face him. "Okay, I was able to get a hold of George, and he's willing to help with the Silas situation. See what he can learn about Silas's financial business dealings. We'll figure out next steps."

"A good start."

"And Shane Winston called." I gave Smoke a synopsis of our conversation then added, "They are mystified—as we all are—how Brett suffered a gunshot wound, but didn't seek treatment," I said.

"Quite the deal all right."

"And he brought up a good point. If Brett thought he might die, why didn't he say who committed the crime he'd witnessed and who shot him? If he'd lived he could've discarded the note and revealed those details when he was ready."

"It's safe to say he wasn't thinking clearly with his brain deprived of oxygen," Smoke said,

"Yes. Now I best get back to attacking my rug."

His baritone laugh caused both Rex and Queenie to sit up at attention and made me laugh too. Just what the doctor ordered after the last couple days' worth of events.

Shane Winston called a while later. "Hi, Sergeant. Sorry to bother you again, but it looks like someone tried to break into the farmhouse. They broke a pane in the front door, and must've unlocked and opened it, but couldn't get very far as you well know."

Oh for heaven's sake. "All right. Are you out there now?" I asked.

"Yeah, Tricia's with me."

"Hang tight. I'll be there in less than ten, and I'll see if the on-duty sergeant can meet us there."

Smoke laid the book he was reading on the coffee table, and rose from the couch. "What?"

"Shane Winston. It seems we have a burglar on the loose that tried to access the Winston farmhouse. I'll call Communications, see if Leo Roth can meet us there," I said.

"Well you got me curious. How about I drive, and you make the call."

10

We pulled up to the Winston house seven minutes later. Shane and Tricia got out of his vehicle as we climbed from Smoke's. Shane looked from me to Smoke then back to me. "Detective. Sergeant, sorry. I didn't recognize you for a minute."

My blonde hair was free from its tight bun and hung to my shoulders. In my jeans and plaid jacket, or other civilian clothes, I'd been told I looked different, as did others who wore uniforms at work. I gave him a small smile. "Some people don't recognize me at all when I'm in regular clothes."

"And when it comes to bad guys, that's a good thing," Smoke said.

I caught Shane's sister's eyes. "You must be Tricia. So sorry about your brother."

She pursed her lips and blinked her greenish-gray eyes a couple times. We meandered to the house. The lower half of the door was solid, the upper half had four window panes. All had been intact the day before. The bottom right one above the doorknob was broken sometime after we'd cleared the scene.

Leo Roth pulled in, and when he joined us, I introduced him to Shane and Tricia. "This call was assigned to Sergeant Roth, so he'll be doing the report," I said.

Roth nodded in agreement. "Let's see what we've got here." The rest of us backed away to give him room. He pulled on vinyl gloves and took photos, then turned the knob, and pushed the door open.

"That stuff laying on the floor in the entry wasn't there yesterday. You can see how it got pulled from the pile on the living room side, off the entry," Shane said.

"That is strange," Roth said.

"Given the fact this house was vacant for a time, and occupied for a few years until Mister Winston died in there yesterday, it is very strange," Smoke said.

"Could someone have seen the medical examiner's van leave from here and decided to burglarize the place?" Shane asked.

"You gotta wonder," Smoke said.

"If whoever came here was looking for something specific, he didn't get very far," I said.

"No," Shane said.

Sergeant Roth's eyebrows lifted. "I'll check for latent prints, but collecting them in freezing temps is far from ideal. And chances are, whoever was here last had warm gloves on and left no prints." He peered into the entry. "Is the electricity on?"

"Yes," Shane said.

"Good. I carry a hairdryer in my trunk for conditions like this. I can warm the area on, and around, the doorknob.

Roth looked at Shane and Tricia. "As a deterrent, we'll nail some boards across the door, if that's okay with you. Not that anyone could enter anyway, given the conditions. But if they happened to return, it would send a message. Or in case someone else shows up."

"That's fine with us, right Tricia?" Shane said.

Tricia nodded in response. I had yet to hear her utter a word, and sensed she was overwhelmed by it all.

"A cleaning company will be here Tuesday, so our family will be around for a while, and we can check on things," Shane said.

"We'll also ask the area patrol cars to swing in from time to time to take a look too," Smoke added.

"Did you have a chance to look in the shed, see if anything is missing?" The second the words left my mouth, I knew it was a dumb question.

"We didn't, but how would we know?" Shane said.

I shook my head. "Sorry, I wasn't thinking."

"We can check for signs that someone has been rummaging around in there," Smoke said, and headed toward the shed.

Thanks for the save, Smoke. Shane, Tricia, and I followed him, while Roth opened his trunk for his latent fingerprint supplies.

"There used to be a padlock on the doors. I don't know why Brett took it off. Especially with all the stuff inside," Shane said.

Smoke pulled open one door, and Shane the other. Tricia took a look inside, and gasped. "Oh. My. Dear. God!" Despite her tone, Tricia had a pleasant middle-range voice. "How will we ever get this all sorted out?"

97

"According to Detective Dawes here, the clean up all boils down to taking it one step at a time," Shane said.

Tricia shook her head. "I think I could walk across the United States in less time."

I turned so she wouldn't see my grin at her comment.

"That's why we're getting a crew who knows how to do it," Shane said, and turned to me. "To answer your earlier question, I doubt anything's been taken. Unfortunately."

Smoke and Shane closed the shed doors, and we joined Sergeant Roth to check on his progress. "You need any assistance, Leo?" Smoke asked.

"I'm good, thanks. I searched with my flashlight and found some partial prints from three different people on the inside doorframe. They've been there a while, so they're not from whoever was here in the last twenty hours, or so. I warmed and dusted and lifted 'em, so we'll see if any are in the system." Roth finished his latent print collection task about ten minutes later when he attached the final adhesive sheet to a latent lift card.

Smoke and I helped him gather his supplies and secure them in his trunk. We were out of the Winstons' earshot when Roth said, "I wasn't on duty when you guys dealt with the situation here yesterday. A glimpse into the house that doesn't have a ground level entrance frankly scares the beejeebers out of me."

"I had pretty much the same feeling entering the second-floor bedroom through a window," I responded with a quiet voice.

"Yep," Smoke agreed.

After Roth took off, Smoke and I joined Shane and Tricia by his vehicle.

"Why would anyone try to get into the house, even break a window to do it?" Shane asked.

"Maybe he thought the house was abandoned. It must've been after dark when he got here. Could be he was looking for something to steal, or maybe needed a place to crash for the night. But didn't know the house was inaccessible until he got into the entry," Smoke said.

I had thoughts along the same line, yet it still came down to the question: how did the burglar know about the farmstead in the first place?

"Shane, you mentioned your brother didn't have a lot of social interactions, but it's possible in the last few years, a friend or two stopped by. Like the detective said, one could've needed a warm place to sleep," I said.

"Do any of those things seem possible to you?" Shane said.

Smoke lifted his hands. "You know the phrase, 'you can't make this stuff up?' We witness stuff you can't make up on a regular basis. Strange things that fit within that category. So yes, any of those things seem possible. But unless we learn the identity of who broke in—and catch that person—we have no way of knowing the reason."

"No." Shane looked at Tricia. "Is there anything else you want to check out here?"

Tricia shook her head. "Shane described the condition of the room our brother lived in for who knows how long. I couldn't go up that ladder and look myself. Now with the break-in, it's about all I can handle for a while."

"Yeah. We'll head back to the hotel and try to unwind," Shane said.

"That might require an adult beverage. Or two." Tricia turned to Smoke and me. "When Shane called me yesterday and told me what happened to Brett, I thought for a minute he was up to his old trickster ways.

"I mean, the house in this condition is the most unbelievable thing either one of us has ever seen. How could we not know how bad off Brett was and abandoned him like this?" Tears sprung from their ducts and rolled down her cheeks.

My heart went out to her and to Brett Winston's entire family.

By the time Smoke and I returned to my place, a little after four o'clock, the sun was low in the western sky, ready to set in within the hour. Fewer daylight hours was one reason investigations seemed more difficult in the winter. Frigid temperatures and frozen conditions added more challenges.

I started to remove my jacket when Smoke lifted his arm in a halt sign. "I just had a thought. How about we head to the Legion Club in Harold Lake for one of their famous burgers."

A date? "Great idea. It's casual so we won't even have to change." I scratched Queenie and Rex's heads, then Smoke let them out while I went to the bathroom to wash up and brush my hair.

When the dogs were back inside, we headed out. "Gosh, we haven't been to the Legion in forever," I said.

"Yep, and it's about time. My mouth is starting to water for a 'build your burger' already."

My stomach growled at the thought. "Smoke, we couldn't say much at Winstons' farm, but what in the world could the break-in possibly be about?"

"You got me on that one. Maybe someone did see the ME's van leave from there and, like most of us, thought it was an abandoned house and decided to check it out. Since the guy actually broke a window to gain entry, I'd propose that he was up to no good."

"Say the burglar knew Brett and didn't know he was dead. What if it was the person who shot Brett, somehow found out where he lived, and came back to finish the job?" I said.

"Whatever it was—I repeat—he was up to no good."

We nursed our thoughts and rode in companionable silence until we got to the Harold Lake Legion Club. The parking lot was nearly full. "So this is what people do on a cold Saturday afternoon in January. They head to a place where everyone knows their names," I quipped.

Smoke released a "hah!" "Let's head inside and see if anyone knows ours."

"That's not always a good thing. When I see people I've arrested, or had legal encounters with, I pretend I don't recognize them. Unless they say hello first."

"They're more likely to recognize me because I'm dressed in plain clothes for work, but you're in uniform. You might look familiar to someone, but they can't always place you. Like Shane didn't recognize you for a minute today," Smoke said.

"Good point."

"Of course you never look plain to me, no matter what."

I rolled my eyes. "Whatever."

We climbed from his SUV and headed to the club's wooden back door. It opened, and an older couple walked out. "Oh, Detective Dawes, long time no see. And that's a good thing. No offense," a wrinkled-face man said with a grin.

Smoke patted his shoulder and smiled. "No offense taken, Jim." He held the door open for Jim and company.

"I will say if this pretty one is with you, you are one lucky son of a gun," the older man said.

All I did was smile, relieved he didn't make a crack about my age. Yes, Smoke was older, and most people thought I looked years younger than I was.

"Don't I know it. Take care, you two," Smoke said, and held the door open for me.

We stepped inside, and it took a moment for my eyes to adjust to the light. Lighter than the dusk outside, that is. Most chairs around tables, bench seats at booths, and all the bar stools, were occupied.

As we headed toward an empty booth I heard, "Corky! Smoke!" My friend Sara stood and waved from halfway across the room. People greeted Smoke and me as we made our way to Sara and John Carl's table.

Sara gave us each a hug, and John Carl nodded with a half-smile. With her outgoing personality, Sara was good for my serious brother. I rested my temple against John Carl's head and reached my arm around his shoulder in a half hug for a moment.

"What a sweet surprise! We never see you guys. I should've mentioned we planned to come here for an early supper. Will you join us?" Sara asked.

Harold Lake was not in Sara's probation agent area, so she was less likely to see any of her past or current clients, and felt fairly anonymous there.

Smoke and I slipped off our jackets, hung them on the backs of the black vinyl padded metal chairs, and sat down.

"It was a spur of the moment decision," I said.

"I had a hankering for one of their burgers, and here we are, twenty minutes later," Smoke said.

"We just ordered so we'll ask them to hold it. Then we can eat together," Sara said.

A middle-aged server with jet-black hair zipped over from another table, pulled menus she had secured between her arm and her side, and laid them in front of Smoke and me. "Evening, folks. Can I start you off with a drink?"

"You still have Castle Danger on tap?" Smoke asked.

She nodded. "Sure do. Short or tall?"

"Corky?" Smoke said.

"I'll take a short one."

"And I'll go for a tall," Smoke said.

"Can you hold our food order, and include it with theirs?" Sara asked.

The server patted the notepad in her apron. "No problem. I haven't put it in yet. I'll be right back with your drinks." She dashed off.

Sara touched my hand. "Gosh, it's been a while since we've hung out. The schedules you two have are hard to plan around sometimes."

"Tell me about it. At least I got some boring household chores out of the way today. Then we had an unexpected call from a friend to check on," I said.

John Carl's eyebrows drew together. "Everything okay?"

"It will be. Nothing to worry about," I told him.

Sara gave John Carl a light tap on his nose with her pointer. "He can't help it. He is your mother's son, when it comes to that particular trait anyway."

Yes, both were devout worriers. But John Carl was more contemplative, and a deeper thinker, than our mother. I tried to keep the most fearsome things at work quiet from them, but that wasn't always possible.

The server returned with our drinks and jotted down our burger order. My toppings: Swiss cheese, avocados, pickles, and mustard. Smoke's: bacon, Swiss cheese, onion rings, tomatoes, pickles, and mayo. Then the server was off to the next table.

Sara raised her glass of red wine. "To friends and lovers."

John Carl's face flushed a bit as he lifted his amber ale. I crossed my eyes at him to coax a smile and got a small one in return. We all clinked our glasses and took sips.

Sometimes I felt a little sorry for John Carl, that he was my big brother. He was less than a year older, yet felt a measure of obligation to protect me. I had given him a run for his money when we were kids. I was bold and curious and daring, too many times. Looking back, I figured I'd survived many narrow escapes in childhood, thanks to a host of guardian angels.

That continued, and multiplied, throughout my years in law enforcement. It seemed my mother and brother—given their avoid risks-at-all-cost personalities and lifestyles—would not need as much divine intervention as I did. That said, bad things happened to everyone, blameless or not.

Over the course of my career, I'd witnessed innocent people get victimized too many times. It was the main reason I continued to serve, what helped me press on, in the times I wondered how it was possible. Victims and their families deserved assurance, resolve, and closure. We did everything we could to catch bad guys and let justice prevail.

11

John Carl's voice interrupted my mental wandering. "Corky, you have that look."

"What look?" I tried to play dumb, but I knew what.

"You know, when you check out, when your mind goes somewhere else," he said.

"Just thinking about guardian angels."

That drew curious looks from all three, and I shrugged in response.

Sara lifted her hand. "Forgot to tell you. The radio station must've talked to the sheriff about the hoarder's death. Corky, you told me a little about it yesterday. Anyway, we heard a brief report over the radio on the way over. They didn't give many details, just that a middle-aged man was found dead from an unknown cause in his upstairs bedroom. And that Oak Lea Fire helped the medical examiner recover his body."

I looked at Smoke. "A citizen likely heard something on their police band that triggered the sheriff's report. I'm surprised he didn't let us know before it aired."

He flicked a drip from his lip. "Yeah, he'd normally send out a message, at least to those involved. But our deal wasn't the only thing that happened in the county yesterday."

"True, but we can agree it was the most unusual," I said.

"Can you tell us more about it? Sara told me what you told her," John Carl said.

"If we keep our voices down, we can give you the highlights without naming names."

John Carl's mouth dropped open when I told him about the ladder, the only access to the upstairs room where the victim lay, how I had climbed it several times, and entered the room through a window. "It was quite the process getting the victim out via the fire truck's utility bucket."

"Even when you're not in danger, you get into the weirdest situations. After all these years, I still can't understand how you can do what you do," John Carl said.

"We all have different callings, dear brother."

"I'm the outlier here. You three brave people work with criminals, and I'm content developing software," he said.

Our burgers arrived, and the only sounds uttered for some minutes were murmurs of gratitude. The Harold Lake Legion was famous for their angus beef burgers for good reason.

After we'd cleaned our plates, Sara asked Smoke and me, "Do you want to join us for a game of Trivial Pursuit?" She pointed at Smoke. "Even though you always win."

Smoke laughed. "Not always."

The truth was, I think he let us win from time to time, so we didn't feel defeated. Because he knew answers to even the most random questions. I smiled at the thought. "Thanks for the offer, but vegging on the couch feels like about all I can manage for the rest of the evening," I said.

Sara waved her hand. "Totally get that, and no worries."

Smoke and I plunked down on the couch like it was our dream destination. Queenie and Rex settled on the rug beside it. I groaned as I stretched out my legs on the coffee table. Smoke rubbed my thigh. "You sound like you're in pain."

"Maybe a little sore from all my trips up and down that ladder yesterday. I used different muscles."

"And you're so fit with all the miles of running you log," he said.

"With the weather we've had, I haven't gone on a decent run in a while. I wish I didn't get so bored running on the treadmill in our work gym."

"As you well know, I don't care for running. Period. Road or treadmill."

I patted his abdominal muscles. "Your workouts keep you in great shape anyway."

"Racquetball is active fun, sit-ups not so much, but they work the abs."

I chuckled. The sheriff's office scheduled combat refreshers every few months, and continual training kept us in shape.

"My mind keeps going back to the attempted burglary at Winstons' place. My gut tells me it wasn't coincidental, " Smoke said.

"My gut agrees with yours. But what my mind questions is: have there been other break-in attempts in the past, minus a broken window, or a jimmied door lock? The place appears abandoned, as we've all noted."

"We have caught teens checking out abandoned properties, looking for a place to party, not thinking they belonged to someone."

"And we've had squatters too. With the Winston property, people wouldn't even need to break into the house. They could open the unlocked shed door, and have their choice of a vehicle to make a bed in," I said.

"Yep. Scary as that building would be to enter and explore, it'd provide shelter, and probably does to a variety of critters."

That thought made what felt like creepy crawlers climb up my spine. "When the team goes in, they'll need hazmat gear and n95 masks on. At least."

Smoke took my hand in his. "The Brett Winston case had a curious little twist to it today. Makes me wonder; if something is inside that the wanna be burglar wants, will he make a second attempt to get it once some of the debris is removed?"

"It'll be easier to explore, that's for sure."

As it turned out, what the cleaning crew discovered inside the house was a first for them—or any before them—in the history of Winnebago County.

Sunday morning, I stepped into the church sanctuary, and spotted my mother alone in a pew. When I slipped in beside her, and gave her a hug, she smiled and grasped my hand. Her almost-fiancé David divided his time between Oak Lea and Texas, the home of his business. He planned to settle in Oak Lea permanently—his birthplace, and where his father still lived—when he had all his ducks in a row.

I prayed for Taylor, and that we'd uncover what Silas was involved with. Also, my for family members, friends, and the Winstons. That reminded me to ask Shane for a photo of Brett when he was younger and healthier to help counteract the sad image I carried of how he looked after death.

Pastor Hobart's message lifted my spirits. I felt stronger and better prepared to face the week ahead, whatever it held. When the service ended, Mother leaned over, "Corinne, I'm bringing lunch to Gramps' at noon. Barbecue ribs. Why don't you join us? And Elton too, if he can."

Ribs, yes. "That sounds great. Smoke is meeting his brothers in Maple Grove this afternoon, but I'd love to. Can I pick up anything for you?"

"Nope, we're all set."

I had over an hour to spare, and checked emails and text messages. I'd missed one from Taylor, sent about the time I'd sent up a prayer for her. *Silas left at 7:15 this morning.* On Sunday morning? I thought for a moment then wrote, *I'll be there early tomorrow - incognito - to check things out.* Her response was immediate. *Thank you!* I sent a smiling face back.

Silas had left home at 7:15 on a Sunday morning, to go where? I'd check with Gramps, see if I could borrow his old Buick for my clandestine operation. He hadn't driven for some time but kept it for me to use when the need arose. My red GTO was not a good undercover vehicle. I paid Gramps' car insurance, despite his protests.

"Queenie, time to go visit Gramps and Mother."

She yipped and wagged her tail. Gramps loved it when I brought her for a visit, and I believed Queenie loved it even more. I pulled in Gramps' driveway and noted Mother had yet to arrive. We'd installed a keyless entry system on Gramps' front door, mostly to ensure his door was locked when he was home alone.

I punched in the code and held on to Queenie's collar as I opened the door. "Hi, Gramps," I called a few decibels above the television's loud volume. I brushed snow from Queenie's feet and slipped off my ankle boots. Queenie bolted over to Gramps' recliner chair but knew better than to jump up on him. He lowered the chair's footrest, and Queenie laid her head on his lap, while her tail wagged to beat the band.

Gramps put his gnarled fingers on either side of Queenie's face. "Hello, you good girl, you. I missed you." It had been a few days since we'd paid him a visit.

I leaned over and gave Gramps a kiss on the cheek. "You been behaving yourself?"

He rubbed my arm and chuckled. "That's a good one, Corky. All I can do anymore is behave myself. Your mother called and said you were in church this morning, so I'd say you're behaving yourself too."

"Pretty much." I sat on the chair next to his. "Gramps, you farmed. Did you happen to know the Winston family that lived over on Davidson Avenue? You seemed to know all the area farmers back then."

"I recall the name, mostly from the animals they brought to the County Fair, but that's been decades ago. Why do you ask?"

"It's a case I'm working on. Just curious."

"Well, I can tell you I never heard anything bad about them, if that's what you're asking," he said.

I heard a car door shut outside and left to help my mother carry in the dishes. She was bent over her SUV's open tailgate. "Corinne, you can grab the gray carrier."

It had three layers to hold 9 X 13-inch pans and seemed to weigh a good ten pounds. Mother also had a soft-sided cooler with drinks and a dessert. We carried the holders into the kitchen. I helped her remove the barbecue ribs, Swiss cheese hash browns, and minted carrots from the carrier, plus salad and fizzy waters from the cooler. We set everything on the table.

"Help Gramps, and I'll get out the plates and flatware," she said.

It took a few minutes to navigate Gramps into the kitchen with Queenie close behind. The more he sat, the more he lost his ability to walk. He often said, "My legs are all played out." I believed after decades of long workdays in the farm, as he approached ninety, he was content to spend days in his chair.

We dished up our plates, gave thanks, and dug in. "We had an unusual case Friday," I said.

Mother's eyebrows lifted halfway to her hairline and Gramps' eyebrows drew together. "What was it? Do tell," he said.

I gave them a few highlights without mentioning personal details, like the note, or the later break-in. "Sad thing is, Mister Winston didn't have good ventilation and died from carbon monoxide poisoning."

"A very sad thing indeed. I've always been afraid of kerosene heaters," said my cautious mother, with good reason that time.

After the delectable dinner, Mother packed up leftovers for me to take home. I thanked her for the food and Gramps for his car. Neither asked me why I needed to borrow it. My answers had been non-committal in the past, so they no longer bothered. "Okay, Girl, time to go home," I beckoned Queenie.

"My girl hasn't stayed over for a while. She can keep me company when you go on your little adventure." Gramps winked at me. He kept a bed, food, and treats on hand for her.

"That's a great idea. We all know how much she loves staying here with you." I bent over and gave Queenie a hug. "Be your sweet self, and I'll see you tomorrow."

I had Gramps' garage door opener in hand, pushed the button, and pulled my GTO inside. The old Buick started without hesitation. I drove it home and parked it in my garage, set for the early morning trek.

Smoke and Rex returned at dusk. I was on the couch deep into research on hoarding disorder. "In here," I called out.

Rex ran around looking for Queenie, while Smoke squeezed my shoulders. "I can only guess why your gramps' Buick is in the garage. And your dog isn't home."

I reached up and laid my hands on his. "Gramps wanted Queenie to stay over, and I'm heading to New Ulm in the morning to check on Silas."

He came around the couch and narrowed his eyes. "Say what?"

"Silas has been leaving the house early, even on weekends. He left at seven something this morning."

"You're going to get up at four in the morning to do that?"

I lifted my hands. "It's not ideal, but we've been on duty every one of the twenty-four hours many times in our careers. I'll take a nap when I get home. Would it be simpler if Taylor had someone local to do that? Yes. But she asked for my help because she trusts me. You'd do the same for one of your brothers."

"That's a given, all right. How about I come with you? Surveillance can be about the most tedious detail there is, so I can both assist and keep you company. I'll ask for a PTO day." Personal time off.

"If you want to. You must have about a gazillion hours in your bank," I said.

"Not quite, but a lot. You planned to take your gramps' vehicle, but given it's a two-wheel drive, and with the threat of snow overnight, we should take my SUV."

"Sounds like the safer option." I gave him a peck on the cheek. "So how're your brothers doing?"

"You know, busy with their families and jobs. Nothing of import or gossipy tidbits to share."

I snapped my fingers. "Darn. No, I'm glad to hear that. With Taylor's deal, we don't need any more drama in either family."

"No."

"I have something you'll enjoy for supper: Mother sent rib dinner leftovers home with me."

"Hallelujah!"

12

Smoke and I were on the road at 4:20 a.m. Monday morning, armed with steaming containers of strong black coffee. He wore a stocking cap that covered his salt and pepper hair—still more dark brown pepper than salt—and donned a long gray beard over his clean-shaven face. I found a reddish-brown shoulder-length wig, and large framed non-corrective eye glasses in my assortment of disguises.

"If the snow holds off, we should be at Taylor's house before six, no problem." I said.

"Yep. Corinne, I never got around to asking what new facts you might have uncovered—no pun intended—on hoarding disorder."

"I'm not awake enough to recognize a pun this early. Okay, well some things I didn't know much about are the biological, the genetic aspects, when it begins in childhood. Studies show there's a region on chromosome fourteen that's linked to compulsive hoarding. In families with OCD, it's likely more than one child will be a hoarder. They can't teach children not to hoard."

"I didn't know that either."

"They've also linked Alzheimer's, and other disorders, to that chromosome," I said.

"Hmm, is there a way to get our chromosomes tested?"

"For Alzheimer's? I'm not sure, but there is what's called a karyotype test for blood or body fluids to check for abnormalities, disorders, and diseases."

"Medical knowledge continues to advance by leaps and bounds," he said.

"And it's leaps and bounds above my comprehension."

"No doubt. So our plan is put a tail on Silas and see where he goes. A shame Silas doesn't take his personal cell when he leaves home. It'd be way easier if Taylor could track him with the push of a button. I'm sure he knows that, and hence, why he leaves it at home."

"Yes, and think of the time we'd save. Taylor could tell us Silas is at XYZ, and we'd head there to see what he was up to," I said.

The miles passed as I sipped coffee, keeping my eyes on the road's white lines and what little I could see off road in the dark. The more rural parts of the state, between cities, had few overhead lights to help guide drivers along the way.

We arrived in New Ulm at 5:56. Smoke parked a block and a half from the Franson's house at 5:58. He shut off the lights but kept the car running. Perfect timing: at 6:03 the garage door lifted, and a silver SUV backed out and drove west on Jefferson Street. We both straightened in our seats.

"Show time." Smoke waited ten beats, shifted into gear, but kept the lights off as he started the tail. When Silas turned north on Tenth Street, I said. "Looks like he's headed to the office. At least in that direction."

"We'll see. Maybe a quick stop for coffee along the way?"

"Speaking of which, it's a good thing we've both got big holding tanks after the large mugs of joe."

"Depending on where he lands, if need be, you can be first to drive to a gas station while I keep watch, and vice versa."

"All righty."

As it turned out, Silas went straight to his office, a convenient block from a gas station. It simplified things when the time came. Smoke drove past it and turned onto the next street. One lone car sat on the south side that faced the building. Smoke did a U-turn and parked behind it. With a good view of both Silas's vehicle, and the back door he'd entered, we'd be able to see if he took his own vehicle or someone else's when he left.

Smoke had down comforters in the back seat. He let the vehicle run for ten minutes, and when he turned it off for ten, we covered our laps to keep warm.

After an hour without a Silas sighting, I told Smoke, "I might as well head to the gas station for my bathroom break."

"Sure."

I climbed out and was at the gas station and back in under six minutes. "Your turn."

"I'll be good for a while. However, if Silas stays at work all day, this is going to be a long one," he said.

We checked our phones for messages and emails.

"Yeah, warm up, cool down, repeat. Why don't you try to get a cat nap? I feel too keyed up to sleep myself," I said.

"I'll give it a shot, and if the hours drag on, boredom will lull you to sleep later."

Smoke moved his seat to a half-reclining position and closed his eyes. At 7:33 Silas exited the building, so I gave Smoke a quick shove. "He's on the move."

Smoke blinked and opened his eyes. He had his seat back in an upright position, the vehicle started, and shifted into gear seconds later. He did a quick face scrub and glanced at his clock. "I can't believe I crashed that hard."

"For a whole seventeen solid minutes. I was afraid you might start drooling on that old man beard you're wearing."

He tapped the steering wheel. "Hah! Sometimes, little lady." I grinned at his grimace.

Silas drove out of the parking lot. We followed him with two vehicles between us. His first stop was a bank's ATM machine. Then he left New Ulm city limits and headed northwest on Highway 68. "Where in the heck is he headed?" I asked.

"Maybe to meet with a client or an investor."

Silas drove the speed limit, and vehicles passed us, then him, on the way. Forty minutes later, Silas pulled into the Jackpot Junction Casino parking lot in Morton. "ATM for some cash, and then off to the casino on a workday morning," Smoke observed.

"To give him the benefit of the doubt, maybe someone connected to the casino is an investor," I said.

"There are cameras all over the place inside, so to look less suspicious, how about I go in alone first to see what he's up to?"

"All right."

Smoke sent me a message with a photo some minutes later. Silas was at a blackjack table next to a female dealer, who had leaned over and given him a kiss on the cheek. *They look mighty friendly. I'll keep them in view.*

My heart beat a little faster. Silas had a small smile on his face yet appeared on the haggard side, older than his thirty-eight years. His sideburns had grayed and his crows' feet had deepened since I'd last seen him a few months before. The friendly female kisser was around his age and looked somewhat familiar, but I couldn't place her. I had never been to Jackpot Junction, so that wasn't it.

I texted Smoke. *I'm coming in.* He sent me a thumbs up back. *Take a left when you're inside.*

The casino was mammoth, filled with patrons and machines and blinking lights in the otherwise darkened space. Some people appeared mesmerized as they pulled slot arms at hundreds of one-arm-bandits. Others shook their heads before they added money for another round. I turned left toward the blackjack table area.

My eyes were drawn to Smoke near a blackjack table. He spotted me, turned his head, and gave me an eye blink signal in Silas's direction. I walked past Smoke but didn't acknowledge him and stopped four tables away from Silas's, where I could glance at him from time to time.

I pulled out my phone and pretended to talk into it as I zoomed it to the max, then turned as I mouthed some words, and snapped a photo of Silas and the dealer. They appeared to be on good terms. I walked to another table and tried to get a read on them—if they were involved or not—but Silas was more interested in the game than the girl.

I sent Smoke a message, *This might be an all day deal with the dealer* 😊.

He wrote back, *At least we can watch other people besides Silas.*

Smoke and I moved to separate areas and took turns checking on Silas, who hung out at the same blackjack table. I wondered if he was money ahead or behind as time passed by. The dealer gave him a discreet nudge here and there, but to his credit, Silas didn't respond with any physical contact in return. Was that because he wasn't interested, or because if someone he knew happened to see him, he didn't want anyone to see them interacting and suspect something?

No one seemed to pay attention to either Smoke or me. I didn't have cash, nor did I want to use a credit card at any machine in the casino, so I moved around and acted like I was checking out the different slot machines. To quell my boredom, I watched people and wondered about their life stories and why they were at a casino on a cold Monday morning in January. Maybe it gave some a warm place to be, with something to do.

My cell vibrated. Shane Winston. It was noisy inside, so I selected the *I can't talk right now, can I call you later?* button on my phone. His reply was immediate. *No need, just wanted to tell you the cleaning company plans to get an earlier start tomorrow. 8 instead of 9.* I sent a thumbs up back.

I wandered over near Smoke and relayed Shane's message. He nodded and walked to a table a few over from Silas's. As if by magic, Silas slapped his deck on the table, lifted his hand in a wave to the dealer, picked his jacket from the back of a chair, and headed toward the exit. He slipped into the jacket and went out the door. It seemed he had gambled all his money away.

Smoke indicated with a head nod I should leave first. We had parked closer to the entrance than Silas did. Silas walked past Smoke's vehicle and didn't look back. I heard Smoke's vehicle locks release and climbed inside. Smoke joined me in a flash, started the engine, shifted into gear, pulled away from the parking spot, and waited until Silas left the lot, ready to follow him.

"Where to now, pray tell?" Smoke asked as we headed southeast on Highway 68.

"It seems it's back to New Ulm, unless he detours along the way. The dealer acted like she has a crush on Silas."

"Either she likes him or his money that he appeared to lose. But from what I could tell, he wasn't interested in her, romantically speaking."

"I agree."

We followed Silas to his office, and he arrived just after noon. The trip to the casino was not a fluke, given the dealer seemed to know him well. I phoned Taylor. "Corky, hi."

"Hey, Taylor. I wanted to fill you in on a couple things. Silas was at his office bright and early, then left at seven thirty-three, stopped at an ATM machine, and drove to Jackpot Junction—"

She cut me off. "The *casino?* Why? He doesn't gamble. Was he meeting someone?"

"It seems he does like to play blackjack after all. He was at a table for over three hours."

"I don't get it. He's been acting strange, leaving early and staying out late, because he's sneaking off to gamble?"

"Taylor, all I can say is we observed him playing blackjack. The dealer seemed to know him well, so he's been there before. He didn't eat, drink, or use the restroom the whole time he was there. Then he returned to his office, and that's where he is now. I wanted to touch base, let you know before I send a photo of him your way."

"Corky, I feel gut-punched about this. Back in his college days, Silas liked to go to casinos. But he told me he gave it up because he hated when he lost. That was before we were married, before we had kids."

"It is curious why he'd start up again so many years later. Was gambling a problem for him back then?" I asked.

"Not that I know of. We never really talked about it. Just that he had gambled, but quit. It didn't seem to cause him any real financial trouble."

"Regarding the female dealer, she gave Silas a kiss on the cheek, but he didn't act like he had any romantic interest in her, at all. He didn't touch her, or look at her in a special way. But he must like her as a dealer because he stayed at her table the whole time."

Taylor sucked in a loud breath. "Is she cute?"

"What?"

"The dealer, is she cute?"

A tough question. "She's a dishwater blonde, attractive, but has a rough-around-the-edges look. Whether it's from a hard life or smoking or drinking or stressors, one can only guess."

"So she seems to like Silas, but he doesn't seem too interested in her?" Taylor said.

"That was both Smoke's and my take."

"What should I do? I don't want to lose him, but we can't go on like this."

"We'll do what we can to help you get to the bottom of things. So you haven't noticed any financial problems? Like overdue household or insurance bills?"

"No, and Silas takes care of them all anyway. They go to his office. Most are paid online, or automatically withdrawn from his account," Taylor said.

"The ones you don't have access to?"

Taylor sniffed. "I'm starting to feel so stupid, so naïve. He's always been a wonderful provider and told me I had enough to take care of, with the house and keeping up with our kids, and all their activities. I budget our living expenses, but he's the financial guy, and I like having him take care of the rest of the expenses."

"Taylor, would you like me to send the pic?" I said.

"Yes and no. Go ahead and send it, please."

After she received it, I got a crying face emoji in return.

Smoke and I kept watch until 5:00 p.m., and Silas had not left the office. We discussed possibilities, what Silas was up to. "What do you think, Smoke?"

"I think whatever your friend George uncovers will give us that answer. Two possibilities. Either he got into a financial bind, tried to get out of it by misusing clients' funds, and got the not so bright idea he could win it back at the blackjack table. Or he got the gambling bug, and when he lost more than he could handle, he dipped into clients' accounts, and is under the false belief he will win it back to replace the money."

"A Ponzi scheme. Which came first, the chicken or the egg? Greed or gambling?"

"Yep. Well Corinne, I think we've done our due diligence for today. We discovered a piece of the puzzle anyway, and Taylor can decide what she wants to do from here."

I sent Taylor a message. *"We need to head home. Silas is still at work. My friend is looking into things, and if you want another tail on S, let me know and I'll find someone.*

It took a few minutes for her to respond. *Thank you. A lot to digest. I'll let you know. Not ready to confront him until I think about it some more.*

Understood, I replied.

13

I woke up at 6:03 Tuesday morning, and it took me some seconds to remember Smoke and Rex had spent the night at his house. I thought of the Winston family and felt a strange sense of both hope and dread. They had a house and shed full of stuff they'd have to deal with, and decisions to make over the next days and weeks. Maybe months. The professional hoarder house cleaners would be on site with a dumpster and portable storage unit at 8:00 a.m.

I rolled out of bed, scratched Queenie's back, and headed downstairs for coffee and yogurt. My shift started at 7:00, and I planned to stop by the Winston property between calls, when it worked out. I'd been in other hoarder houses before and after they'd been cleaned. Still, I felt a particular draw to the Winstons'. It was more than my natural—maybe a little morbid at times—curiosity. Victims, whether due to accidents or crimes against them, held special places in my heart.

Brett Winston had died under preventable circumstances, had his family recognized his decline and living conditions. No question they cared about him and would carry a measure of guilt the rest of their lives, like many others who'd witnessed a loved one go down a bad path and had tried to intervene, sometimes over and over. When their efforts fell short, when the one they tried to help didn't want help, they felt responsible, nonetheless.

In Brett's case, his wife had made a misguided effort she thought would help him. After it failed, she'd given up on him and taken off for parts yet unknown. His friends may have tried to do something else, but in his grief it seemed Brett focused more on hoarding than on personal relationships. Had Brett been my brother, even though he wouldn't let me in the house, I would have sought professional help, staged an intervention. Brett's junk-filled house and kerosene heater in the bedroom where he lived were a health hazard, and proved to be fatal in the end.

No question Brett was desperate when he called his brother to deliver needed supplies. I wondered if he had a deep-down hope that when Shane saw his living condition, his family would step in and rescue him, get him help. It did no good to obsess over what might have been, what could have been had Brett Winston received treatment. I rubbed my temples to help shift my thoughts.

I arrived at the office an hour later and sat down at the computer in the squad room to review reports from the past three days. Not one had the same magnitude as the Winston case. Vince Weber joined me a while later. "Sergeant Corky, hey."

"Hey yourself, glad you're better."

"Yeah well, they say every day you can get up and take nourishment is a good one. I get that now that I finally licked that cold," he said.

"For sure."

He sat down at the next computer. "Heard you had a bad case, huh? Poor guy trapped in a room and died there. Who'd a thunk anyone even lived in that place?"

"None of us. Tragic, for sure. We've seen hoarder houses before, but none like this one. The Winston family hired a cleaning crew. They're going to start the junk removal process this morning, and I plan to swing out there when I can."

"Huh. Well hey, let me know when you're heading that way. I'd like to take a look see myself, if I'm not tied up."

"Will do."

Smoke poked his head in the doorway. "Morning, Corinne, Vincent. Glad to see you're back among the living."

Vince blew out a breath. "Yeah well, it's not the first time. And nothin' compared to the last time." His near-death experience we'd never forget.

Smoke lifted his hand. "Sorry."

"Don't be. Best thing that could've happened to me."

"I can't begin to imagine," Smoke said.

"Me neither, before I died. And someday, something like that will happen to you—to all of us. I got a pretty awesome preview."

We were silent a moment before Smoke nodded. "I guess. Change of subject. To let you know, I've tried to get a lead on Deena Winston's whereabouts. Seems she's done a good job of disappearing. I got her phone number from Shane Winston, but like he said, she must've gotten a new phone and number. Shane also gave me names of her brother and two of her friends. She and her brother have been estranged for years, and I haven't been able to track him down either.

"I located the friends and left messages. One got back to me, said Deena had told her she was in love with a guy but wouldn't say who it was. They planned to get married; start a new life. That was last August. Deena said she'd be in touch, but the friend hasn't heard from her since," Smoke said.

"Sounds like Deena was serious about starting a new life. One that didn't even include her friends or her former in-laws," I said.

"I'll get a hold of motor vehicle registration in Minnesota and ask staff to contact departments and registered drivers in the other forty-nine states. It might take a few days, but we should get a hit, find her somewhere."

"Winnebago County, Seven fourteen?" It was Communications.

Vince pressed his radio button. "Go ahead, County."

"We have report of an erratic driver in a red Nissan headed east on County Thirty-four, by Target."

He jumped up. " Ten-four, en route from the station."

"Copy."

"Doubt if I'll catch up to him, but glad I left my car running." Weber hustled off.

"What would we have done without him?" I said.

"Good thing we didn't have to find out," Smoke replied.

"Yeah."

I finished with the reports, and with no calls pending, I went on patrol and monitored traffic behaviors until I got called to a dispute between some boys at the Emerald Lake High School parking lot, reported by a fellow student. When I pulled in five minutes later, I spotted two teen boys a few feet apart, with a girl between them.

They all looked at me when I climbed from my squad car. "Hi, I'm Sergeant Aleckson. Everything okay here?"

One boy looked down, and the other one shrugged. The girl said, "They're fighting over me. I'm friends with both of them, and don't want to go to the dance with either one. Not as a date."

When neither boy responded, I said, "A verbal disagreement? No punches?"

Both boys reacted with almost identical looks of surprise: their mouths and eyes opened wide, and they shook their heads.

"All right. I know it's about time for school to start, and we don't want you to be late." I pulled a memo book and pencil from my pocket. "Since I got an official call here, I'll need your names and birthdates."

I jotted down the information as they gave it to me. "Okay, if you each agree to let this go, I'll tell Communications that no report is needed. I need you each to say, 'I agree' out loud."

They all did. "Thank you." I said, and pressed my radio button. "Six o eight, Winnebago County."

"Go ahead, Sergeant."

"No report needed on the school call. I'll be here for a bit on another matter."

"Ten-four, at eight-fifteen."

The school bell rang as I turned to the teens. "Sounds like you got five minutes to get to class. I need to check on something in the office, so you can escort me in."

The hallways were filled with students and staff, and everyone's eyes appeared to fall on me. *Why was a deputy sheriff in our school?* was audible in the whispered murmurs. I smiled and greeted the masses on my way to the administration office.

The older administrative assistant smiled a little when I stepped up to the counter.

"Good morning. I'm Sergeant Aleckson."

"Morning, Sergeant. How can I help you?"

"I'm working on a case, and the victim was a student here. Should've graduated twenty-six years ago. I wondered if you have yearbooks from back then?"

"Oh. Well, sure. I'll be happy to get them for you. It'll take me a few minutes," she said.

"Thank you."

She headed through a door, returned with three yearbooks, and laid them on the counter. "I hope you find the person you're looking for."

"Is it okay if I go through the books here?" I asked.

"Of course. Take your time."

I opened the first one and found Brett Winston in the sophomore class. He had a lean face and longer hair, but not as long as at his death. I snapped a pic, then found his junior year photo in the next book and took a shot of that. In his senior yearbook, I paged through pictures of activities and events, then went to his class photos. I studied his face a minute.

Brett had always been on the sensitive side, according to Shane. His greenish gray eyes had a sparkle in them, and his smile was natural, not too wide, not too narrow. I checked the student directory in back to see what sports or activities he'd been in: choir and track. A singer and runner. I took a photo of his senior picture, closed the book, and put it on top of the others.

"All done, thank you," I told the assistant who'd moved to her desk.

"You found what you needed?" she asked.

"Yes. Thanks again."

Back in my squad car, I pulled out my phone, and saw Shane Winston had sent me a message, *The crew is here and hard at work.*

I wrote back, *Good to hear. I'll be by in a bit.*

I looked at Brett's photos in my phone again. At age eighteen, like all of us, he had no idea what paths his life journey would take him on, the joys he'd experience, or the physical and emotional pain he'd suffer.

I set my phone in the center console and pressed the sheriff's radio button. "Six o eight, Winnebago County."

"Go ahead, Six o eight."

"I'm clear from Emerald Lake High School."

"You're clear at eight twenty-nine."

With no calls pending, I headed to the Winston farmstead. The boards nailed across the front door were gone. The cleaning crew was on site and had started to remove some clutter. I spotted Shane's SUV, with a utility trailer connected to it, on the north side of the house. The portable storage unit and a dumpster sat between the house and the shed. I phoned Communications with my location, climbed from my car, and met Shane near the storage unit.

"Morning, Sergeant. Well, here we are." He lifted his arms.

I nodded. "Yep. Looks like they've removed a fair number of items already."

"Given the scope, it's one needle in the haystack of needles, but each one they remove is one less inside," he said.

"No Tricia?"

Shane shook his head. "She'll be out later. She sent me a message, said she hadn't slept last night and needed a few hours. I haven't slept much myself since we found Brett. In fact, I drove home and picked up my trailer for certain things."

Four men and two women carried out filled boxes, and smaller pieces of furniture and set them on the ground. "What's the process here?" I asked.

"Broken pieces go in the dumpster. Same with baby car seats—there have been three so far—believe it or not. With the regulations, people don't want used ones anymore. I guess Brett couldn't resist anything he saw by the side of the road. Or maybe he dumpster dived. Seeing what he had in there, I no longer doubt that he must've. Damn.

"Anyway, after each load, they help me empty the boxes so I can decide what to keep and what to throw. Things I have a question about, we put over there." Shane pointed at a tarp on the ground next to the storage unit with several boxes on it.

I walked with him over to the new loads the crew had. Three boxes of newspapers, another infant car seat, a card table with broken legs, and four folding chairs in good condition.

"Let's see if there is anything besides newspapers in these boxes," Shane said.

It took the crew a few minutes to look through them. Nothing besides newspapers.

"All right, the three boxes, car seat, and card table in the dumpster. We'll put the chairs in my trailer to donate to the Salvation Army or another nonprofit group that wants them," Shane directed.

14

"**W**innebago County, Six o eight," Communications Officer Robin called over the radio.

"Go ahead, County."

"Deputy Zubinski requests assistance at her location. I'll send the info to your laptop."

"Copy, and I'll be en route." I called out "bye" to Shane and crew, jumped in my car, started the engine, and read the message. *In progress disturbance at the Emerald Lake Cafe.* I was four miles away. When I cleared the driveway, I activated lights and sirens and was back in Emerald Lake five minutes later.

"Six o eight, Winnebago County, I'm Ten-six at the Emerald Lake location."

"Ten-four, you're Ten-six at nine thirteen." Was there something in the Emerald Lake air that morning? I wondered as I jogged into the café.

A group of people had gathered on one side of the café. A table and some chairs had been overturned. Broken dishes lay on the floor. An older man was seated in a chair, his hands cuffed behind him. He moved his head back and forth in a "not me" gesture. An older woman sat alone in a booth, her face in her hands. I glanced from him to her, then scanned the others' faces. I recognized a few of them.

Mandy joined me and spoke at a low volume. "All I've got so far is the man in cuffs had some kind of episode, started pushing dishes off the table, then the chairs, then the table itself. No one was assaulted or hurt." She nodded at the woman in the booth. "That's his sister. She was in the bathroom when it started.

"From what I can tell, something's wrong with his cognitive abilities. If you'll transport him to jail, I'll get witness statements then release them. I'll interview his sister, see if anything like this has happened before, and determine what the next step should be."

"The charge is criminal damage to property?" I said.

"Yes. I'll charge him with that to hold him and request a mental health evaluation." She picked up a wallet from a table and handed it to me. I slid it in my back pocket. "His name is Kirby Sawyer, and his ID's in there. There was nothing else in his pants pockets, or his jacket pockets, except his gloves." She pointed at the jacket hung over the back of a chair.

"I'll help escort him to your car in case he acts up again," Mandy said.

We moved to either side of his chair, and Mandy said, "Kirby, this is Sergeant Aleckson. We're going to help you stand up and walk to her car. The sergeant will give you a ride to our jail where you'll stay for a while today."

He looked up at her like she was speaking a foreign language. "Jail?"

"Yes. The officers will take good care of you there."

His sister lifted her tear-stained face. "He didn't mean it. He's never done anything like this before."

Mandy turned to her. "Like we talked about a minute ago, that's why we need to find out what happened."

I picked up Kirby's jacket on the way by, and we got him into my squad car without incident. Mandy buckled his seat belt, and I laid his jacket on his lap.

"Thanks," Mandy said as she closed the car door.

"Later." I slid into the driver's seat, started the car, and radioed the county I was 10-15 by one male, en route to the jail.

"Copy, Sergeant. You're Ten-fifteen at nine twenty-one," Officer Randy responded.

I glanced at Kirby in my rearview mirror. He had a blank look on his face as he stared out the window. "Kirby, do you live in Emerald Lake?" I asked to engage him. When he didn't answer, I left him to his own thoughts.

Ten minutes later, I pulled up to the jail's garage door. "Winnebago County, I'm Ten-six at the jail." Central Control heard me, and the overhead door opened as Randy said, "Ten-four."

Communications and Central Control in the jail had the same cameras set outside the jail doors, and the grounds around the campus. I pulled into the garage sallyport. As the garage door closed behind me, the man door opened, and Corrections Officer Rick came out to meet us.

"We're at the jail, Kirby." I climbed from my vehicle, unholstered my Glock, secured it in a gun locker, and opened my back car door. Officer Rick and I can help you out." Rick reached in and unbuckled the seat belt.

"Okay," he said.

Rick reached his hand around Kirby's arm, and Kirby leaned into it as he stepped out. "Never thought I'd get arrested or ride in the back of a squad car," he said.

We left the garage and walked down the hall to the elevator. Central Control opened the door, and the elevator took us to the next floor where Booking Officer Tony waited behind a counter.

"You'll be cooperative if I remove your handcuffs, Kirby?" I said.

He looked down then nodded. "I'm sorry for what I did in the café. I got so mad when that woman told me my son was the biggest loser she'd ever known. I went off the deep end, didn't even know what I was doing until I heard my sister yell at me to stop."

"Who is the woman who called your son that?" I said.

"I never saw her before. I don't know why, or how in the world, she'd know me."

"Did she leave the café after that?"

"I didn't see which way she went, or anything else till the deputy handcuffed me," he said.

"Can you describe her?"

"She had dark hair, and a scary mean look on her face is all I remember."

"Maybe the woman mistook you for someone else. Where is your son?" I asked.

Kirby drew in a long breath. "He died in a fire in Minneapolis last year, the apartment building that exploded. You know, caused by that gas explosion."

"Yes, that was a tragic incident. I'm very sorry, Kirby."

Tears glistened in his eyes. "And then that woman had the nerve to call him a loser. He was a good man, a high school counselor, who lost his life for no good reason."

"A horrible accident."

"The worst. His girlfriend—her name's Brooke—she's the one who called and broke the news to me. She said Jay was visiting a friend there when it happened. She didn't know Jay's friend, didn't remember his name. Just like I didn't know Brooke's name until then. Jay said he'd met someone special, and he seemed happy. We got to talking, and I forgot to ask her name. He'd had some not so good relationships prior to that.

"Anyway, I thought Brooke would come out to see me. You know, so we could mourn Jay together, but I never heard from her again. When I called the number she'd called me from, it didn't go through. I thought maybe it was too painful for her to see me so sad, but I don't know.

"I contacted the police right after she called. They told me no woman named Brooke had reported her boyfriend had been in the building, and we didn't have his friend's name to verify the visit. But since Jay never returned home, he must've been among the missing. They said the investigators were sifting through everything, looking for human remains. They took my DNA sample for comparison but still haven't matched it to my son's," he said.

"The fire was last August, wasn't it?"

He nodded. "August twenty-first."

"That's a long time to wait for an answer."

"You know it. Jay was closer to his mother than to me. Just one of those things. After my wife died, the two of us got closer, but he was busy with his life in the city, and I was still working." Kirby waved his hand. "Didn't mean to get into all that, but it gives you a little background of why that woman's comment provoked me the way it did. Not an excuse, just a reason."

Officers Tony and Rick and I were all ears.

Kirby went on, "Again, not an excuse, but a factor: I'd just heard an old school buddy of Jay's died over the weekend. The two of 'em lost touch at some point. Anyway, I got to thinking about Brett and feeling sad he'd died so young, like Jay. And then that awful woman disrespected my son like that."

Brett? "You're talking about Brett Winston?" I asked.

"Yes siree. He was Jay's best friend in their school years, and beyond. Brett had that tragedy with his family, and he kinda shut Jay out, and other friends too, after that. I don't mean to speak ill of the dead," Kirby said.

"You're not."

"I heard Brett had moved back to the farmstead a while back, but I didn't know about that either till a couple days ago. People with their gadgets always seem connected to what's goin' on, but I sure seem to miss a lot. We used to phone people to let them know when something happened. Now about everyone thinks we'll find out on social media, or the news, I guess."

I pointed at a bench across the corridor from the booking desk. "Kirby, have a seat for a bit until the officers are ready for you."

"I need to talk to Zubinski," I told the officers and walked down the corridor, past empty holding cells, and phoned her.

"Sergeant?" she said.

"Mandy, can you talk?"

"Yep. Just got in my car. I'm about to clear, and head to the jail."

"Okay. So you know, Kirby Sawyer has all his faculties. He gave us a rundown of what led to his behavior. Is a younger woman with dark hair still inside?"

"No. She left right after I got her name."

"What's her name?" I said.

"Let me look in my memo book." A moment she said, "Rose Ebert."

"Did she tell you she said something to provoke Kirby?"

"No. In fact no one noticed anything before he went berserk."

"I suppose Rose wouldn't want to admit it after he had such a dramatic reaction."

"Probably. So what did Kirby say?"

"I'll tell you the whole story when you get here. Aside from some broken dishes that I'm sure Kirby will be happy to pay for, there was no other damage, was there?"

"No," she said.

"My advice is to charge him with disorderly conduct, instead of criminal damage to property, and see if we can get him into court this afternoon."

"I'll be there in about ten minutes, and we'll figure it out."

"Thanks." We disconnected, and I returned to Booking. "Deputy Zubinski is on her way to fill out the arrest intake form. I'm going to talk to the county attorney, tell him the circumstances, see if he can get him into court sometime today, and recommend he's given a fine and released on his own recognizance," I said.

Both officers nodded.

I went over to Kirby. "Deputy Zubinski will be here shortly, and we'll follow the process from there."

He looked at his folded hands in his lap. "My sister's gonna kill me for being such a horse's behind in the café today."

"I think she'll forgive you when she hears the story," I told him.

He shrugged and circled his thumbs.

Mandy had entered via the sheriff's office sallyport and filled out the arrest intake form with the charge I'd suggested. The booking officers took over from there. I rode the elevator down to the ground level, entered the garage, retrieved my service weapon, and when I was in my car, Central Control opened the overhead door.

I drove the short distance to the sheriff's parking lot, and once inside, met Mandy in the squad room. "Do tell," she said.

I shared what Kirby Sawyer had told the booking officers and me. "He knows he screwed up. I checked, and he doesn't even have a speeding offense on his record."

"I know, I ran him too. If you want to plead his case to the county attorney, I'm fine with that. It won't take me long to write the report," she said.

I phoned County Attorney Ray Collinwood, and left him a detailed message, along with Mandy's number. When I hung up Mandy said, "It's in their hands now."

"Winnebago County, Six o eight," Officer Robin said.

"Go ahead, County."

"There's an incident at Davidson Avenue, and they've requested you to respond. Detective Dawes is on his way to that location also. I'll send more info to your laptop."

My heart rate increased as I pressed the button. "Ten-four, I'll be en route from the office."

Mandy's shoulder lifted. "The cleaning crew is there, right? Maybe something happened to one of them with all that stuff. You could get buried alive in there if you weren't careful."

I hurried to my car, curious as all get out what the incident was. I started the engine and turned on the laptop. When I read the words, they blurred for a moment. I blinked and read them again. *Cleaning crew found bodies in the living room. The ME is responding.*

Bodies, plural? "Dear Lord," I uttered and high tailed it back to the Winston farmstead.

15

Smoke had arrived a couple minutes before me. He stood by Shane and Tricia near the front entrance. All three stared at me as I approached. The expressions Shane and Tricia wore were similar to many others I'd seen over the years. Tricia had collapsed against Shane. His straight posture made him look as though a jolt of lightning had surged through him. Tricia was pale, Shane was flushed.

The cleaning crew members paced around by the storage unit and the dumpster, no doubt trying to process what they'd discovered in the living room. One clutched her collar and stared, another moved his fingers like he was striking keys on a piano.

Smoke walked over to meet me. "It's easier to show you than it is to tell you." I followed him into the now partly-accessible house. The cleaning crew had laid large canvas matting on the floor from the entry to as far as they'd gotten with the removal process in the living room. Overturned boxes and their contents were strewn around on the floor. We got as close as we could on the canvas without stepping on the exposed carpet.

"Looks like the cleaners were about to take those last stacks of boxes, between them and the couch, when they spotted this terrifying sight," Smoke said.

My eyes fixed on the beige cloth couch where two skeletonized bodies perched. A male and a female, evidenced by their physical appearance, and the clothing that clung to their bones: summer outfits and sandals on their feet. The female's head was tipped back into the couch cushion. The male was leaned to the side against her, his arm laid across her midsection.

The couch and floor had stains around their bodies and feet from the putrefaction, or goo, in the decomposition process. Darker-colored stains were visible on the female's shoulder and breast area and by the man's groin.

"Looks like there's a mushroomed bullet stuck in the male's right hip bone," I said.

"Yeah. The bullet tore through his shorts, and is visible all right," Smoke said.

"How about the female? There was so much blood on her shoulder and chest area."

Smoke moved to the right, and I moved to the left. From the new angles we saw a bullet in her neck bone. "Damn. You see what I see?" Smoke said.

"Yes." Tears formed in my eyes, and I blinked them away. "Who are these people? Must be victims of the crime Brett said he tried to stop. But why would he leave their bodies here? Even after however long it's been, there's still a faint foul odor from the seepage in the carpet and the couch. It must've been horrific as they decomposed."

"Must've been. Maybe that's when he got the ladder, moved upstairs where the smell wasn't as bad, and he didn't have to come down here again. Brett had been in a bad place, mental health-wise, for some time." Smoke waved his hand in a semi-circle. "And it seems filling his house with more and more stuff was the way he coped."

"The logical part in this whole illogical ordeal is that he confined himself to the second floor because dead victims were here on the first," I said.

"Who was the shooter, and why did he do it? Same one who shot Brett?"

"If Brett wasn't an accessory to this crime, why didn't he report it?"

"You mean like he didn't report the person who shot him?" Smoke said.

"Like that, yes."

Smoke's eyebrows lifted. "Two possibilities: he was scared, or he was the shooter. The ME couldn't rule that out. Now we have two more victims. When Brett wrote that he couldn't stop it, he may have been referring to himself. Couldn't stop himself."

I stared from one body to the next. "Why were they sitting on Brett Winston's couch, and how did they get here in the first place?" I braved another perusal of the bodies. "It looks like the female had a ring on a right finger that slipped off. It's on the couch beside her."

"I see that. Could be a good identifier." Smoke took a closer look and shook his head. "I don't spot her handbag." He checked around the carpet's surface. "Nor do I see any shell casings. So either the killer had a revolver, or he picked up the casings."

"When the ME and crime scene team get here, process all this, and examine the bodies, they're bound to locate their IDs," I said.

"Should, yes. And that couch is full of DNA evidence, if one or both are in the system. Meantime, we should check on the folks outside, see how they're doing."

"Did they see the remains in here?" I asked.

"I think all the cleaners did. Shane took a quick look. Tricia couldn't."

Shane and Tricia stood with the cleaning crew by the storage unit.

"I thought I'd seen it all. Those skeletons on that couch was the last thing I would've wanted to see, ever," a woman told Smoke and me when we joined them. Maggie, her name patch said.

Smoke nodded. "It is an awful fright to behold, no doubt about that. A couple things. First off, I will arrange a debriefing for all of you. We do them after every critical incident. They're very effective in helping us reset our brains.

"You folks have seen a lot in your cleaning careers, but like Maggie said, the bodies were the last thing she, or any of you, would've expected or wanted to see. So how about we have a session later this afternoon? Let's say around four. Would that work for everyone?"

Some nodded, others said, "Yeah."

"Second, I need to ask you not to talk to your friends and families about this yet. We've just opened a homicide investigation, and the sheriff will determine what he wants to make public, and when."

I heard a few utter, "Okay."

Smoke continued, "Word has gotten out about Brett Winston's death in the house, and our patrol deputies have caught a few curious people on the property. We want to respect the family's privacy as much as possible. That said, the house has gone from a cleanout project to a crime scene. We'll be taping a perimeter around the entrance until we've finished the investigation."

Some murmurings sounded among the crew.

"Can I ask a question?" A cleaner named Pete asked.

"Go ahead. Not sure if I can answer it though," Smoke said.

"About how long do you think the investigation will take?"

"I have no idea at this point. I'd say our crime scene team, and the medical examiner's officer, will likely complete their part of the investigation in a day or two. In the meantime, if you can give Sergeant Aleckson your names and contact information—cellphone numbers preferred—we'll let you know the confirmed time and location of the debriefing by early afternoon. Tentatively plan for four p.m. in a government center conference room. All right?" Smoke said.

They all agreed. I pulled out my memo pad and pencil—graphite wrote in freezing temps when ink did not—and got each person's information. The six crew members had ridden together in a van to the site. They climbed back in for a relief-filled ride away from the unexpected crime scene.

Smoke turned to Shane and Tricia. "We'll arrange a separate debriefing for you and your families."

Shane nodded, and Tricia stared straight ahead.

"Do you have any idea who the deceased victims are?" Smoke asked.

"No. I mean I only took a quick look, but no. You said it's a homicide investigation, and I don't understand this at all. It was a shock when we heard Brett had been shot at some point. And now we find out there are two people dead on his couch. I don't get it. Brett actually stayed in this house with them on the couch like that. And he didn't call the cops?" Shane said.

Tricia started to cry.

"We'll need the medical examiner's office to complete their examinations, and hopefully we'll learn their identities and cause of death, sooner rather than later," Smoke said.

"Brett is the least violent person I know—knew. Since he got shot, maybe the others did too."

Yep.

"That's what we intend to find out," Smoke said.

"Why didn't he call the cops?" Shane asked again.

The unanswerable question we all grappled with. "We might come across more information as the house gets emptied. Brett may have written something more detailed about it, more than the short note we found," I added.

Shane dug his toe in the snowy gravel a moment.

Smoke closed the gap between them, put one hand on Shane's shoulder, and the other on Tricia's. His voice was smooth when he said, "You two should head back to the hotel. The medical examiner and crime scene team will be here any minute. We'll keep you apprised as best we can, and get that debrief in the works. Sound like a plan?"

Tricia looked at Shane to answer.

"As you said before, Detective, one step at a time," Shane said. The new mantra he must've repeated to himself a hundred times by now.

After the siblings left, Smoke said, "Ready to brave another look?"

I nodded. "And take photos. Ones I will never carry on my person, of course. I'll wait till we find out who they are, and get photos of what they looked like in life. And that reminds me, I was at Emerald Lake High School earlier."

"I heard you get the call. Kids fighting?"

"A verbal dispute we got settled. What I wanted to tell you is, I went into the office afterwards and looked at Brett Winston's high school pics." I pulled out my phone and showed him.

Smoke took it from me and studied the photos. "Good looking kid. Really sad how his life took a nose dive, how it ended."

"I know. I think about Taylor's mother—probably too often— how her life came to a tragic end. She was with the wrong person, and her jealous ex-boyfriend flipped out and killed them."

"I think about that a lot myself. Has Kristen been able to move on and accept Taylor as your sister?"

"More or less. You know how betrayed Mother felt when she learned my father got involved with Wendy after they broke up, and before they were back together again. Even though the breakup was Mother's idea in the first place."

"Still, I can't blame her for that. Your dad was my best friend, and it surprised me he went out with Wendy a time or two. Not to speak ill of the dead, but she was on the wild side, and Carl was anything but."

"Taylor is the special someone from their brief tryst. It seems like a twist of fate Taylor's mother was on the wild side, and now we're concerned Taylor's husband is caught up in something on the wild side himself."

"And when you play with fire—"

"Yeah."

Smoke and I entered the house and stopped about eight feet from the couch. I counted five boxes that looked like they'd been dropped. "The crew must've been in mid-move when one of 'em spotted the bodies, and they all let 'em go," I said.

"That'd be the natural reaction, no doubt. I hope they'll be able to verbalize, share everything they experienced in the debrief."

I moved my head from left to right around the room to absorb all I could, what was evident in the piles, and to figure out where the stairs to the second floor and down to the basement were located. Somewhere between the kitchen and living room, I imagined.

I had my phone in my hand and clicked on the camera icon, snapped photos of the room and the two victims on the couch. I studied the male's arm laid across the female.

"Looks like an impulse move to protect her," Smoke said, as if he'd read my thoughts.

"They're in a sitting position, so it doesn't look like they tried to make a run for it. Unless they were moved to the couch after they were shot." My eyes scanned the carpet's surface. "I don't see darker stains that would indicate blood on the floor, in the immediate area anyway."

"No. So how long have they been here? Given his shorts and her summery dress, they should be able to narrow down the time of deaths within a few months."

"Last summer, or the summer before?" I said.

"You got me stumped on that one. The ME said Brett's bullet wound was months old. That said, we don't know whether Brett and this couple got shot during the same incident."

"That's true. What a conundrum."

"That it is."

We heard the Winnebago County Mobile Crime Unit come to a stop on the driveway and went out to meet them. Deputies Todd Mason and Brian Carlson, the week's assigned team, climbed out. They looked at the in-process—now halted—cleaning operation. Mason whistled, and Carlson said, "And I thought my parents had too much stuff."

Smoke's phone buzzed. "Detective Dawes. . . . All right, thanks." He disconnected. "The ME's ETA is about ten."

"We can't begin our work till they get here, so how about you show us the infamous entrance to the upstairs room?" Carlson said.

"Prepare yourselves, and follow me," I said.

Carlson, Mason, and I headed around the house. The ladder lay on the ground. "If you want to take a look at the upstairs room, we need to set the ladder up." I pointed. "It's the south window."

The two lifted the heavy ladder into position. Mason was the first one up. He spent a moment checking it out, then came down again. "That is super sad. Before I got into this line of work, I had no idea how many people hoarded. Not all to that degree, of course."

Carlson climbed up and spent a little more time than Mason had. Back on the ground he said, "All I can say is it's a good thing he called his brother when he did, or who knows how long he might've been there before he was found."

"Not as long as the two on the living room couch below," I said.

"We should take a look at the scene, then get into our hazmat suits before the ME gets here," Mason said.

I waited with Smoke by his car while the two went into the house, spent a couple minutes inside, emerged with grim expressions, and climbed into the mobile unit. The medical examiner's van pulled in behind the mobile crime unit.

Dr. Calvin Helsing and Roy Swanson got out and joined us. "The plot thickens, eh?" Helsing said.

"And it's as clear as mud," Smoke said.

"Crime scene team inside?" Swanson asked.

Smoke pointed at their van. "Putting on their suits."

"As should we," Helsing told Swanson.

Mason and Carlson resembled astronauts on a space mission when they stepped from the van, covered from head to toe, along with eye goggles, n95 face masks, and vinyl gloves. Shoe covers hung from their pockets. Carlson held their equipment case.

They nodded at Helsing and Swanson, then Mason said, "Why don't you suit up in our vehicle?"

Swanson retrieved their things from the ME's vehicle and went into the other. He and Helsing were suited up minutes later. They looked like four astronauts ready for their mission. Smoke and I got jumpsuits from our trunks, took off our jackets and suited up, ready to assist.

16

When Smoke and I stepped into the entry, we saw Mason and Swanson snapping photos of the overall scene and the remains on the couch. We pulled on shoe covers and went in. Carlson had started to sketch the scene on a legal pad.

"My my my," Helsing said as he surveyed the room. "There are dozens of wet gravel and snow-mixed boot tracks on the canvas they laid over the carpet. Whatever evidence from past perpetrators may still be present on the carpet below."

"Could be," Smoke said.

"The couch and their clothing have plenty of DNA evidence on them."

"Provided they're in the system, we can get matches and identify them," Smoke said.

"Provided," Helsing agreed.

"It's a small miracle the cleaners got this much removed in short order," I said.

"May have to hire a different cleaning crew after they got this major shocker," Carlson said.

"Doctor, any idea how many cleaners find bodies in hoarder houses?" I asked Helsing.

"From all the cases in Minnesota I know of, it's when they suspect a person has died inside and go in to check. I haven't heard of a case where it was a surprise like this one. Usually a family member or neighbor reports they can't get a hold of a person, or haven't seen them for a while. As you all know, they go in with law enforcement to search, and the smell often gives the location away. Sometimes they use a cadaver dog if they have trouble zeroing in on what room the deceased is in," he said.

"It's the same in non-hoarder houses or apartments. Someone reports when they haven't seen a neighbor in a while, or they catch that unforgettable smell," Smoke said.

Mason's face screwed into a grimace. "Don't remind me of the one case we had where the woman died on the floor in her apartment, but for some reason neighbors didn't smell her. Maybe because the whole place had a bad odor, in general. A few days later, the putrefaction process started, and the fluids leaked through the ceiling to the apartment below."

"One of the worst scenes we've been at," Carlson said.

I cringed at the thought and I wasn't even assigned that case. However, I would never be able to unsee their photographs, like I would never unsee Brett Winston dead on his upper-level couch, or the two who'd died in his living room, along with many, many others.

"It's sad when something like that happens, bodies not found for a while." Smoke glanced around then pointed at the upended boxes a short distance from the couch. "Looks like there was more open space in this room, with access to the couch and other furniture. Then when Brett started filling it with stuff, he left about five feet between the victims and his closest piles."

"Out of respect, to give them a little unnecessary space?" Carlson said.

"If only we could ask Brett. And get answers to a list of other questions besides," I said.

"No organs to check for body temps," Swanson quipped.

Helsing looked from one victim to the other, then he leaned in for a closer view of the female's remains. "An important thing to note: both victims died from gunshot wounds, and the evidence is here to prove it."

Helsing pointed at the female's neck. "A bullet is stuck in the female's cervical spine. C-seven. Given the massive dark stains on her dress, it's safe to say the bullet struck her left carotid artery."

He moved to the male's remains next and pointed at the groin area. "The bullet is imbedded in his pelvic bone. Like with the female, the blood stains are massive, so the bullet no doubt passed through his femoral artery."

"You're saying the killer was either a sharpshooter who knew kill shots, or was damn lucky," Smoke said.

Helsing shrugged.

"From what we've gathered, Brett Winston struggled to organize his thoughts, along with his things. As we can see all around us. His brother said he didn't think Brett even owned a gun. I don't see him as the shooter," I said.

"From what little I know, I have to agree with you," Helsing said.

"Doctor, how long do you think they've been dead? It seems like it must be a *long* time," I asked.

"A human body can be reduced to a skeleton in less than two weeks under certain conditions," he said.

"I didn't realize it could go that fast. The closest we've gotten before this were ones in earlier stages of decomp, like the one Carlson mentioned."

Helsing lifted his hand to the victims. "Putrefaction, or decomposition, has five main stages: Autolysis, or self-digestion, where the cells break down, followed by Bloat, Decay, Active Decay, and Skeletonization. Each stage involves different microorganisms and bacteria. Environment plays a key role.

"Given what the victims were wearing, we can presume it was warm, maybe hot out when they died. Insects thrive and reproduce faster in warm conditions. Fatal wounds, such as these two suffered, would've been a big draw to house flies, then blow flies, then beetles. A fly will lay over two hundred eggs in a body's orifices and open wounds. The eggs hatch into first-stage maggots within twenty-four hours."

We'd all witnessed how maggots appeared on bodies soon after death.

"Dust to dust, a process that's downright difficult to comprehend," Smoke said.

We were silent a moment, then Smoke turned to Mason and Carlson. "Get close up shots of the bullets, team."

"No pun intended?" Carlson said.

I groaned, but his comment helped ease the tension.

"The bullets mushroomed when they hit bone, which makes it more of a challenge to read the bullets' surfaces. But experts should be able to tell us more about them. It appears they both have hairline fractures around the bullets," Smoke said.

"We'll take X-rays and measurements of those at autopsy." Helsing lifted a hand. "Detective, normally our office would remove the bullets at autopsy, but there's no reason we can't remove them here, give them to your team to enter into evidence, and get them to the crime lab."

"Sounds like a plan. Next project, team," Smoke said.

Mason and Carlson took turns at their case. Mason removed a set of pliers and Carlson picked up evidence bags. With eyes of five witnesses on him, Mason used the pliers and clenched the bullet in the female's spine. He twisted it a few times to loosen it. When it released, he removed it, and dropped it in the bag Carlson held open.

Carlson pulled a sharpie from his pocket and filled in the required information on the bag. A photo of it in the female's cervical spine would be added when it was printed. "If you can all add your initials, or signatures," he said.

We each took a turn with the sharpie to add ours.

As Carlson put it in the case, he told Mason, "I can remove the other one."

Mason nodded and handed the pliers over. We kept our attention on Carlson as he worked the bullet from the male's pelvic bone. Mason opened the evidence bag, Carlson dropped it in, Mason filled in the info, and we all signed it as before.

"Go ahead and collect the female's ring lying beside her," Smoke said.

Mason got tweezers from the case and picked it up. A gold band with a large sapphire gemstone surrounded by a circle of small diamonds. He did a visual scan. "No inscription inside. An engagement ring?" he said.

I shrugged. "Could be, if she wore it on her right hand. Or maybe it's an heirloom."

Carlson opened a bag, and Mason dropped it inside. He entered the info, and we each initialed it.

"As far as personal items, in addition to their clothing, all we've spotted is that ring. No other jewelry on either one. No necklace, bracelet, watch, or what have you. Hopefully his wallet is in the male's back pocket so we can learn his ID. As far as the female's goes, if it's somewhere in the house, it should turn up," Smoke said.

"In a year or so," Carlson murmured.

Smoke went on, "Sergeant Aleckson posed good questions earlier. In addition to who are they, why were they in Brett Winston's house, and how did they get here? One thought is someone dropped them off. Another is, maybe one of the covered vehicles in the shed belongs to them. After the crime he said he couldn't stop, Brett decided to hide it in there."

"Like it would never be found?" Mason said.

Carlson pointed at the sets of remains. "That'd be small potatoes compared to this."

"No doubt." Smoke's eyebrows lifted. "All right, next steps. We've got a couch and carpet saturated with putrefaction and blood. After we collect what we need to, we'll get a biohazard waste company to remove and dispose of them."

"Yes, we need to do that," Helsing agreed.

"Doctor, after we've removed the remains, we'll take a closer look at the couch, see if there are any fibers or hairs worth collecting. God only knows where Brett got this couch, or if it's ever been cleaned. You'll get hairs and fibers from their clothing too."

"Of course. I'm not a forensic anthropologist and I'm not certain we'll need one. We can make that determination later. I can however estimate the ages of the remains based on the fourth sternal rib end, joints, cranial sutures, and teeth," Helsing said.

"The sheriff's office will look at the reported missing persons around the state. Get any pertinent info to your office," Smoke said.

"Doctor and Detective, are you ready for the gurneys?" Swanson asked.

Helsing looked from one face to the next and nodded. "Yes, and bring some clean sheets too."

Mason and Carlson left with Swanson and returned with two gurneys, the bags, and some sheets. All three changed their gloves to avoid cross contamination. Swanson opened one body bag, Mason opened another, and they laid them on top of the gurneys.

"All right, this is a first for me. Their clothes should help, but if we find the skeletons don't remain intact when we move them, we'll figure out a way to get the sheets under them and then lift the sheets," Helsing said.

"Who first?" Carlson said.

"Left to right, the female," Helsing said.

"Least the fluids are all dried up," Mason said.

Swanson went around the couch, reached his arms behind her spine, and lifted so Mason and Carlson could get hold on either side.

Smoke assisted with her legs, and they laid her on the gurney.

Helsing zipped it up while the team prepared to remove the male. He was inches taller with heavier bones. Swanson and Mason had his upper body, and Smoke and Carlson took the lower part.

"I don't feel a wallet in his left pocket," Carlson said.

"Nor in his right pocket," Smoke said.

I assisted by lifting his calves and feet. We laid him on the other gurney, and Helsing zipped it up.

I'd had trouble with that action since my Grandma Brandt died, and I'd watched the funeral directors zip her in. From then on, when they got up to the decedent's neck, I looked away. It seemed silly I was still affected, especially when flesh was no longer present, but I suspected my visceral reaction would be with me for life.

With the gurneys in the van, Helsing and Swanson waved their goodbyes, and we watched them drive away with the mysterious remains of a male and female recovered from a hoarder house.

"Corky, you like to write, right?" Mason asked out of the blue.

"Yes, but I haven't written much besides reports for a long time." I elbowed his arm. "What brought that up?"

"I started thinking you should write books about some of the crazy cases we've had. Like this one," he said.

"Todd, do you think anyone not involved in this world would believe it?" I said.

"That's why they call it fiction. You'd need to make up names to protect the innocent and the guilty," Carlson said.

"In your spare time when you're not solving crimes and helping family members," Smoke said.

I knew he wouldn't say more, but I shot him a slight head shake anyway. "Back to the business at hand. Detective?"

"Yes. Let's see if there's anything we should collect. And push the couch back, in case there's something under it," he said.

"We can hope the bullet that went through Brett Winston is there," Carlson said.

"Dream on," Mason said.

We pulled off our used gloves inside out, and put them in the small trash bag Mason picked from their case. We kept extra ones in our pockets and put clean ones on.

I heard a vehicle on the driveway. "Now who's here?" I headed for the door, but all I caught was the tail of a small SUV before it disappeared. "Must've been some curiosity seeker," I told the guys when I returned. "In a very dirty vehicle, couldn't tell the color for sure, and didn't see the plate."

"Makes you wonder if we need to keep someone posted here around the clock until this place is cleaned out," Smoke said.

"The thing is, you don't get a full view of the house and yard until that last little curve. The person likely got close enough to see the mobile crime unit and our squad cars, turned around, and left in a hurry," I said.

"So it wasn't a delivery guy with a package," Carlson said with a chuckle.

"Good one, Brian, and heaven forbid," I said.

"We could park a squad car in the driveway as a deterrent. I don't get creeped out too easy, but if I had to help guard the place at night, I'd worry about angry spirits," Mason said.

"Do tell," Smoke said.

"Two people—that we know of—were killed here. We've all heard stories about restless spirits."

Carlson narrowed his eyes. "I think Todd should take the first night shift for trying to scare us."

"Let's concentrate on the physical world and the task at hand," Smoke said.

"And pray we don't find any more bodies," Mason added.

"Someone put a muzzle on that guy," Carlson said.

I shook my head in an effort to lose the images Mason's words had fabricated in my mind.

Smoke pointed. "Couch," and pulled his flashlight from his coveralls pocket. We gathered around him as he flashed over its surface. "No bullet hole, so Brett Winston was not seated by the other two—at least not on the couch—when they got shot." He nodded at a nearby chair with two boxes on it. "He could have been sitting there."

164

"Or, in all this rubble, the bullet that went through Brett's shoulder may be stuck in a wall, or in another piece of furniture, or laying on the floor somewhere," I said.

"We've sifted through things before. Usually soil or sand, however," Smoke said.

"There is a fair amount of dirt in here too," Mason added.

"Any fibers or hair on the carpet in front of the couch would've been covered with body fluids after the shootings. Again, how long would they have been there before that?" I asked my question out loud knowing there would be no answer.

"The ME will send the clothing from the skeletal remains to the regional crime lab for testing. But given the variety of stains on the couch, we'll cut some fabric off the back and seat and send samples to the crime lab as well. More people could've been here before—even during—the shooting. We have no idea," Smoke said.

With eyes, noses, and mouths covered, Mason and Carlson got on either end of the old tan couch. It looked like it weighed a ton the way they struggled.

"The fluids might not have dried inside the cushions yet. Corky, let's help them out," Smoke said.

We slid our eye protectors from the tops of our heads, and pulled our face masks up from our necks. Smoke moved in next to Mason, with me beside Carlson. We bent over and grasped the front feet and helped move it back.

"No bullet under it," Carlson said.

The carpet was less dirty beneath the couch than the rest of the room, but not by much. A golf ball was the lone object there.

"Somebody golfed in here?" Carlson said.

"Another random item in a house filled to the brim. I noticed a box full of various small sports balls the cleaning crew carried out," I said.

"Why a whole box?" Carlson said.

Mason shook his head. "Why ask why?"

"Team, you got big paper evidence bags, right?" Smoke asked.

"Yeppers, in the van," Carlson said.

"We'll cut the fabric tops off the cushions and the back of the couch, and from the carpet with the fluids. Scientists can get a sample of Brett Winston's DNA from the ME as a known person," Smoke said.

"There are sharp knives in our case. I'll get the bags," Mason said.

"Grab five or six, " Smoke said.

When Mason returned, he laid papers on the carpet, opened the bags, and set them on top. Mason and Carlson cut fabric from the areas Smoke directed, and wiped the knives with an alcohol pad after every cut to avoid cross contamination. Each section went into a separate bag, and were marked as such.

"Detective, we've collected a lot of evidence from the crime scene. Now to identify the victims and find the killer," I said.

"That's our goal. I'll have Communications contact the biohazard removal company to pick up the couch and the rest of the fluid-soiled carpet. They've got good tools to cut it out." Smoke walked away to make the call.

17

We had pushed the couch back to within two feet of the piles behind it. The cleaning crew would need to clear out more so we could examine the walls. Mason moved a couple boxes to access the nearby chair in question. Carlson joined him, and each one removed a box from its seat.

"See any bullet holes?" I asked.

"Nope," Carlson said, and they set the boxes back down.

Smoke returned. "The biohazard crew will be here about two-thirty. On a separate note, I talked to Sheriff Kenner, and he'll reserve a room in the government center for the debrief. Then he'll be on his way here."

"Didn't he have deputy interviews?" I asked.

"He did. Just finished. Communications briefed him on what we got out here, and I sent him photos of the victims. He couldn't believe it, said he had to see the scene for himself."

"He missed the scary part," I said.

"After he views the scene, he plans to head to the Midwest Medical Examiner's Office and witness the examinations later today. I don't suppose you want to join him, Corinne?"

"No thanks. But since the two are skeletons, it'd be less traumatic than others I've been at," I said.

"Detective, we took a close look, and there's no bullet hole in that chair." Mason waved his hand that direction.

"All right."

Deputies Todd Mason and Brian Carlson put the rest of the evidence in the mobile crime unit and headed back to the office. "I'll send a text to everyone on the cleaning crew with the meeting details," I said and took care of it.

Smoke and I met Sheriff Mike Kenner outside when he arrived at 1:12 p.m. He'd served with Winnebago County for over twenty years. He stood six feet tall with broad shoulders, a long torso, and military haircut. I'd seen his brown eyes soften with compassion and harden with anger in different situations.

A neatnik by nature, Kenner glanced inside the dumpster and the portable storage unit, and shook his head a few times. "Kinda makes me feel itchy thinking about living in a house surrounded by all that stuff."

"I had to brush aside my claustrophobic tendencies as best I could and *make* myself crawl into the room where Brett Winston died," I said.

"Hard to imagine. I've meant to get out here to check on things before this, but it's been one thing after the other the last few days," Kenner said. True. Ours was not the only case in the county.

"Mason and Carlson hadn't seen the room, and when they got here this morning they went up to see for themselves," Smoke said.

Kenner nodded. "I need to do the same."

We led the way to the back of the house, then Smoke pointed at the ladder and lifted his arm. "Be our guest."

Kenner sucked in a breath, blinked a few times, and paused on the first rung before he went up. He spent a couple minutes looking inside before he climbed back down. The rosy tone on his face displayed his emotional reaction, one I'd seen at prior scenes.

"Unbelievable. I heard the verbal reports, read the written ones, saw the photos, and it still baffles me how anyone could live like that. And how did a big guy like Roy Swanson climb through that window?" he added.

"I made it, and I'm not much shorter than Swanson," Smoke said.

"Good thing we train for those kinds of entrances," I said. "Sheriff, back to Brett Winston. A supposition, given the horrific find today, maybe he confined himself to the second floor because of the dead bodies on the first," I said.

Kenner's eyebrows lifted.

Smoke said, "Without knowing the whole story, it seems like a reasonable explanation. Scratch the word reasonable and change it to *an* explanation."

"I get that. Especially now. Let's go check out the living room," Kenner said.

When Kenner entered the house and looked around, his shoulders lifted in short twitches. "Un-be-freakin-lievable. I'm trying to get a handle on this. Two people who must at least be acquainted with Brett Winston arrived here. They are perhaps conversing, the couple on the couch and Winston in maybe that chair." Kenner pointed at the one we'd checked. "Was someone else here already, or did they burst in and shoot them all?"

"We didn't find a bullet hole in the chair. Brett may have opened the front door for the killer, they had a confrontation, Brett got shot, maybe played dead. The two on the couch, not so fortunate," I said.

"We also haven't come across any shell casings. Like I said before, the shooter must've collected them, or he had a revolver. As much as Brett Winston doesn't seem to fit the profile, we have to remain open to the possibility he was the shooter," Smoke said.

I had to remind my brain of that because my gut didn't agree.

"Sheriff, the cleaning crew was pretty distraught, as you can imagine. So it'll be a good thing to debrief them today."

"It surely will. Almost no one comes across a skeleton in their lifetime, much less two, in any line of work. A debrief is just the ticket. Thanks for handling that, Dawes."

"Glad to do it. I saw the same scene they did, but I was prepared for it. They weren't."

Sheriff's phone buzzed with a message, so he checked its face. "I'll get back to them in a minute."

"Sheriff, we'll need to check the missing persons cases in Minnesota and the surrounding states, unless something shows up here that reveals the victims' identities."

Kenner nodded. "Doesn't hurt to get on that right away. I'll have staff take care of that detail. And thank you for doing a standup job with this complex case, Detective Dawes and Sergeant Aleckson."

After Kenner left, Smoke and I sat in our cars to check work messages and emails while we waited for the biohazard team. I phoned the two crew members who hadn't confirmed they'd gotten my message about the time and location of the debrief. They apologized and said they'd be there. After I'd responded to a few messages, I climbed into Smoke's car. He checked the time on his watch. "Biohaz should be here any minute. It's way past lunch time, if you want to go get something to eat. I'll wait for them."

"I may not have an appetite the rest of the day. You go ahead, feel free to take off. I can wait for them," I said.

"I'll stay. By the way, Shane had some extra house keys made. He gave one to the cleaning crew leader and one to me. After we string the crime scene tape, we can lock up." He pointed at a tall, free-standing yard light close to the shed and faced the house. "Shane said the switch is in the entry. Remind me to turn it on when we leave."

"Good plan. Also, you told the Winstons you'd set up a debrief with their family, right?"

"I did, and I'll see what works for them. Shane told me they'd planned a memorial service for Saturday when they could get the whole family together. He may want all of them to take part in that too. At least give them the choice to say yay or nay."

"It's difficult to realize the impact something like this has. It spans from this generation to the next. And probably the next one after that."

When Biohazard Professionals arrived in their transport truck, Smoke turned off his car, and we met them in front of the house. They had their jumpsuits on. "Greetings, Detective," one said.

"Hi, Sam. I see they sent the A-team."

Sam chuckled. "I guess you could say we're all on the A-team. This is Ian."

Smoke nodded. "Ian. And Sergeant Aleckson."

We exchanged greetings.

"So you got a contaminated couch and carpet that needs to be removed," Sam said.

"That we do. Two victims likely died on the couch last summer, and their skeletonized remains were discovered this morning. The clean-up project came to an abrupt halt," Smoke said.

"That would do it," Ian said.

"No doubt. As you can guess, when the bodies decomposed on the couch the fluids leaked into it. Same thing with the carpet where their feet rested. The surfaces of both are dry, not sure if the couch is dried all the way through, however," Smoke said.

"We'll follow our usual safety and required protocol. We got giant bags that will accommodate the couch, and whatever size containers we need for the carpet," Sam said.

"We'll leave you to it. The sergeant and I will wait outside. Saves us having to suit up again."

"Sure. No reason you need to be in there for our part," Ian said.

They put on their industrial respirator masks, eye protectors, and chemical resistant gloves. Next, they gathered bags, an equipment case, and a flat dolly with wheels. They brought everything inside.

Smoke and I sat in his warm squad car and checked reports on our work email accounts. Thirteen minutes later, Sam and Ian emerged pushing the dolly with the bag-encased couch marked with biohazard stickers on it. When they got through the entry, they lifted the couch, and slid it into the back of their vehicle.

"That was fast," I said, as we climbed out of Smoke's car.

"Like I said, they're the A-team," he said.

Sam explained, "We cut out more of the carpet than needed, to be sure. It's rubber backed and had a waterproof pad underneath it besides. When we removed that pad, we found it had done its job. No leakage on the sub floor. Still, we put super-duper germ killer on it anyway."

"And sprayed the rest of the open area, so let it dry a while before you go in there," Ian added.

"Will do. We weren't planning to do any more here today. We'll need the cleaners to haul out more stuff. Then we can look for potential evidence and any clues of how this all went down, what happened," Smoke said.

"Like you guys always say, it takes a witness, a confession, or evidence to solve crimes." Sam looked at Ian. "Let's get the bags of carpet pieces, then we can vamoose."

They went back inside, carried the bags out, and loaded them in the truck.

Smoke lifted his hand in a wave gesture. "Appreciate you taking care of this so fast."

"Sure thing. See you again sometime." Sam waved back as they climbed into the truck and "vamoosed."

"Let's go ahead and lock up, attach the crime scene tape, and head back to the office. I'll work on my report until I need to get materials ready for the debriefing," Smoke said.

"And turn on the yard light."

"Right."

"You know that ring we found on the couch? Wouldn't hurt to show the photo of it to Shane and Tricia, see if they recognize it," I said.

"Wouldn't hurt."

I was in the squad room finishing my detailed report when Todd Mason and Brian Carlson came in. "We got the couch and carpet pieces delivered to the Midwest Crime Lab for DNA testing," Mason said.

"They're making the samples priority number one," Carlson added.

"Nice." I studied their faces. "You guys doing okay?"

"Yeah. The scene was beyond weird. Even though we had a sense of what to expect before we got there, it was still a shock," Mason said.

"Todd's right. It had a high creep factor. Like something you'd see in a horror film," Carlson said.

"Hard to believe it was real," Mason added.

I nodded. "And the great unknown is how the whole thing went down. We have victims and the bullets that killed them. There hasn't been an unresolved missing person's report in our county in the last year. Few years. Where are they from? The female's ring is valuable. Very valuable, if the gemstones are genuine. So we can't deem them homeless. Plus Brett Winston must've known them."

"You'd think. Pray their DNA is in the system, or we find their IDs among the rubble," Mason said.

"Sheriff's witnessing the ME's examinations, huh?" Carlson said.

"He is. It'd be a different process on skeletons, for sure," I said.

He nodded. "Different, all right."

"We heard Dawes is doing a debrief with the cleaning crew," Mason said.

"Yes, at four. You guys gonna join them?"

"Not sure. You?"

"I'm thinking about it, mostly to see how they're doing. Like you said at the scene, Brian, they might have to get a new crew in after the shocker they got," I said.

I stepped into Room 118 at 3:53 p.m. The six cleaning crew members, along with another man, had arrived for the debriefing session. I glanced at the names on the sign-in sheet. Seven names and phone numbers. The group stood by Smoke as he handed out papers, ones that listed coping skill tips and some space for them to record their thoughts and feelings.

Two tables were pulled in to face each other, a few feet apart. "All right folks, if you'll find a seat, we'll get started in a few minutes. Sergeant Aleckson has joined us. You met her at the scene." Smoke lifted his hand toward the man I didn't recognize. "This is Bud, the company's owner. He's here to support his team, learn more about their experiences, and how this session can help them."

I nodded at him. "Thanks for being here."

Bud nodded back. "I needed to be. We want to take good care of our people. They perform tasks a lot of others can't."

"For sure," I said.

Over the next hour, the four men and two women recounted details of their individual reactions, how some thought the remains were plastic posable Halloween decoration skeletons. Until they took a closer look.

Maggie had first spotted the stains around the remains on the couch and screamed, "They're real!" Soon they were all screaming, and those with boxes dropped them and ran out. A couple collided and almost fell down in the process. Pete called their boss, headquartered in Plymouth, a Minneapolis suburb, who called the Winnebago County Sheriff's Office. Detective

Elton Dawes was on the scene in seven minutes, and I'd arrived three minutes after he did.

Smoke said, "After a traumatic event, our thoughts keep returning to it time and again. Each one of you expressed normal, expected reactions to a very unexpected incident. A key step is to gain control of your thoughts, move them from the front of your brain to the back, for your peace of mind.

"You have each other, you have a boss who cares. Talk about your feelings. I know that isn't always easy, but it's important. We're still early in the investigation, but Sheriff Kenner plans to release a media statement sometime this evening.

"No details, just that the remains of an unidentified male and female were discovered in a rural county home today. As big a shock as it is to those of us who didn't know the man who lived and died in that house, it's nothing compared to what his family members are going through."

Pete raised his hand and looked from his crew leader to Smoke. "Mick, what should we do? Do you want us to go back and finish the job?"

"If you're able to, sure. If not, we've got others we can send instead. Detective, when will our crew be able to go back in the house?" Mick asked.

"Unless I hear different, tomorrow if you're able," Smoke said.

Mick stood. "Who thinks they can make it tomorrow?"

Along with Mick, three others raised their hands and two shook their heads.

"Tomorrow won't be too late to change your mind if you wake up and decide you need more time or don't want to go back at all," Mick said.

Some nodded in response.

Smoke rubbed his chin. "The biohazard cleaners removed the couch and contaminated carpet. We'll also tape a cover over the area. Let's plan on your return tomorrow, unless something changes on our end. Thanks again for the difficult work you do. It takes a lot of stamina."

18

The cleaners thanked Smoke and cleared from the room. "I don't know how they do what they do under the best of circumstances," I said.

"No." Smoke's phone buzzed and when he checked it said, "Shane Winston. I left him a message earlier." He pressed the accept button. "Detective Dawes. . . . Yes, Shane. . . . We have no clue yet. Staff is, or will be, checking missing persons' records in the state, hopefully will find potential matches. The ME will need to compare them to the remains after they've completed their examinations. . . . I get that.

"There are hundreds of people, adults and children, reported missing every month in Minnesota. Fortunately, the majority are found and their cases are cleared. . . . Right. One reason I called earlier was to let you know the couch and soiled carpet have been removed. If you're okay with it, the cleaning company will resume their duties in the morning. . . . Sure. We'll set up the debriefing when you know what works best for your family. We'll be in touch."

Smoke hit the end button and puffed out a big breath. "In a nutshell, you know the Winstons are planning a memorial service for Brett on Saturday. It'll be in the afternoon at Anderson's Chapel. The rest of their family members plan to arrive by early Friday afternoon: Tricia's husband and kids, Shane's boys. If we can arrange it on our end, they'd like to meet with me, you, and maybe the sheriff. Shane and Tricia hope we can share with the rest of the family what we know and have a debrief of sorts."

"I'm sure the kids have gotten bits and pieces from their parents, but I agree that it'd be helpful to hear the details we're able to give, so they all hear the same info."

"Yep. I'll phone Kenner, see if he's able to take my call." The sheriff did answer. Smoke gave him the updates and asked if the medical examiner's office had more information about the victims. Smoke grabbed his memo pad and said, "What was that?" He was silent as he scribbled something down. "Got it. Thanks, Sheriff."

"What?" I asked when they disconnected.

"The male measured six foot even, with a medium body size index. The female was five-five, with a small body size index."

"How do they calculate body size index?"

"According to what Kenner said, it's the person's height divided by the circumference of their wrist," Smoke said.

"Okay then. Well that narrows it down when they compare any listed missing persons to the remains."

"Yep. Sheriff also said if they can't learn their identities another way, like DNA, they're considering using a computer-generated facial reconstruction program."

"I've seen examples of that. I read that they also call it facial *approximation,* which may be a better term," I said.

"Probably a more apt one, all things considered."

"It's amazed me over the years how forensic anthropologists and artists can make a sculpture and construct a face, based on skull remains."

"I agree. They are quite accurate in many cases. A little less so in others," he said.

We were silent a moment. then I glanced at the time. "You about ready to wrap it up for the day?"

"Close. I got the bulk of my report written, but need to finish it before I sign off. How about you? You're on OT," he said.

"I officially went off duty at sixteen hundred. The debrief was something I needed to witness, and to show my support for the cleaners."

"It helped me having you here. You, and the sweet supportive look on your face."

That coaxed a smile. "You did a top-notch job, as usual. Still, I wonder how many of today's crew members will actually return tomorrow. You know, when reality sets in, and they wake up in the middle of the night in a panic."

"The goal is the debriefing model will kick in, and help calm their anxiety. The older ones said they'd be there. The younger ones, no. We shall see. On a related note, I sent a message to the area night sergeant and deputy, asked them to swing into the Winston property every hour or so."

"That bright yard light should help discourage those who like to commit crimes in the dark of night."

Instead of turning on Brandt, my road, I continued to Davidson Avenue and the Winston farmstead. As I approached the house, a few clouds in the otherwise clear sky drifted across the crescent moon. The overhead light shone bright on the yard and dispelled much of the darkness. It gave the false appearance that either someone was home, or expected in the next hour or so, had the crime scene tape not been stretched across the front entry, that is.

The house and property had screamed "abandoned" to deputies who took an occasional trip down the driveway. When I thought about the couple on the couch, and the person who had attempted a burglary the day after Brett's body was discovered, a chill ran through me. A coincidence? What if the burglar had gained access and found the skeletons? Many would call that poetic justice—me included—and it might've even scared the would-be burglar straight.

The sheriff's office had no clue how many attempted burglaries there may have been over the years—and the last three in particular—given Brett Winston hadn't reported a single crime, not even ones he was required by law to report. He'd gotten shot. So had two others in his house. Instead of calling EMS and the authorities, he dealt with both crimes in his own way. Avoidance. *Man.*

I took a last look at the house and the shadows cast by trees around it. The sense of loneliness it produced made me long for my own home, to see Queenie and Rex. But most of all, I longed for Elton Dawes and his warm, strong embrace.

It felt like a weight lifted from my body when I left the property. As I drove home, a sense of relief calmed me. I whispered, "thank you," because I wasn't the night sergeant responsible to ensure either he, or the area deputy, did their hourly checks on the Winston property.

I pulled in my driveway, pushed the remote garage door opener button. As the door lifted, I locked my squad car doors and headed inside. Queenie and Rex barked their greetings and pleas to release them from the kennel. I closed the overhead door against the cold night air and freed them.

When I leaned over and hugged each one, they sniffed my uniform, as per usual. I had a good sense of smell, developed over the years, but it wasn't close to theirs at 10,000 to 100,000 times more acute than humans. Given that, how could they roll around on a dead fish and other smelly things I'd questioned over the years? I wondered how the dogs would've reacted at the crime scene today. In addition to the trace decomposition odors, they may have appeared crazed in their quests to smell one pile of various items after the next.

"All right, my furry friends, I need a shower, as you can tell. Then I'm going to climb into a lavender scented hot bath and soak for a long time."

I slipped off my boots on the garage rug. The dogs followed me into the kitchen and waited for their big dog size milk bones.

Queenie and Rex chomped away as I stepped into the laundry/bathroom area. I hung my duty belt on a hook, emptied my pockets, and stripped off my clothes and Kevlar vest. I removed the brass from my shirt, threw the clothes in the washer, and started the cycle. One thing I loved about winter was the ability to hang things outside to freeze away germs. My vest and boots would be on the deck later.

I stepped into the shower, and as the water pounded on my body, I had to remind myself it was still Tuesday. A helpful aspect after a debriefing was the ability to put a traumatic incident in perspective, for each person to accept that no one at the crime scene today was responsible for what had happened in Brett Winston's living room months before. I hoped and prayed each cleaner would be able to move forward without much difficulty.

Young Brett's yearbook photo came to mind, the one I'd intended to print until I got waylaid by the crime at his house. I turned off the shower and wrapped a towel around my body. On my way to the upstairs bathroom, I spotted a note on the kitchen counter from my mother.

Hi dear, I put a meatloaf in your fridge. Enjoy!

My favorite caterer. I retrieved my phone from the laundry room and called her.

She answered with an upbeat voice. "Hello, dear. Are you home?"

"Yes." I opened the fridge and looked inside. Beside the meatloaf was a bowl of mashed potatoes and a tossed green salad. "Thank you times one hundred. It was a long day, and your meal is a much-appreciated surprise."

"I know you don't always have time to prepare a home-cooked meal, and you know how much I love to cook. especially in the winter."

She was being kind. Cooking was not in my top ten favorite activities, and I didn't often *take* the time to prepare any kind of meal. "Again, much appreciated. Sorry to cut you off, but I was about to hop in the bathtub when I found your note."

"Okay, dear. I love you, and hope you have a relaxing evening."

"I love you too, Mom. Bye."

We disconnected, and I scurried upstairs for a long winter's soak.

The frigid breeze caught my breath when I opened the deck door. I slipped into my wool clogs and stepped outside, set my boots on the deck floor, and hung the vest over the back of a chair. All germs would dissipate in no time. I went back inside and plopped on the living room couch.

Smoke phoned me just before 7:00 p.m. "Sheriff Kenner released a statement to the media. I'll read it to you: The unidentified remains of a male and a female were found in a rural home in Emerald Township, Winnebago County today. They were victims of a crime and had been deceased for several months. If anyone has any information about the crime, please contact the Winnebago County Sheriff's Office."

"That sounds good. There is someone that knows something. Maybe the killer has a guilty conscience and will feel coaxed into a confession."

"Think so?"

"No, but I can hope so."

"See you in about a half hour." He liked to clean up at his house and check on things.

I opened the photos on my work phone and scanned through them. The female's ring was stunning. The male's wallet wasn't on his person, and we hadn't found the female's handbag. If the two were killed during a robbery gone wrong, why hadn't the perpetrator taken the ring? Maybe it was too tight to slide off her finger.

Queenie and Rex perked up their ears and ran into the kitchen when they heard the garage door open. Smoke. I met him as he stepped into the kitchen. He set his duffle bag on the counter, petted the dogs, and then we embraced. I turned my head into his neck to inhale his clean, woodsy scent.

"Mmm, lavender. I could appreciate that fragrance all night long." He bent his head and nibbled on my ear, then his lips captured mine in a long, toe-curling kiss.

"Any idea how good that felt?" he said.

"I believe I do, and I'd love another stab at it later."

He chuckled. "At the end of a crappy day, there's no place like your body close to mine, little darlin'."

I gave his chin a light pinch. "It was different, in a spooky sort of way, that's for sure. Hear any more from the sheriff about the autopsies?"

"Nada. You know how he likes to leave his staff alone when they're off duty. As much as possible."

"True. I guess in this case, no news means no news," I said.

"Yep. I stopped by the Winstons—"

"So did I. Sorry, I interrupted."

He poked my shoulder. "Couldn't stay away either, huh? Shoulda known."

I poked him back. "The yard light is great, but the place still feels eerie."

"It is officially an abandoned house, and probably is haunted besides, like Mason said."

"Could be. You know people actually pay money to spend a night in haunted places," I said.

"To each his own. You'd have to pay me a *lot* to be there at night, and I'm not afraid of ghosts. A hoarder house filled with things from unknown origins however . . ."

"Smoke, I've thought more about the victims and their missing wallets. Could the shooter have given them a ride to Winston's house? They had some type of altercation, and he shot the three. Maybe Brett played dead, like we'd mentioned as one scenario. Then the killer robbed them, but he couldn't get the female's ring off her finger. That's why he didn't take it."

"You do come up with intriguing possibilities, Corinne. One that makes about as much sense as any other theory, given the only clue we have so far is Brett's cryptic note. Which provided no answers at all."

"Maybe we'll find a journal, or some other information among his stuff," I said.

"That would help." He clasped his hands together. "All right. No more shop talk for tonight."

"We can't seem to help ourselves. On a personal level, Mother sent over her famous meatloaf and mashed potatoes for supper."

"Be still my heart. Reminds me, I brought a six-pack of Castle Danger from my fridge, but forgot it in my vehicle."

He went into the garage, and I pulled the dishes out, set them on the counter, and got plates and flatware from the cupboard and drawer. Smoke carried in the beer, found a bottle opener, popped off the top, and held it up. "You want one, right?"

"You bet."

He opened a bottle for himself, and we clinked the necks together. After a nice long draw, I set the bottle on the counter. "Dish up, and we'll zap our meals." We filled our plates with meat and potatoes, heated them in the microwave, and added the salad on the side. We sat down at the dining table, gave thanks, and dug in. I hadn't eaten since breakfast, and the food tasted even better than I'd dreamed it would.

"Heard anything from Taylor?" Smoke asked between bites.

"No. I'd planned to check in, see how things are going, but haven't yet."

"Given her situation, no news *is* good news."

"True. Have some more meatloaf, Smoke. There will still be enough for at least another meal," I said.

"We keep talking about cooking, try it for a while, then go back to our old non-cooking habits."

"One reason is because Mother keeps spoiling us. I think cooking is like therapy for her."

"If enjoying the results of her therapy sessions helps her out, who are we to complain?"

I finished my food and beer and leaned back in the chair. "I am stuffed and content to do nothing but veg out for the rest of the evening."

"How about later tonight?"

"I'm open to suggestions."

"I'll come up with some things for you to consider."

I smiled at the thought. "You're near genius with what you come up with."

19

Smoke's phone rang in what seemed like the middle of the night. I rolled over and glanced at the clock: 5:03 a.m. Wednesday morning. When I roused him, he said, "Hmm?" He heard the phone's second ring, sat up, and snatched it from the bedside table. "Dawes . . . *What?* . . . All right, I'll be there in fifteen, maybe less."

My heart had started pounding the moment he shouted "what." It was my turn to ask, "What?"

He rubbed his arms. "A break-in at the Winston farmstead."

"*What?* An actual break-in? You have got to be kidding me."

"After I brush my teeth and hair, and throw on some clothes, I'll be on my way. Roth said I should phone Communications my location when I get there." He leaned over for a quick kiss.

"I'll bring some coffee out there." He started to shake his head, so I added. "As an off-duty cop."

He shrugged and headed to the bathroom. When I climbed out of bed, both dogs perked up. I slipped out of my nightwear, and pulled sweats and undies from drawers. I went on duty at

7:00 a.m., but felt compelled to check out Winstons' house beforehand.

I had a cup of coffee in a covered mug ready for Smoke when he came into the kitchen. He retrieved his badge, wallet, memo pad, pen, and pancake holster with his Glock from the duffle bag, and put them where they belonged on his person in under a minute.

I handed him the coffee. "Thanks," he said and headed for the door.

"Where's your jacket?"

"In the car."

The kitchen door shut, and I heard the garage overhead open. I put another pod in the coffee maker, went to the front closet for boots and outerwear, and by the time I was ready, so was my coffee. When I went to the laundry room for my wallet, it hit me that I'd left my work boots and vest on the deck.

I jogged to the sliding door, grabbed the items, set them inside, got my keys from the kitchen drawer and coffee from the counter, told the dogs to be good, and was on the road in minutes.

I pulled in behind Smoke's car at the Winstons'. The yard light was off. Sergeant Leo Roth shined a flashlight on the door as Smoke inspected it from afar. The crime scene tape had been ripped away and the boards over the entry window smashed. The door itself stood ajar.

Add criminal damage to property to the charges.

Roth and Smoke glanced my way as I approached.

"Ghosts didn't do this," I said.

"Ghosts?" Roth said.

"From the haunted house."

He half-smiled then shook his head. "I must be tired."

"Leo, so fill me in here," Smoke said.

"LeVasseur was here a little before four. Nothing. I got here at four fifty-eight, saw the mess, radioed Communications that I'd be at this location to check things out and asked them to call me. When they called, I said I'd phone you so citizens with a radio that have craved information on this property since the hoarder's death wouldn't hear about this latest deal."

"Brett's death, and the remains found in his living room, have certainly seemed to spark an interest in the place. And led to break-ins," Smoke said.

"Not the first time something like that has happened. But more common are those bad guys who check when a person's funeral's going on if family members of the deceased are home, or their doors are locked," Roth said.

Not uncommon. "Yeah, we've had enough of those reports. Question. Do you think anyone was aware the place was being checked on a regular basis?" I asked.

"Aside from our deputies, or the family? All I can say is neither LeVasseur nor I saw any vehicles idling in the area, and we drove down Davidson Avenue more than our hourly checks." Roth flashed his light on the driveway. "There's a fair number of tire tracks there, and on the yard. I'm not sure we could separate any of them out at this point."

"We're better off looking for trace evidence outside, and inside, the house," Smoke said.

"Agreed. Forgot to mention, Communications said they'd call the sheriff around seven. They contacted Mason and Carlson, the crime scene team, who should be here within a half hour," Roth said.

"Probably not the assignment they wanted after all the time they spent here yesterday," I said.

"We have to let the cleaning company know that we'll need to either delay, or to cancel, today's detail. I'll take care of that," Smoke said.

"Something to consider. If we need to block the front entrance and living room off for a day or two, the cleaners could move their operation to the side entrance, or the shed," I said.

"That might work. When Mason and Carlson get here, we can assess. The cleaning crew may have another job they can go to today," Smoke said.

"I need to go home, take care of our dogs, and get ready for work," I said.

"It surprised me when Dawes said you were on your way out here, over an hour before you went on duty," Roth said.

Smoke lifted a hand. "Corinne, I told Roth you feel a sense of responsibility to the family. After all, you took the original call, found Brett Winston dead, had to tell his brother the sad news, and have been here about every step of the way," Smoke said.

"I guess. I do feel a certain obligation to families who need answers when tragedy strikes, like we all do. They're the ones we work for, right? The victims and their families," I said.

"Yep," Roth said.

"That we do," Smoke agreed.

"See you later," I said and climbed in the GTO. It choked me up to think someone, or maybe a different someone, had attempted a break-in the day after Brett Winston's body was found, and succeeded in a second attempt the day the remains of two people were discovered in his living room. Did Brett Winston have something among his thousands of possessions that someone knew about and wanted?

The Winston siblings had a lot to deal with: their brother's death, two unknown people killed on his couch, a house and shed stacked to the hilt with stuff. Add to that, the burglaries.

After I'd attended to things at home and was ready for work, I climbed into my warmed squad car, and pressed the radio button. "Six o eight, Winnebago County."

"Go ahead, Six o eight."

"I'm Ten-eight." In service.

"Sergeant, copy you're Ten-eight at six fifty-seven. You have one call pending."

I checked my computer screen. The Winstons' burglary. "Ten-four. I'll be en route to that address."

"Copy that, Sergeant."

Another message popped up on my screen from Communications. *Evening and overnight officers have fielded dozens of calls about the remains found at that residence yesterday.*

I sent back, *Copy that.*

On the way I wondered if people called to question, or to comment, on the crime. Probably a mix of both. Some might remember a suspicious vehicle driving around last fall, or something similar.

I tried to mentally calculate how many hours I'd spent, either at their property, or writing reports about the incidents I'd responded to there. The horizon had lightened, and the sun would rise in about a half hour. Winter's frigid temperatures posed one challenge, fewer daylight hours posed another.

I parked behind the Winnebago County Mobile Crime Unit at the farmstead. "Six o eight, Winnebago County. I'm Ten-six at that location."

"Copy, Sergeant. You're Ten-six at seven-o-four."

I joined Smoke outside near the front entry. "The team is inside," he said.

We stepped onto the front stoop and gazed in the living room. Overhead lights in the entry and living room lit up the areas. Mason and Carlson had their jumpsuits, gloves, and shoe covers on and stood near where the couch had sat.

"Any clue what the motive might be for something like this?" I posed the question for Smoke.

"No. There's a fair amount of damage on the floor by where the team is standing. Whoever it was displayed a lot of anger. It doesn't seem like it'd be kids, but who knows. Would teens be out at four something this morning on a school night?"

"Communications said they've gotten tons of calls since Sheriff Kenner issued his statement. Maybe that prompted this."

"Could be. If they've seen activity here, and figured out where the scene of the crimes was. Hard to know."

"Okay if I put on shoe covers and go in?" I said.

"Sure, but you don't need shoe covers, not with the tarp still in place. The team is about done taking photos. And the cleaning crew will *not* be here today. We'll shoot for tomorrow instead."

"Sounds like the better option. Have you talked to Shane Winston about this?"

"No. I thought I'd wait till eight."

"Hi, guys," I called to Mason and Carlson as I entered the house with Smoke behind me. We took note of the tipped over boxes and things strewn around. "What a mess," I muttered.

"Bigger mess, you mean," Mason said.

I nodded. "You were right, Detective. The person, or persons, showed lots of anger in here."

"Used an axe in the floor where the couch used to be, of all things. What's up with that?" Carlson said.

Seriously?

"If I had to hazard a guess—and it might seem crazy, because it is in no way logical—I'd say the killer returned to the scene and did it," Smoke said.

"He came to check on his victims, saw they were gone, so it set him off?" Mason guessed.

"Like I said, it makes no logical sense. There had been no reported incidents at this property since Brett Winston moved in here. Then his body was found, word got out about it, and we had an attempted burglary last Saturday. Now a successful one during the night, after the remains were found and removed. The two incidents might not be related at all; not committed by the same person. It's one big damn puzzle," Smoke said.

"Looks like we need to talk to the sheriff about security here," Mason said.

"At least get motion detection cameras on the house and shed," Carlson said.

Smoke nodded. "The shed. That's what's rolled around in my mind. It doesn't appear the shed was entered either time. That supports the theory that whoever it was, they were only interested in the house. And for a specific reason, like the one that played out when they broke in early this morning."

"As far as security here is concerned, what do you think, Detective? Will that person ever come back?" I said.

"My opinion? I tend to doubt it. They broke in, chopped up the floor, knocked over boxes. They had no way of knowing we were doing regular checks, so they probably came in, thought they had plenty of time before daybreak to do their thing, unleashed their anger, said a final goodbye to the scene of their crime, and fled to parts unknown," Smoke said.

"That actually makes some sense," Mason said.

Carlson nodded. "It does, in a crazy kind of way."

"I agree motion detection cameras would be good, and I'll mention that to Shane when I break this latest news to him. He can tell Tricia and the rest of the family. There are probably valuable things here, in the shed for sure. I'll reiterate to the family they should put a heavy-duty lock on that door until everything gets sorted through," Smoke said.

"We'll get our maintenance guy out here to fix the door again," Mason said.

"I'm sure they have an extra door in the shop," Carlson said.

20

I was in the sergeant's office when Communications sent me the message, *Kirby Sawyer requests you to call him when you have time. He said you have his number.* I responded, *I do, thank you.*

In all the chaos the day before, I hadn't checked to see if he'd been released from jail. I found his number in my memo book, and as I punched it in my phone, wondered why he'd requested a call.

"Hello?" he answered.

"Hi, Mister Sawyer, it's Sergeant Aleckson."

"Thank you for calling me, Sergeant. I need to apologize and don't even know where to start. I can't tell you how embarrassed I am about my behavior in the café. I didn't sleep much last night thinking about it."

"I appreciate that, and when you told me about your son, and what the woman said about him, I could understand why you got angry."

"Thank you for saying that. I normally don't lose my temper and never act like I did in the café. My mind keeps going back to the hateful way that woman looked at me. Kind of evil like."

"Did you figure out who she was?" I asked.

"No. I went into the café to tell the folks how sorry I was. They told me it was all right, and I was welcome back there any time. So I asked if they knew who that woman was. One of the gals said she'd seen her there another time, like last week, but the woman didn't seem to want to talk, so the gal left her alone."

"I'm glad you made amends at the café, and it sounds like the woman who insulted you must have some major issues."

"I think she does. Makes me wonder if she got me mixed up with someone else. She acted like she knew who I was, who my son was. But I didn't know her, so how would she know me?" he said.

It was a day of mysteries, no question there. "Mister Sawyer, this might seem like a strange question, but do you have any of your son's school yearbooks?"

"Why yes, I believe they're still in his closet with some other high school stuff he never got around to taking. If not, they're among the things we cleaned out of his apartment. Thankfully, not too many boxes of stuff I needed to keep.

"Some books, personal papers. When his school got the news, and when kids were back from summer vacation, it seemed like a hundred of them sent me cards and notes. I look at them from time to time when I need a little pick me up."

"It shows how much your son was loved. The reason I asked about the yearbook is, how about you go through the class pictures, see if one of the girls looks like the woman in the café," I suggested.

"Oh. Now that's an idea."

"She'll look a little different, twenty some years older. Her hairstyle and color likely have changed."

"I'll do what you said, and look through the books. Maybe I can figure out who she is. I don't think it's anyone Jay took out on dates back then, but I guess it's possible."

"I'm curious to hear what you find out," I said.

"Okay, sure. I have your number now, so I'll be sure to let you know. And thanks for being so nice."

Nice? He made my day. "I appreciate that, and the same to you."

After we hung up I realized he didn't mention court, so it must have gone well.

I headed to the squad room to check my mailbox and saw Deputy Vince Weber writing at a computer. "Hey, Vince."

"Hey, Sergeant. So I hear you got caught up in more drama out at the Winston place today."

"It just won't quit."

"Yeah well, I saw photos Mason and Carlson took of the victims yesterday. The whole scene, them on the couch and all, didn't seem real. The team was right: it sure ranks near the top on the creep factor scale."

"One way to put it. Vince, we talked about you tailing along when I was there."

"Yeah, I planned to check it out yesterday. Instead it was back-to-back calls. You musta seen my stack of reports," he said.

"Yes I did. Now you should go out there for sure, see if the place is haunted. Inquiring minds want to know."

His eyebrows shot up. "Me?"

"You had that spiritual experience," I said.

"What I saw in heaven doesn't mean I can spot ghosts here on earth. And I don't wanna be able to either."

"I'm in that camp right along with you."

"So whadda we plan to do to keep people outta that spooky house?" Weber asked.

I told him what Smoke had said at the scene, that it may have been the killer who unleashed his final anger and won't return again.

"Sorta makes sense, if the guy is demented enough to think choppin' up a floor would make him feel better."

"To answer your question, they're getting another door with a lock. We believe the two burglaries are related but don't have the proof. Dawes questions whether there'll even be another one. The sheriff will have to make the next call, decide what level of security he thinks is needed."

"Yeah well, if they want deputies campin' out there after dark, they need to send teams, not singles," Weber said.

"That'd help. I feel sorry for the family. Look at all they've had to deal with in less than a week. If somebody trustworthy came along, said they'd handle sorting through everything, I think they'd be tempted to take them up on it and return to their home states."

"I probably would be too. I'm not the neatest guy in the world, but even I don't like a lotta junk around."

"The thing is, there are no doubt treasures hidden among the trash. The cleaning company should be back tomorrow, and if they doubled the size of their crew, they could get the job done in a week, maybe ten days," I said.

"A week? Think it'd take that long?"

"At least. The big shed is packed too."

He shook his head. "Oh, man."

"Vince, the haunted house theory aside, I think you'd be a good one to go out to Winstons' house, meet the siblings when they're there. At least Shane will be there tomorrow, directing the crew where to put stuff. You have even more of a calming aura about you now than before. I'm sure the family would appreciate someone besides me and Dawes hanging around."

He chuckled. "I don't know about any aura around me, but I've been kinda curious, trying to imagine what it's like at the place. I'll make a point to stop by tomorrow, maybe take my lunch break out there, if nothing else."

As I reviewed deputies' reports in the Sergeant's Office, I heard Smoke tell Communications he was Ten-ten, at the office. I waited a few minutes then made my way to his cubicle. He'd hung his jacket on its hook and was about to take a seat.

As Smoke sank down on his chair, he uttered, "Corinne." He squeezed the bridge of his nose, a sign he felt stressed. The burden he carried was apparent.

I touched his hand and took a seat myself. "This too shall pass."

"Ya think? Right now it seems like we'll be forever stuck in hoarder house hell, along with all the horrors that go with it." A good way to put it.

"It's not like you to get stuck, Detective."

"I know, but it's the way I feel about now. I phoned Shane a while ago, when I was still at their place, told him about the latest deal, asked if he wanted to check it out, then advised him not to."

I let his words sink in a moment. "Good advice. There's no reason for them to see it."

"They'll be installing the new door sometime today, so that should help the family feel less violated," he said.

"Did you talk to the sheriff, get his opinion on whether we need security out there?"

"Yeah, and he decided we'll install the alarm system. If anyone tries to break in, the sheriff's office will be alerted. It's not cheap, but a lot cheaper than posting security there until that place gets cleaned out. In retrospect, we should've done that after the first attempt, but who knew?" Smoke said.

"The office will pay, instead of the family?"

"Yep. Sheriff says he can justify it since it's become an active crime scene."

"He's right about that."

Smoke's work cellphone rang. He looked at its face and sucked in a breath. "Shane Winston." He hit the accept button and the speaker feature. "Detective Dawes."

"It's Leah Winston, Shane's wife. On his phone." She sounded frantic.

"Yes Leah, what is it?" Smoke said.

"Shane had some sort of spell, and we're in the emergency room now." Physical? Psychological?

Smoke stood, and my heartbeats sped up.

"Tell me what happened," Smoke said in his calming bedside manner voice.

"He fainted. For the first time *ever* in his whole life. I called nine-one-one, and the ambulance brought him here. They don't know if it's his heart, or if he had a stroke, or what," Leah said.

"They'll figure it out. Meantime, anything we can do to help?"

"Oh, um. Not that I can think of. Tricia's here too."

"Thank you for letting us know. Take care of yourselves, and we'll keep you in our thoughts and prayers," Smoke said.

"That's the best thing you can do for Shane, for us. I'll give you an update when we get one."

"I'd appreciate that," Smoke said and they disconnected.

"What were you saying, something about being stuck in this deal forever?" I said.

"The family's drama continues. Poor Shane, especially. He's borne the brunt of the burden. Guilt over his brother's death, two people killed in the house filled mostly with trash, then got burgled and axed. All in under a week."

"More than enough to cause either a heart attack or a stroke."

"We'll see how this plays out. Either Tricia will have to step up to the plate, or they might have to cease operations at the house for a while," Smoke said.

At 1:15 p.m., I was on patrol when Smoke phoned. "Shane Winston called with some good news."

"What?"

"After multiple tests, both the ER doctor and a cardiologist have declared Shane to be in good health. His blood pressure was a little high, but not bad. The docs figured given the stress he's been under, either his blood pressure shot up, or dropped suddenly, and caused his fainting episode. They prescribed an anti-anxiety med for him."

"That is good news. Not that it happened, but that he's getting treated," I said.

"Yep. The family: Shane, Leah, and Tricia want to meet with us this afternoon, hash things out, come up with a plan."

"They're looking to us for direction?"

"Sounds like it. They've been sailing in uncharted water for days with no land in sight," he said.

"Your description sounds like a line from a poem. Alexander Pope?"

"Not that I know of."

"An Elton Dawes original then," I said.

"Hah! Anyway, the family will come to the sheriff's department at fifteen hundred and we'll meet in Kenner's office, per his suggestion. Sheriff told me he has agonized over the whole thing since he saw the state of the Winston house. And then he witnessed the victims' examinations at the ME's office besides."

"What'd he say about the exams?"

"Not much. Said the anatomy class he had in college helped prepare him for it. A little bit, anyway. It was the crime itself, and the fact it wasn't reported, that got to him big time," Smoke said.

"Like for the rest of us."

"Oh, and I got the okay to have a security system installed. It won't be the whole shebang, just the two entry doors."

At 2:55 p.m., I heard voices in Kenner's office before I knocked on the doorjamb and stepped inside. Chairs were pulled into a semi-circle by the window.

"Come in and join us, Sergeant. You know everyone?" Sheriff said.

I zeroed in on Leah Winston. "I haven't met you yet."

Shane reached his arm around her back. "My wife, Leah."

I nodded and smiled. "Hi."

Leah half-smiled back. "You've been a big help through all this. It's good to meet you in person."

"Thanks, glad to do everything I can."

Sheriff cleared his throat. "All right. I know we're planning to get you, and the rest of your family, together to discuss everything that's happened. So you can each put things in perspective, help you to move on."

"The debriefing?" Shane said.

Sheriff blinked his eyes. "The debriefing, yes. But in the meantime, I think it'd help the three of you to talk about your brother and the victims in his living room. Any questions or comments you have, whatever."

Tricia started crying. "Shane and I wonder how we'll ever be able to forgive ourselves."

I leaned forward. "My therapist and my loved ones saved me, helped me heal after a tragic incident I believed I could have—should have—prevented. If I'd had all the information, I would have. But I didn't, like you didn't."

Tricia stopped crying and locked my eyes with hers. "I'm so sorry for whatever you've been through."

"Thank you."

"The longer you live, the more 'what ifs' you have to deal with. In our personal lives, and as deputies, we see families like yours go through things that are about impossible to imagine. And like Sergeant Aleckson did, don't hesitate to get the help you need," Smoke said.

We ended up having a mini debrief. All said they felt better after they'd unloaded some guilt, then went on to discuss what seemed like an impossible clean-up project.

"Detective, you mentioned how your office was checking missing persons records," Shane said.

"Yes. Sheriff?"

"Staff has discovered two possible female matches and one possible male match. The medical examiner's office will take a close look, see if they can match them to the victims' remains," Kenner said.

All three nodded.

I pulled out my phone. "Detective, have you shown them the photo of the ring?"

Smoke shook his head. "Not yet."

"Ring?" Shane said.

I located the photo. "It was on the couch, next to the female's remains. We wondered if you might recognize it. Maybe saw it on one of Brett's friends. Maybe at a party." It sounded like I was grasping at straws as I passed my phone to Shane.

He stared at it a long moment. "We haven't socialized with Brett in years, but I might remember a ring like that. It's beautiful." He shook his head. "No, I don't." He passed it to his wife.

Leah studied it. "Shane's right, it is beautiful. Very much so. I would remember if I'd seen it, like on one of Deena's friends. But it's been years since we had any social events with them." She handed the phone to Tricia.

Tricia took a quick glance and shook her head. "Since we lived so far away, the only get togethers we had with Shane and Deena were at family gatherings."

Tricia handed me the phone. "Thanks. We didn't expect you'd know the owner, but had to check," I said.

"To let you know, the security system will be installed before the end of day," Kenner said.

"Thank you. That will make us feel better. Not that we can understand the sudden interest in the house," Shane said.

"Or if there were incidents in the past Brett didn't report," Tricia said.

Shane lifted his hand. "So the cleaning crew plans to return tomorrow?"

"Yes. I talked to Bud, the company owner, and he said they'll have ten workers, instead of six, on site. The goal is to gain access to the side entrance as well as the front one. Bud said he didn't want to overwhelm you, trying to decide what you want done with things, so two crew members will be assigned to help you specifically with that task. They're experienced in assessing what to throw and what to keep," Smoke said.

Shane released a breath that sounded like it was the first good one he'd had in days. "God knows we need every bit of help we can get."

It surprised me when Tricia said, "I'll be there too. I need to get over my angst about this whole thing. Brett's our brother, and maybe we couldn't help him before, but we're the best ones to take care of his stuff now."

21

I met Smoke at the Winston farmstead Thursday morning at 7:00 a.m., forty-some minutes before sunrise. He and the Winston siblings had gotten the code to arm and disarm the security system. The yard light was still on, and no one had tried to enter the house after the system had been installed late afternoon on the previous day.

Smoke nodded as I climbed from my car. I followed him to the entry. He disarmed the system, opened the new door, and turned on the entry and living room lights. "It will seem a little friendlier now when the crew and the family arrive," he said.

"I agree. Want to take another peek at the axe job?"

"I guess. We shoulda thought to bring a rug to put over it," he said.

"The cleaners lay those tarps down anyway."

"True. I'll check back throughout the day when I can."

"Same here. I told Weber he'd be a good one to meet with the family, to help calm them."

"You've got a point. He's always had that secret sensitive side, but now he doesn't try to hide it. Unless he needs to put on his tough guy demeanor."

I chuckled. "I pray all goes well today, and there are no more, shall we say, unusual finds."

Smoke rubbed his brow. "Speaking of which, I asked crew leader Mick to tell his team to be on the lookout for any shell casings or bullets on the floor, or stuck in a wall, or a piece of furniture."

"Hope that doesn't freak any of 'em out."

"Hope not. Didn't actually occur to me that it might," he said.

When we stepped back outside, Smoke locked the door, set the alarm, and we left in our squad cars ready to respond to whatever duties we'd be assigned.

Calls kept me busy until late morning. When I knew Vince Weber wasn't tied up on a call, I sent him a message. *Heading out to the Winstons if you want to stop by.*

See you out there, he sent back.

When I arrived, the place was alive with activity. Crew members carried things out from the front and the side doors. Shane, Leah, and Tricia appeared focused on their tasks. It seemed like they were in a race against time. I debated whether to interrupt their rhythm when Mick called out, "Break time in five minutes. Finish up with your last loads."

The Winstons spotted me as I made my way around the dumpster and storage units. "Hi, Sergeant," Shane said, and the women smiled. All had rosy cheeks and were dressed for the cold in quilted coats, stocking caps, and insulated gloves.

I exchanged greetings with crew members as they wrapped up before their break. "It's like a well-oiled machine around here," I told the Winstons.

"For sure," Shane said.

"We're very impressed with how efficient they are. Amazing," Tricia said.

A pizza delivery truck pulled into an open area by the front entry. "Will some of you help the guy?" Mick hollered. "We got a table set up and wiped off in the kitchen. You can carry the pizzas in there. Everyone, grab as much to eat as you want. We'll get the vans warmed up, so you can sit down, take a load off, and enjoy your meal."

I figured the cleaners brought their lunches, so it was a nice surprise to see the boss had provided it instead. Several crew members carried in stacks of pizza boxes. Mick called out, "Winston family, help yourselves. There'll be more than enough. You too, Sergeant."

Shane looked at his wife and sister. "We'd planned to run into Emerald Lake for lunch, but this'll save us a trip, if that's okay with you two?"

They both nodded and Leah said, "Why not?"

I followed them into the kitchen and looked around. The walls were a pale lemon shade, a cheery color, even in the midst of the chaos which had been drastically reduced. Boxes and whatever else had blocked the door were gone. Cupboard doors stood open, with several shelves emptied.

Crew members filed in, lined up at the white porcelain sink, washed their hands, and dried them with paper towels from the roll. They loaded plates and carried them out to the vans. A few stood and ate off to the side. Maybe hoping for a second helping.

The Winstons pulled off their gloves and washed up too. "Seems strange to be back home on the farm, washing up in this old sink," Shane said.

Vincent Weber poked his head in the kitchen. "Yo, Sergeant. Party goin' on?"

Tricia's eyebrows lifted, but Shane laughed.

I waved him in. "Deputy Weber, come in, and I'll introduce you." When everyone had given him their names, he focused on the family members. "You have my condolences. I know Sergeant Aleckson, and Detective Dawes, along with the sheriff, have been here for you.

"Still, I wanted you to know that us deputies, and communications officers, and office staff have been thinking about you, and a lot are praying for you. A good friend of mine was killed a few months ago, and I almost died about the same time. It gave me a different perspective on life.

"I know that Brett wore a cross around his neck and what that means. I hope it helps when I tell you I *know* your brother is in a better place. A place you can't begin to imagine."

Shane, Leah, and Tricia all teared up. So did I. Some crew members sniffed behind me.

"Can I give you a hug?" Tricia asked Weber.

He snickered. "If you don't try anything funny."

She caught the joke and smiled as they hugged. "Thanks," both said as they stepped apart.

Shane brushed his tears away. "Why don't you have some pizza, Deputy Weber?"

"Nah, I already ate. But thanks. I should say hi to the rest of the cleaners. Sergeant?"

"Sure." We headed outside and waved at people in one van. The woman in the driver's seat opened the window.

"Just wanted to say thanks for doing what you do," Weber said.

They thanked him back, then the man in the front passenger seat leaned over and said, "We haven't found no bullets, Sarge."

When someone speaks, expect the unexpected. I nodded and told him, "You might not, either. I hope that didn't worry anyone on the team, thinking about that."

He shook his head. "We find all kinds of weird stuff."

I bet they did, and will. I smiled. "Thanks again."

Weber and I walked to the second van, thanked the crew members inside, and made our way toward the house.

"Long as everyone's occupied, I'm wonderin' if I can go up the famous ladder and take a look at the room?" he said.

"Sure." We headed around back. The ladder laid on the ground next to the house. "I'll help you position it."

Weber bent over and lifted it. "It's a heavy bugger, isn't it?"

"Heavy enough to withstand strong winds, although it's pretty sheltered here with the trees close behind."

We set the ladder against the house. Weber stared a moment, scooted up the rungs, and visually searched the room for a while. He climbed back down and caught his breath. "Mandy told me about all this, and I got kind of a picture, but it is way worse. I gotta say, my heart goes out to the guy I never knew.

"When I told the family Brett was in a better place, I had no clue the kind of hell he lived in here on earth. Not till I saw that room. Once he got to heaven, he musta felt like a thousand pounds got lifted off his back, unbelievably relieved he could leave all that stuff behind."

When he put it that way it made me feel better about Brett, no longer trapped and surrounded by clutter. We laid the ladder back on the ground and headed to the front door. The cleaning crew still had time before their break ended. We went inside, and I pointed at the chop marks in the floor.

"Ah geez, someone displayed a lotta anger in here. What'd the old floor do to deserve that?" Weber said.

"We can only speculate, but it's very strange all right."

"And still no sign of the bullet that went through Brett Winston."

"Not so far. Like the cleaner said, they haven't found it," I said.

"Could be Brett put it somewhere himself or threw it away."

"I'd vote for 'put it somewhere' instead 'of threw it away.'"

Weber let out a short laugh. "I'll go say goodbye to the family, then get back on the road."

"I appreciate you coming here. I could tell your words gave the family comfort."

His chin jutted out a tad as he grinned.

We went out the front door and around to the side. The Winstons and crew members had finished eating and were putting their plates in a garbage bag. "I'll go collect trash from the others," one said and left with the bag.

Weber pulled a couple business cards from his jacket pocket. "Hang in there, Winston family. If you ever wanna talk, I'm all ears. Okay?"

They took the cards and thanked him again. Weber lifted his hand in a wave. "Until next time."

After he left, Shane said, "He kinda looks like a professional wrestler, and seems more like a counselor or minister than a deputy sheriff."

"He said he almost died. It seems that might've given him a new perspective," Tricia said.

Rather than telling Weber's story, and opening a complex discussion, I said, "Vincent Weber has a sensitive side, and he likes to help people."

They were silent a moment until Leah pointed at an open box filled with a chicken alfredo pizza. "You didn't get any, Sergeant. Have some. There are other choices too."

My stomach made a small noise that sounded like "please." "That one looks great, thank you." I pulled off my gloves, grabbed a piece with a napkin and took a bite. "Mmm." It hit the spot.

Back at the office mid-afternoon, I found Amanda Zubinski pulling envelopes from her mailbox. She turned to me. "Is all better on the western front?"

"Better than yesterday, and way better than the day before. Not better than early Friday morning, before we found Brett Winston, of course."

"Yeah. Vince called after he got back from talking to the family. He said he was glad you asked him to go meet them and check out the place, although it shocked him, like it has everyone else," she said.

"You have to see it to believe it. The family really did appreciate meeting Vince, hearing his words of comfort. Shane said he seemed more like a counselor or minister than a deputy."

Mandy giggled. "Totally, sometimes."

"Wrapping it up for the day?"

"Just about to head home. By the time I get there, it'll be fifteen hundred. You?"

"Yeah. The last two days were long ones." My cellphone buzzed. "It's Smoke." I pushed the accept button. "Detective? . . . What'd they say? . . . Not that we didn't have our hopes up. Too high anyway. Thanks." I disconnected. "The medical examiner's office confirmed the two victims did not match the photos of the people reported missing."

"Now we know anyway," Mandy said.

On the way home I considered swinging by the Winstons' place, but I'd started to feel like a stalker. The thing about unresolved issues and unsolved crimes is they were like magnets that drew me back again and again.

Did that hold true with the person who shot Brett and killed his two guests? After Brett's death was reported, the killer had to get to the scene of his crime but couldn't access it until some debris was cleared. After he committed the crime, he would have watched and waited for news of the dead victims to be reported.

When that didn't happen, he must have believed Brett was dead too. In that case, the killer must not have known Brett or that he had family who would've checked when they hadn't heard from him in a while. It was one explanation that made sense all these months later.

Or was it a senseless, random crime after all? Several elderly people who lived alone had been killed in Winnebago County over the years, and we still had no viable leads, little evidence, and no suspects. The Winstons' house was isolated, a mile from the nearest home. Someone with evil intent—maybe who had a partner—could have showed up and found an opportunity to kill.

Brett had survived. A man and a woman died—vanished— yet no one who fit their descriptions had been reported missing in Minnesota. Where were they from, why were they at Brett Winston's house, and why had they been killed? Those questions bubbled in my mind time and again. We needed answers soon, for everyone's sanity.

I'd been home for an hour when George called.

"Hi, Sergeant." His voice was an octave lower, and he sounded congested.

"George, you don't sound so good."

"The flu hit me hard Sunday, and I finally felt revived enough to give you a ring."

"So sorry. My sister's issue has been on my mind, of course. But we've had a big deal case that's taken higher priority the last few days," I said.

"Just wanted to let you know I haven't done much on my end, except to check Silas's company. It's got high ratings, happy investors, so no red flags at the upper level."

"That's good to know. Detective Dawes and I did a little undercover work and tailed him on Monday. Seems longer ago. Anyway, Silas went to work early, then left about ninety minutes later, stopped at an ATM, and went to the Jackpot Junction Casino in Morton, played blackjack for a few hours, and headed back to the office."

"Hmm. Seems odd. I don't know him, but leaving work to gamble doesn't seem like a good idea. Was Silas with anyone?" George asked.

"No, but the female dealer seemed to know him well enough to give him a kiss on the cheek."

"Hmm. He kiss her back?"

"No, he mostly seemed interested in the game. The thing is, he had a gambling problem years back, and my sister was shocked when I told her he was at the casino. My primary concern is, besides their marriage and family, if he's losing money, he might be tempted to borrow some from clients' accounts and go down that dark hole."

"I agree. He'd be looking at prison time, and that's not a fun gig."

"I'm on a six-three work rotation, and my next day off is Monday. Let's play our next steps by ear. You need rest to recuperate. Taylor's been dealing with this for a couple months. I'll keep her in the loop, let her know my investigator is ill."

"Thanks." He started a coughing jag.

After a moment, I said, "Take care, George," and hung up. Poor guy.

I sent Taylor a message, *How are you?* She responded, *Better. Busy week. Let's talk this weekend.* I sent a smiling face emoji back.

Her words were cryptic and didn't give any personal details, but I held onto the word *better*. Plus, she hadn't called with more concerns since the last time we'd talked. It gave me hope things had improved.

22

Friday dawned bright and clear. I thought about Smoke's report the previous afternoon. He'd stopped at the Winston farmstead and discovered the cleaning crew had made substantial progress. They had created a wide path between the kitchen and dining room and into the living room. People no longer had to go out the front door and around to the side door to access the kitchen, and vice versa.

They'd also exposed the bottom of the stairway to the upper level. When they cleared piles away from the basement door, they discovered the stairs were clear. No stuff on them. Tricia said it was a dream come true in the midst of a nightmare.

The cleaners and family went down and found only the washer, dryer, furnace, water heater, and water softener in the entire space; a huge relief to all. Shane told Smoke the softener had been unplugged before Brett moved in and hadn't been used in years. It was anyone's guess the last time he used the washer and dryer, but he had a working furnace and hot water anyway.

Smoke also relayed what Shane had told him. "Brett had been scared of the basement since he was a kid. He was down there alone one night when the power went out in a storm. It got pitch black and Brett couldn't see anything. He screamed until his father found a flashlight and went down to rescue him.

"Brett had wrapped himself up in a ball on the concrete floor. His father had a helluva time calming him down. Shane said he'd kinda forgot about that, but it made him wonder if Brett ever went down there again."

Shane told us the day Brett died he had always been sensitive. *Brett.* He'd suffered a childhood trauma he hadn't known how to deal with, and a fear he hadn't overcome.

Shane and Leah's boys and Tricia's husband and children would arrive that afternoon. Smoke planned to meet with the family around five. The meeting we had with Sheriff Kenner turned into a mini debrief for Shane, Leah, and Tricia, and helped lessen part of their guilt. Shane carried the largest load, but Tricia suffered right along with him.

The cleaners had not yet discovered bullets, or shells, or a note from Brett that shed light on the shootings. On the positive side, the family had put more items in the dumpster than in the portable storage unit. Even better, a local thrift store said they'd pick up any furniture, dishes, tools, books, etc. they didn't want. They'd be by later in the day for a load. Shane's trailer was full of giveaway items.

I was in the sergeant's office when Kirby Sawyer phoned. "Hi, Mister Sawyer."

"Hi, Sergeant, and call me Kirby."

"Kirby, how can I help?"

"I wanted to let you know I went through Jay's yearbooks a few times, even used a magnifying glass, but couldn't connect the face of that woman in the café to any of 'em."

"Sorry to hear that. It'd be good to figure out who she is, find out why she said what she did. But it was worth a try, right?" I said.

"The worst part about it, aside from my tantrum in the café, is that it really did a number on me. Ripped open the wounds of losing my son. The authorities still have a lot to go through in the apartment debris, but the way it was blown to smithereens, who knows how many more months that will take."

"When something unexpected happens to a loved one, it's human nature to want closure. I hope you'll get an answer soon."

I heard him sniffle. "You are so right. Thanks, Sergeant."

Kirby Sawyer's call reminded me I hadn't printed Brett Winston's high school senior photo. I located it in my phone, emailed it to my work address, found a photo sheet in the squad room's cupboard, and sent it to the printer. When I picked up the photo, Brett's young face pulled at my heartstrings. I found a scissors in the supply drawer, cut around the photo's border, and slipped it in my breast pocket.

I responded to a traffic crash with minor injuries that required a great deal of paperwork, measurements, photos of skid marks, and interviews with the drivers, passengers, and witnesses. No one required hospitalization, fortunately. The state and insurance companies needed detailed reports to settle claims or in the event someone reported an injury that showed up later they said was caused by the impact.

I submitted my report minutes before my shift ended at 3:00 p.m. and tracked Smoke down in his cubicle. "Detective."

He looked up and slid his readers to the top of his head. "Sergeant. Finish your reports?"

"Yeah. I think I'll head home and come back in civilian clothes when you meet with the family."

"No civilian clothes in your locker here?" he said.

"Nope, just another uniform. I'm not planning to stay for the meeting. I just want to meet the rest of the family; give them my sympathies. I'll be on duty during Brett's service tomorrow and might be tied up on a call."

"True. Saturdays can get pretty busy."

"I also plan to swing by Mother's shop before the meeting. She loves it when I do and I've barely talked to her all week." I gave him a small wave. "See you in a bit."

Queenie and Rex were happy to see me and disappointed I didn't release them from the kennel. "Sorry, just here for a quick change." They barked as I headed into the house. I went through my usual routine at a faster pace: disrobed in the laundry room, showered, towel dried. I pulled jeans and a burgundy sweater from hangers on the rack above the dryer. I dressed, released my hair from its ponytail, brushed it out, put on mascara, and was ready to go.

I hadn't driven my GTO for a few days, and it was pleasant to turn the ignition and not hear all the sheriff's radio chatter.

On the other hand, at times off duty, I wished I could activate my lights and pull over someone who ran a red light or was speeding. Not then. I even turned off my car radio and appreciated the relative silence on the drive to Kristen's Korner, my mother's dress and accessory shop.

"Corinne!" She dropped the pile of tops she was folding and met me with a big hug. "Done with work, I see. Or are you undercover?"

I chuckled. "No, off duty."

"Gramps and I kind of wondered when you used his car Monday what kind of secret operation you were on."

I didn't use his car after all, but no need to get into the details. "I needed to help a friend. You know how people notice my car, and I wanted a lower profile," I said.

"It's sweet you love your father's car like you do. He'd be so proud of you. And John Carl and Taylor. And his grandchildren too, for heaven's sake." But not hers, sad to say.

"So how's business? Picking up, as we approach February next week?"

"January tends to be slow, but it gives me time to order spring and summer stock, work on my books," she said.

"Yes. Any plans for the weekend?"

"The shop's open tomorrow, but it's Candy's turn to work this Saturday. And David is flying in . . ." she looked at her watch. . . "any minute now. He wants to take me out for dinner tonight, so I don't have to cook."

"It's good to let him do that for you once in a while. Relax with a glass of wine in a nice atmosphere."

She smiled with a look of love in her eyes. "It is."

Two young women stepped into her shop. "Afternoon, let me know if you'd like help finding something." They nodded and thanked her. "Corinne, how about you? You need a new outfit?"

"I'm good at the moment. I either wear my uniform, sweats, or pajamas most of the time." I lifted my knee. "Or jeans. The thing I love most about my uniform is, I never have to agonize over what to wear to work."

The women heard me and laughed. "I never thought of that," one said.

I chuckled. "It's a nice perk."

"Corinne is a Winnebago County Deputy," Mother said.

Their eyes widened. "Oooh, it's big news around town how you guys found bodies in a house somewhere out in the country. Did you figure out who they are?" one asked.

"Not yet, but we will." I hoped against hope.

"Well, thanks for what you do," the other said.

"I appreciate that. Have a good evening, and bye, Mom."

"Bye, dear."

Conference Room 118 was reserved for the Winston family gathering. When I walked in, it appeared everyone had arrived. They stood in small groups in the open area.

The sheriff waved his hand at me and said, "Sergeant, we're just about to get started. Everyone, this is Sergeant Aleckson. Like your folks told you, she was the first deputy on the scene after your uncle, and brother-in-law, died."

I got a range of looks, from blank to contemplative.

"Hello. I'd like to know who you are." I went from one to the other, and as I shook their hands and offered my sympathies, Tricia's husband, Brett's niece, and nephews told me their names.

"This session will be helpful for you to learn more about what happened, talk about it, and get the support you need."

Smoke clasped his hands. "Thank you, Sergeant. I know you can't stay, but we surely do appreciate all you've done."

Shane started to clap, and the rest joined in. I felt a warm blush start in my chest and creep to the top of my head. "Thanks, everyone." I waved and headed out the door.

That was unexpected and embarrassing, I mused on the drive home.

Smoke returned to my house later that evening and leaned against the kitchen counter. "I decided to take Rex home for the night. With all the odd things going on at the Winstons', I'd feel better knowing that if someone tries to break into my house, I'll be there to stop them."

"Activity around a place does help keep bad guys away. So how'd everything go with the extended Winston family's debriefing?"

"It went as well as could be expected. It's been difficult for them to process the whole thing, to believe it. The kids are beyond troubled that two corpses sat on their uncle's couch for months," he said.

"Of course. We all are."

"Sheriff has staff checking with other states to see if they have missing persons who are possible matches for the two at the ME's office."

"Good."

"The other thing, the cleaning crew will be back in the morning to make up for one of the days they lost there this week."

"Saturday morning, without the family?" I said.

"Yep. The Winstons agreed the crew has a pretty good handle on how to sort through stuff. They won't peruse drawers of papers, or what looks like personal items, that sort of thing."

"How long do Shane and Tricia plan to stay?"

"At least through next week. Both have lots of PTO built up, between vacation and sick leave, so that's not an issue. Shane's boys may come back when they tackle the shed. Vehicles, tools, you name it, to look through."

Smoke took me in his arms for a farewell kiss. "Have a restful sleep tonight, my love."

"You too. See you sometime tomorrow."

Saturday I was tied up with call after call until things let up a few minutes before 2:00, the time of Brett's service. I let Communications know my location and slipped into the chapel after the service had begun. It was a small gathering with family and a few others—friends I presumed—and included Kirby Sawyer, a surprise. He must have contacted the family to extend his sympathies and if they hadn't heard, would've told them about his son's death.

Sheriff Kenner, Elton Dawes, Vincent Weber, and Amanda Zubinski sat in the row behind the groups. When I slid in next to Mandy, she gave my arm a gentle nudge.

A thin, elderly man with hair like spun cotton stood behind the lectern. His voice was weak and on the gravelly side, so the microphone helped project it to those gathered. "Brett Winston was one of my favorite students." He nodded and lifted his hand toward Kirby Sawyer. "Along with Jay Sawyer. They were a fine pair. Brett on the serious side. Jay just the opposite."

I heard chuckles among Brett's siblings and Jay's father as they exchanged looks.

"When I got word Jay had died in an apartment explosion last August, it broke my heart. Then Brett died accidentally too. It just doesn't seem real. I hadn't seen either man in ages. It's one of those things in life. We go our separate ways but still carry people we love in our hearts and minds. Thank you for letting me say a few words."

Shane helped the man to his seat, then went to the lectern himself. "Many thanks, Mister Baker. You were Brett's favorite teacher, and we appreciate you being here with us today. You too, Mister Sawyer. We mourn the loss of your son along with you."

Kirby pulled a tissue from his pocket and wiped his eyes.

Shane went on to tell stories about Brett, how he rescued injured critters, and nursed as many back to health as possible. How he cherished loved ones, especially his wife and son. How he struggled to cope after he lost his son and it disabled him. Brett started to collect things. More and more until his death.

Shane concluded with, "After Aiden died, Brett and Deena purchased a beautiful granite monument and had all their names engraved on it. It doesn't seem Deena will be buried there, but we can bury Brett's ashes next to their son."

The pastor preached a short message to give them hope and closed with a prayer.

23

After the service, we were invited to gather for refreshments in the social room across the hall. Kirby Sawyer gravitated toward Smoke and me. "It's good to meet you, Kirby. The sergeant told me about your loss, and you have my deepest sympathies," Smoke said.

Kirby nodded. "I appreciate that. It's about impossible to believe. Every step we took after we got the news didn't make it any easier to accept. Jay was living in an apartment, and my sister and I had to take care of the furniture and such. It appeared a woman had been staying with him.

"Actually, it looked like she had just moved some things in, not a lot. We figured it was his girlfriend. The one who seemed to disappear off the face of the planet after her one and only call to tell me about the explosion."

"Nothing in the apartment with her name on it, like a bill?" Smoke asked.

"Nothing."

Smoke's eyes narrowed a tad. "The apartment building that exploded was in a higher crime neighborhood, known for illegal activities. Any idea who Jay would've been visiting?"

"Not a clue. He was a counselor at North High School. I thought maybe he was trying to help someone there. When I talked to people at his school, they didn't know either. It happened right before school started. Everyone there was pretty shocked by it, I can tell you that much," Kirby said.

"No one knew his girlfriend?" I asked.

"That's the thing. They said Jay was secretive about it and thought maybe she was married. At the same time, it was not like Jay to do something like that. The whole thing is a big mystery, and not one I like at all."

After Kirby left, Shane joined me. "I feel so bad about Jay Sawyer and can't believe we didn't hear about it. He was Brett's best friend back when. I guess we know Brett had been in a different place for a while. Still I'm surprised no one told him. Mister Sawyer said he didn't have Brett's number, didn't know he'd moved back to the farm, or he would've told him. Too many things—important things—fell between the cracks."

Kenner, Smoke, Weber, Zubinski, and I talked to family members and friends for a while longer, then we gathered together. "It's nice you all came," I said.

"Yeah well, I hope three of us here in uniform, plus the sheriff, didn't get anybody riled up. No offense, Sheriff," Weber said.

Sheriff Kenner smiled. "Didn't seem to. The family said they appreciated it."

On the drive home, I gave in to temptation and continued past my road to the Winstons' place. It was 4:26 and the cleaning crew was ready to shut down for the day. It seemed all eyes turned to me when I climbed from my squad car.

"Sergeant, you work Saturdays too?" a small Latina asked.

"Oh, yes. So how are things coming along?"

Mick waved his hand from the house to the storage unit, to the dumpster. "Well, you can see we filled up the thirty cubic yard dumpster. We got another one coming on Monday. The main level is pretty much cleared out, and we got about halfway up the steps. We don't want to get into the room Brett Winston occupied until the family's here with us. Probably personal stuff they should see first."

"You have an efficient crew, that's for sure," I said.

"They are the best." He nodded at the shed. "Some are a little concerned about potential *unusual* finds in there."

Like another body or more? His words, and the way he said them, made chills dance up my spine. "Some critters likely have made comfy little homes in there."

"I'd say. We have a division that takes care of animal removal. Mice, rats, squirrels, raccoons, birds, snakes. It'd be more common to find bats in the house attic where it'd be warmer, the way they like it."

I didn't mind any of those creatures in the great outdoors, but not loose in a house, or garage, or other structures. "Thanks again, Mick. I'll be off duty Monday when your crew returns, but I'll be in touch with the Winstons, get updates from them."

"I gotta say, they've been real fine to work for, and work with."

"Have a good day off tomorrow."

"Will do. I'll turn on the yard light and set the alarm system before we go," Mick assured me.

I had showered and was about to check emails and messages when Smoke arrived with Rex and takeout from our favorite Oak Lea authentic Mexican restaurant. I took the bag of food from his hand and set it on the counter. Queenie barked with excitement until Smoke scratched her head and Rex gave her a lick.

Smoke gathered me in his arms, and we embraced for a long moment, kissed for a longer one, and embraced again.

"This has been an eventful week," I said with my face rested against his chest.

He gave my hair a gentle yank. "Ya think? The good news is, we can kiss it goodbye in a few hours, and start a new, less eventful one. I hope."

I stepped back. "Maybe we should crack open a beer, toast to that, and see what's in that bag. Smells delicious."

Smoke got the beers from the refrigerator, and I unwrapped shrimp fajitas, mango chicken burritos, and a container of a steak and pepper dish. We toasted to a better week ahead, especially for the Winstons and filled our plates with the best Mexican food around.

Smoke swallowed a bite then said, "You've mentioned Kirby Sawyer and his loss. Another sad tale. It takes a long time to sort through debris, find bits of remains, and work to identify people. I remember when it happened, authorities had no clue about the number of people in the building. So many were otherwise homeless, couch-hopping.

"When they interviewed residents who weren't home at the time, they didn't know who was or wasn't in their apartments when the building exploded. They'd see people in hallways and had no clue who they were. Families of the deceased may not have heard from them for months or years, and lost track along the way, had no idea if they were in the building."

"Sad how many that entails. And it brings up a good point, people in those situations are rarely reported as missing, so no one's looking for them. Then other people, like Kirby, are waiting for confirmation."

We finished our meal, put the leftovers in the fridge, and settled in for an evening with a light romantic comedy on TV.

It had snowed overnight, not enough to plow, but enough powder to cover my squad car. I started the engine and brushed off the snow. While the car warmed, I went back inside and met Smoke as he came into the kitchen, followed by Queenie and Rex. "Mornin' little darlin'." He leaned in and nuzzled his nose against my cheeks. His lips captured mine, and it warmed me from head to toe. "Thanks again for last night. I slept like a log after all our fooling around."

I laughed and gave him a quick peck. "A memorable night, but I need to shift my focus to whatever my duty will call me to do today."

"The warrior mindset?"

"Mixed in with compassion as needed."

"Yep."

As it turned out, Sunday at work was steady, but not crazy. Toward the end of my shift, I cruised down Winstons' driveway. No one was around. I sat for a moment and watched the leafless branches sway gently in the northerly breeze. What would happen to the property once it had been cleared of debris, and cleaned?

If I were a family member, I'd vote to tear the house down. Shane and Tricia had not lived there for many years, yet held on to it, perhaps for sentimental reasons. It seemed the tragic events from the past months had lessened their desire to keep it. They would retain happy memories of their childhoods whether the house was there or not.

Their father had built the pole shed not many years before. It was a beautiful piece of property with room to roam; a good place for a family to build a nice house and create their own memories.

Taylor and Silas and George came to mind. It was my day off tomorrow, and if Taylor needed me, I would do what I could to help. I'd discovered along the way that taking care of a task was often less tiring, less stressful, than thinking about it.

I woke up Monday morning and remembered it was my first day off of three. When I shouted, "Yes!" Queenie stood from her spot on the bedside rug and let out a little yip. I rolled over, reached down, and petted her. "No appointments or commitments on the calendar today. Smoke must've taken Rex home when he left, and I was too zonked out to hear them." Queenie yipped again.

I glanced out the window at the gray day, but it didn't dampen my spirits. With no particular plans in mind, I sat up and stretched. My thoughts traveled to the Winstons as they began week two of their major house project.

With ten crew members on removal detail, they had made great progress. By Saturday afternoon they'd removed large, medium, and small furniture pieces, along with boxes filled with random—often strange—items. Lawn ornaments and lawn chairs, plant stands, flower pots, aquariums, file cabinets, pet carriers, bird feeders, children's toys, pictures, lamps, some with shades.

The thrift store was happy to take some loads, other items went into the dumpster, and the family had yet to decide about things in the portable storage unit. I stood, shook my arms and legs, then rolled my shoulders and head, in hopes it would release thoughts about the Winston family's ordeal for a while.

Queenie followed close behind on my way down the stairs to the kitchen. "You need to go outside, Girl?"

She gave her single bark signal, and we trooped into the living room. I slid open the glass door to let her out, then returned to the kitchen and made a cup of coffee. When Queenie barked to come in, I had her treat ready. I set my coffee on the end table, and we nestled on the couch.

My phone dinged and woke me with a start. I hadn't planned to fall asleep: proof the last six work days had taken their toll. I picked the phone up from my stomach and read the text message from George. *I feel like I'm going to live after all, but still don't have much voice, or energy. Sorry.*

I wrote back, *No worries. Take care of yourself. We'll talk when you're well again.*

If he wasn't better soon, Taylor might want to hire someone else.

Taylor's kids would be in school, and Silas would be wherever, I thought as I phoned her. "Hi, Corky." Her voice was soft, her words slow, like she felt defeated.

"Hi. You okay?"

"Yeah. A little down, I guess. I try to think about anything other than Silas's behavior and activities," she said.

"So sorry about that, Taylor. And I hate to tell you, but George is still pretty sick."

"I wondered how he was doing. One of my friends has the flu bug, and it's a nasty one this year."

"My friend just got over a bad cold. It may have been the flu, but he didn't get tested. Taylor, to let you know, I'm off the next couple days, and I'd be happy to help you, with whatever," I said.

"I appreciate your support and I'll let you know."

"Please do that. I'll ask George to recommend someone if he's not better soon."

"Thanks, Corky. We'll figure that out, if we need to. I signed up to help over the lunch hour at school, so I better get moving."

"All righty."

Smoke was at a Sheriff's Association meeting with Kenner and wouldn't be back until late afternoon, or early evening. I had the day to myself, with Queenie, that is. The temperature had climbed to the mid-thirties by late morning, and a run would be a good way to release both toxins and stress.

I puttered around the house, did laundry, and some half-hearted cleaning. Queenie and I went on a three-mile run early afternoon and stopped in to see Gramps on the way back. We all cherished the hour we spent together.

Home again, I showered, and was on the couch reading a book mid-afternoon when Taylor phoned me.

She sounded a little out of breath. "Corky, I followed Silas to the casino to confront him, talk to him about his gambling problem. I waited a few minutes to work up my courage, and when I went into the game room, I saw that hussy throw her arms around him and give him a big kiss. She wasn't working, she was just hanging around there."

That brought me to my feet in a flash. "Then what happened, where are you now?"

"I went up to them and stopped myself from slugging them both. Instead, I shook my finger in their faces and said, 'You can have him, you home wrecker.' I ran out, and heard Silas calling for me, saying it was all a mistake, but I kept going. Just got in my car and started driving. I think Silas is following me."

School had let out by then. "Where are your kids?" I asked.

"At home. At lunch today, I told the kids I had an errand this afternoon and might not get back until suppertime. I asked Katie's friend to ride the bus home with them. They're watching the other two."

"All right. I know it's a bit of a distance to my house, but I want you to come here. We can figure out next steps. If Silas follows you all the way, I'll do my best to mediate."

"Okay. I should be there in less than two hours. I'll let Katie know I might be late," she said.

"Good. And Taylor, if anything makes you scared along the way, call nine-one-one first. Then call me. Also, take note of your location before you do."

"Corky, the way you said that is scaring me."

"I'm sorry. We have no reason to think anything unusual will happen. I just want you to be aware of what to do, in case. Concentrate on the road and drive safe, okay?" I said.

"Okay."

I thought of something else. "You're hands-free, on your Bluetooth, right?"

"Yes, Sergeant Aleckson."

I smiled at her answer. "Good. See you soon."

After we disconnected, I started to pace, and prayed for Taylor's safety.

24

Taylor phoned a half hour later. "Silas is still behind me."

"Are you doing okay?"

"Yes. He tried to call me twice, but I won't answer. He's not driving crazy, hasn't tried to pass me, or anything like that. Corky, this whole situation is the most bizarre thing ever. Nothing about it seems real. It's like we're in some kind of alternate reality."

"I've been in those kinds of situations. What you need to do is relax as best you can, and concentrate. You've got family who loves you and we'll do all we can to help and support you," I said.

"I do know that. It's what's helped me press on the last couple weeks."

"Focus on your driving and call me whenever you need to."

"Thank you." She ended the call.

Taylor didn't want other family members to know about their situation until the whole truth—whatever it turned out to be—was brought to light. She'd decide how to tell them. Taylor had a complex family history she'd learned about a few years ago.

In a nutshell, her unmarried teenage mother Wendy put Taylor up for adoption. No one, except her parents, knew she'd been pregnant, and given birth. A few months later, homecoming night her senior year in high school, Wendy and her boyfriend Toby disappeared. The belief was they'd run away together.

That assumption was negated over thirty years later when a couple's remains—Wendy's and a boy named Sheldon's—were discovered in an old Dodge Charger at the bottom of a lake. It was Toby Fryor's vehicle, but Toby was not the victim. Instead, he was responsible for the deaths of Wendy and two boys, Sheldon and Rudy. Rudy's remains were never found.

When his Dodge Charger surfaced, it prompted long-lost Toby Fryor to do the same, posed as someone else. Had Wendy's friends known about her baby, they would've figured Toby was the father. Instead, Taylor's father was my father, conceived during a one-night stand.

The Evertons had lost their daughter decades before and were overjoyed to meet their beautiful granddaughter decades later, as were Grandpa and Grandma Aleckson. The added twist: my mother's almost fiancé David was Toby Fryor's brother. I'd killed Toby in self-defense, and neither his father nor his brothers blamed me in any way.

I worked off nervous energy—stirred by memories and questions about Taylor's husband—dusting and vacuuming. I wasn't afraid of Silas, but Silas under pressure might present himself in a different manner. Why had he followed Taylor from the casino, and what did he expect to say, or do, when he caught up with Taylor?

After I considered how unpredictable his behavior seemed, what state of mind he might be in, I retrieved my personal sidearm, a Smith and Wesson, ready in its pancake holster, from my safe. I carried it when I went for runs on country roads, and on many other occasions. Off duty or on, I felt both safer and better equipped to help others if the need arose.

Smoke and Sheriff Kenner's meeting was in Crow Wing County, about one hundred miles north of Oak Lea. For some reason, or for no reason at all, my internal tension grew as the minutes passed. I clipped my holster onto my jeans waistband and zipped my hoodie partway up to conceal it.

Taylor phoned again. "Taylor?"

"Corky, I'm almost to your road and will be there in a couple of minutes. Silas is still behind me."

"Okay, I'll walk out to meet you," I told her.

Dusk had closed in, and the temperature hovered at the freezing point. "Queenie, you need to stay inside and no barking." A command she couldn't always obey.

I slipped on a light jacket over my hoodie and headed out the front door. Taylor pulled into the driveway, parked, and got out. Silas drove in, parked beside her, and climbed from his vehicle. Her eyes darted back and forth; worried. His skin was stretched tight, and he looked both haggard and scared.

A blue subcompact Suzuki, its headlights off when they should've been on, pulled in. We all turned toward it as a woman I recognized climbed out. The blackjack dealer. She wore brown ski pants and a bulky camel cable sweater. No jacket. Her face was a deep red beet color, her expression livid. In the cold air, her exhalations looked like steam as they rose above her head. My body tensed, prepared for a showdown.

"What in the hell, Misty?" Silas said.

Misty.

"That's what I want to know," Misty spit back and pointed at Taylor. "You followed that bitch all the way here to this podunk county full of losers."

Losers?

"Do *not* call my wife that. She is anything but, and she's the love of my life besides," Silas said.

"But you *have* to love me," she yelled back.

Things had gone from bad to worse in a nanosecond and needed to be brought under control in the next nanosecond.

I waved my hand. "Misty, it's cold out here. How about we go into my house and discuss this." I had more equipment inside: handcuffs, a baton, taser gun. I'd call 911 in a heartbeat if Misty's anger escalated. I brushed my elbow across my holster.

Taylor followed my lead. "Misty, you can talk to Silas in private, if you'd like."

Silas frowned and shook his head a tad before he caught himself.

"*No!*" Misty screeched, and my eardrums pulsed against the assault. Her hand moved toward her pocket, and mine went for my gun. "Other side of the car," I yelled at Taylor and Silas, but they didn't budge.

"Misty, hands up where I can see them. *Now!*"

She looked like she was in a trance and didn't comply with my orders. Maybe she didn't hear me.

"Misty, I'm a deputy sheriff. Hold up both your hands where I can see them," I directed, my voice at full volume.

The next instant, she drew a handgun with her right hand and used her left hand to get a good grip. I caught a glimpse of Silas as he pulled Taylor down and laid his body on top of hers. As Misty started to lower her gun I yelled, "Stop," and shot her in the right forearm before her finger reached the trigger.

Misty's gun dropped to the ground. She screamed then started to kneel like she was determined to pick her gun up with her good arm. I reached it first, handed it to Silas, and jumped on top of Misty who'd landed face down. I holstered my S&W.

"Taylor, call nine-one-one, tell Communications I need help here *now*."

I heard Queenie barking as I grabbed Misty's upper arms, wrestled them behind her, hooked them together with mine, and held on. An earthy blood scent rose from her wound. She shrieked and shrilled like a banshee until she ran out of air, then started to pant instead. Our combined breaths looked like short bursts of steam.

"That hurts, you crazy bitch," she yelled.

I somehow restrained myself from an unprofessional response and pulled her uninjured left arm back a little more instead. Taylor had the phone to her ear and held up three fingers. I nodded and shifted. "Can you get a clean dishtowel to wrap Misty's arm?"

Taylor handed her phone to Silas to stay on the line with Communications and sprinted off while Misty wiggled and struggled against me. A few more minutes to maintain my hold seemed like a month away. Resolute willpower, fueled by anger, would see me through until help arrived. Taylor returned with the towel and managed to work beside me as she wrapped the towel around Misty's arm over her sweater.

When a squad car pulled into the driveway, immense relief coursed through my body. I had mentally counted to ninety seconds after Taylor finished wrapping Misty's arm and knew I couldn't hold tight much longer. As the car door opened, I heard Sergeant Leo Roth tell Communications he had arrived on the scene.

Silas held Misty's gun in a lowered, ready position. "Silas, lay Misty's gun on the Kia's hood," I said.

Roth dashed to my aid.

"She threatened us with her gun. When she refused to drop it, I was forced to shoot her. Silas held her weapon until you got here. It's on the Kia," I said.

Roth leaned over. "Okay. First off, let's take a look at the wound."

I eased my hold on Misty's right arm. Blood had seeped through her sweater and was visible on the towel. Roth pulled the sweater from her right shoulder and slid it, and the towel, off her arm.

Misty didn't resist. She had an elbow-length wool top on underneath, and it enabled us to visually examine her wound.

246

"Appears the bullet missed bone, and went right through," was Roth's cursory assessment.

It didn't look as bad as I'd imagined, but I said nothing. Roth kept further thoughts to himself as well.

"Taylor, run in and get a bottle of distilled water from the laundry room shelf to rinse off the wound. Sergeant, you got your kit?" I said.

"Sure." Roth left, returned with his case of first aid supplies, and knelt down beside us. Taylor was back a moment later.

I rolled away from my position on Misty's back, kneeled beside her, and interlocked my right arm in her left. Roth pulled on vinyl gloves. When he reached for the water, Taylor twisted the cap off, and handed it to him. "This might sting," he said.

Misty jerked a little but remained silent. In the cold air, the room temperature water likely felt warm on her skin.

Roth withdrew a roll of hemostatic gauze tape that had agents to help clot blood and a blunt nose scissors. He handed the scissors to me. Misty didn't struggle as he wrapped the tape around her wound. He took the scissors from me, cut the gauze from the roll, put the supplies back in his case, and stood.

"Misty, I need you to work your way into a kneeling position. Then hold your hands out in front of you." Given her injury, he'd opted to cuff her hands in front, instead of behind, her back.

When Misty was on her knees, Roth applied the handcuffs. She groaned at that. "Okay. Now put your right foot on the ground, and we'll help you stand up," Roth said.

I had her left arm, and he slid his hand around her back to steady her as she struggled to her feet. "Anything on your person; drugs, weapons like a knife, or nail file?" he asked.

"F you," was her reply.

Roth patted each front pants pocket. Nothing more, after her gun was confiscated. "Sergeant, if you can help me with the pat search."

I did, and when I'd finished said, "All clear."

She dropped another F bomb.

"What's your name?" Roth asked.

Misty spit in place of an answer.

Roth gave her his most serious frown. "Spitting on someone is a crime of assault in Minnesota, so consider yourself fortunate your germ-filled spittle didn't land on any of us."

Misty jutted her chin out in a defiant way, like a rebellious child might.

"Where's your ID, your phone, Ms. we don't know your name?" Roth asked.

She growled, but at least didn't spit again.

I figured Silas had heard the conversation, and would tell Roth, but he must've had reasons not to.

"I believe her first name is Misty," I said.

Roth nodded. "Okay. We'll get it all sorted out."

Misty turned to Silas and yelled, "The last one didn't get away from me, and you won't either."

Was that a threat, and what in the world did she mean? It led me to question if she was delusional, in addition to having a personality disorder, or two, or three.

"Let's get her into my squad car," Roth said.

He had parked in the middle of the driveway, a good ten feet behind the other vehicles. Roth clasped Misty's upper right arm in his, and I took her left. Although her hands were cuffed, she still tried to pull away from my grip. Roth and I tightened ours in kind.

Misty delivered a string of expletives. Aside from the offensive verbal assault, I was a tad bit impressed she had such an extensive vocabulary. Albeit a vulgar one. Some words I hadn't heard used in years and didn't know they were still in use.

Roth opened the backseat door, placed his hand on Misty's head, and tucked it down so she wouldn't knock it on the way in. When she was seated, he said, "I'll hold her, if you'll buckle her in."

He put his finger on the sensitive nerve under her nose and lifted. She whimpered, and her eyes watered as her head tilted back against her will. She could neither head butt nor bite us, and that was the goal. I snapped the belt around her in short order.

Roth released his grip, shut the door, opened his driver's side door, climbed in, and started the car. He turned and slid the hard plastic shield over to cover the open metal cage behind his seat. "In case you get the urge to spit again."

25

Roth pressed his radio button. "Six seventeen, Winnebago County."

"Go ahead, Sergeant."

"There was a confrontation at the residence. The suspect sustained an injury, but we have things under control."

"Copy. Need EMS to respond there?"

"Negative, I'll provide the transport. We will need our crime scene team to report here, however."

"Ten-four. I'll get them rolling."

As we walked away we heard Misty yelling, kicking the seat, and banging her body against the door.

"And she called me a bitch," I said.

Roth shook his head. "Who is she, and what about the other two—Silas and Taylor—why were they here today?"

"All I know about Misty is she's a blackjack dealer at Jackpot Junction, and I just learned her name when she got here." We walked over to Taylor and Silas. I waved my hand from one to the other. "This is my sister Taylor Franson, and her husband Silas. Sergeant Roth."

They exchanged nods.

Roth lifted a hand. "Our crime scene team will be here shortly to photograph the scene and collect evidence."

"My motion detection camera should have picked up and recorded most of this," I said.

"Sweet," he said.

When my phone buzzed, I pulled it out and checked: a text from Smoke. *Communications called Sheriff and reported a call to your house. Said Roth's there, things are under control.* I sent a thumbs up back. I hoped it was enough reassurance because it was all I could give at that moment.

"Sergeant, I need to get Misty to the hospital, but let's check her vehicle for her ID and phone." Roth handed me a pair of protective gloves. "You take the driver's side, and I'll take the passenger's." We opened Misty's front doors. Her pink-cased cellphone and a small black purse lay in plain view on the passenger seat.

Roth picked up the purse and looked inside. "You're my witness. Not much room in here. I see a wallet, comb, lip gloss, and bottle of pills, minus the prescription label. For what, is to be determined."

I walked around to his side and glanced in her purse. "Won't be much for the jail staff to inventory."

Roth pulled out the black bifold wallet, unsnapped it, spread the bill holder open, and thumbed through it. "No big bills. Looks like three twenties, a ten, two fives, and six ones." Her driver's license was in the front card slot. Roth withdrew and held it up.

"Her name is indeed Misty. Misty Lee Bayner with a Chaska, Minnesota address."

"Chaska? That doesn't make sense. The casino must be ninety minutes away, a long commute, especially in winter," I said.

"She probably moved, and hasn't changed her address yet. Forty-one years old. Old enough to know better, but not old enough to care, huh?"

"Who knows? She seems obsessed with Silas. What she said about the last one not getting away, and the hateful way she said it, sounded ominous. She's after Silas now, so what happened to the other guy who didn't get away? She got him locked up in her basement?" A facetious comment, yet stranger things happened.

"We'll see what we can get out of her. That, and what possessed her to do what she did here today. I'll have her vehicle towed to the sheriff's garage, and we'll do an official search for other weapons and incriminating evidence," Roth said.

We shut Misty's car doors, and Roth dropped her driver's license into his breast pocket. "I'll seal her purse in an evidence bag, and the corrections officers can inventory the contents. If you'll add your witness initials to the evidence bag." We completed our tasks, and he closed the trunk.

Misty howled some more from inside the car as we walked back to Taylor and Silas, who held hands and stayed put by the garage. Both looked like they were stuck in a bad place and had no clue where their escape route was.

"We'll get her treated at the hospital, then booked into jail. Hopefully the doctor won't want to keep her overnight," Roth said.

"If they do, that'll be another cluster for our office to deal with," I said.

Taylor surprised me when she blurted out, "When that maniac held her gun on us, I have never been more frightened in my entire life. Corky yelled at her, and then there was a loud bang. I didn't even know Corky had her gun and thought for a second Misty had shot Silas. When Misty's gun dropped, Corky picked it up in an instant, and handed it to Silas. I was frozen to the spot, couldn't move for a while."

Silas reached his arm around Taylor's shoulder and squeezed.

Roth's eyes narrowed. "You've been through a lot of trauma here. Now you can rest assured Misty is in our custody. After the investigation, and the list of offenses she'll be charged with, the court will decide what happens after that."

Taylor and Silas nodded.

"I'll need your statements, but that will have to wait. We're a deputy short on this shift—one went home sick. Others are tied up, or they would've been here to assist. I'll be back when we have things under control with Ms. Misty. In the meantime, hang tight."

"Sergeant Roth, I'll check the video footage."

"As protocol, wait for the crime scene team to witness when you do," he said.

"Sure. I've got legal pads. If you want, we can each write down the details of the incident from our own perspectives. That'll save you time," I said.

"Good idea, thanks Sergeant. I'll let you know what happens at the hospital."

When Roth opened his car door, Misty's squeals escaped from within.

I muttered, "I hope he doesn't have to listen to that commotion the whole way there."

Taylor and Silas stayed by the garage door. I was about to tell them they could wait inside when Deputies Vincent Weber and Amanda Zubinski arrived in the Winnebago County Mobile Crime Unit and parked behind Misty's vehicle.

When they got out Weber shook his head, "Ah geez, Sergeant. Don't get enough excitement at work, huh?"

"Guess not."

Zubinski rolled her eyes at him, then turned to me. "You okay?"

My shoulders lifted. "A little shaken, but otherwise fine. The important thing is, my family didn't get injured."

Weber nodded in Taylor's direction. "Huh. That your sister?"

"And her husband."

"Sounds like there's a story there," he said.

"I'll tell you the background later. For now, the condensed version is, Taylor's husband Silas followed her to my house. He was followed by a woman named Misty who got here right behind him. Seems she was obsessed with Silas, didn't want

Taylor to have him, and pulled a gun on them. I drew mine, shouted a warning, and shot her in the arm."

"Ah geez, that brings up bad memories of Darcie."

"Flashes of that incident ran through my mind when Misty started her rant. But she didn't try to run them over, like Darcie did to us."

"Yeah." Darcie had stalked Weber and mistakenly thought we were involved.

"Let's focus on this case, Vince," Mandy said.

I pointed at the motion detection camera on my garage. "My camera should've captured most of it, at least. Roth said one of you should witness it when I download it to a thumb drive."

"Sure," Mandy said.

"Smart thing when you finally installed it," Weber said.

"I'll grab evidence bags, and we'll start with your gun, Corky. Sorry, but you know the drill," Mandy said. Yes I did.

Mandy returned with bags stuffed in her front pockets. She and Weber slid on the vinyl gloves.

"Least the cold makes it easier to pull these buggers on," Weber said.

Mandy lifted a bag. I unholstered my Smith and Wesson, held it by its butt, and handed it to Mandy. "You'll find I fired one round at Misty. After the bullet struck her arm, it landed in Taylor's Kia." She unloaded it and handed the bullets to Weber who dropped them in an evidence bag. My gun went into another.

"Okay." Weber recorded the info on the evidence bags and carried them to the van. He returned with a pair of small pliers he'd stuck in his back pocket. "Come and meet Taylor and Silas." After introductions, Silas's hand shook as he pointed at Misty's weapon on the Kia's hood. "That's her gun," he said.

Weber moved closer and snapped photos. He picked up the gun and unloaded it. Mandy opened a bag for the bullets, and another for the gun. They sealed both bags. Weber pulled the marker from his pocket, noted the date, time, and contents.

I pointed to the ground where Misty and I had struggled. Weber handed the evidence bags to Mandy and snapped photos of that spot. Weber turned his attention to Taylor's Kia. "Ah, the bullet in question."

He and Mandy studied the imbedded bullet a moment. Weber took several photos before he withdrew the pliers and a bag from his pocket. He clamped the pliers on the bullet, twisted to loosen it, pulled it out, and dropped it in the bag. He jotted the identification info on it. "Should have our suspect's fingerprints on it," he said.

"Yes. About her gun; there will be at least three sets of prints on it. Hers, mine, and Silas's," I said.

"So noted," Mandy said.

"I'll secure these in the van, then we'll grab the video, and wrap things up here," Weber said.

"Do you two want to go inside?" I asked Taylor and Silas.

Taylor shook her head. "We'll wait till you're done in there."

The rest of us headed toward the front door. "Just stomp the snow from your boots, no need to take them off." That's when I realized I still had my wool slippers on. They wiped their boots on the outside mat and followed me to the office den, with Queenie behind them.

I sat down at the computer, selected the web browser, entered the camera's IP address, and logged in. I checked my phone for the times Taylor called me on her way. "All right, they arrived at just after sixteen forty. Let's capture the video from then until now." I inserted a thumb drive, selected the time frame, and sent that portion to the drive. When it had transferred, I removed it and handed it to Mandy.

"Not gonna watch it?" Weber said as he slipped the drive into an evidence bag.

"Sometime, maybe." I elbowed his arm, then inserted another thumb drive into the computer. "But I'll save one for Dawes. He'll want to see it."

"I think we got all we need, right Deputy Weber?" Mandy said.

"Yeah. We can be on our way," he said.

We headed outside, and they called out their goodbyes to Taylor and Silas.

Weber pointed at Misty's SUV. "What about her vehicle there?"

"We'll need to have it towed. Let's check with Roth on that," Mandy said.

I managed a small smile. "Thanks, you two."

Mandy nodded, and Weber said, "Later then." And off they went.

I joined Taylor and Silas, then pointed at the hole in her vehicle. "Sorry about your Kia, Taylor. Insurance should cover it, or the judge can make it part of Misty's restitution."

"Corky, are you *kidding*? Do not feel one bit sorry about my car. You saved our lives." She touched my shoulder and lowered her voice. "Can I ask why you even had your gun with you, when you aren't working?"

I didn't want to admit Silas's unknown and questioned state of mind was the core reason. "It's my personal weapon, and I often carry it. Like the old Boy Scout motto, 'Be prepared.' I think of it as situational awareness, expect the unexpected."

She raised her eyebrows. "You must always feel like you're on duty then."

"No. More like I tune in as the need arises." A chill ran through me. Maybe from the night air, maybe from a "could've been worse" thunderbolt. "Let's go inside and warm up."

Taylor, Silas, and I trooped into the house. Queenie begged for my attention and assurance after all the excitement she'd been excluded from. I scratched her head. "It's okay, Girl. Everything is just fine."

They left their shoes on the entry rug. Silas took Taylor's coat, hung it in the front closet, then hung up his own. He turned to Taylor. "I need you to know I didn't have any kind of personal relationship with Misty. I liked playing blackjack at her table because she's one of the better dealers."

"You didn't know how much she liked you, that she had a crush on you?" Taylor said.

I think *obsessed* was more like it.

"She was flirty, but I figured she acted like that with all the guys. I was interested in the game, not the girl." He raised his right hand. "I didn't do a single thing to encourage her, and I swear I had *no* clue she had some kind of weird thing for me. Or that she was off her rocker." Silas reached for Taylor's hands.

The way Taylor's brows came together when she looked into her husband's eyes reminded me of an almost identical expression on John Carl's face when he was troubled. I zoned out a moment and thought about the father we never knew.

I tuned back in when Taylor said, "What is it then? What have you been hiding from me all these weeks? Something besides trucking off to the casino when I thought you were at work."

She'd known about the gambling piece for a while, but with George out of commission, we had yet to learn anything about Silas's business dealings.

Silas glanced down at their joined hands. "I'm afraid it's something pretty serious."

My heart skipped a bunch of beats as my imagination went wild. I waited for Taylor's reaction and/or response. Her frown deepened.

Silas turned to me. "Can Taylor and I go somewhere to talk in private? I have a lot to explain."

It took me a few seconds to find my voice. "Of course you can. Go in the office den and close the door. You'll have total privacy."

26

Taylor led the way, and when the door latched, I started to pace. I needed to work off the adrenaline dump I'd ignored since first Taylor, then Silas, then Misty arrived at my house. When Misty pulled out her gun, I had my own unholstered and pointed at her in an instant, before my brain fully registered the whole scenario. Muscle memory training had saved at least one life.

I paced some more until Queenie whined. "Sorry, I know it makes you nervous when I do that. Let's find a big milk bone for you to chew on while I get cleaned up after that unexpected encounter with a most unwelcome intruder."

I pulled the treat from Queenie's food cabinet, and as she took it from my hand, I glanced at the kitchen clock. Smoke would be on his way home soon. Not soon enough. As I undressed in the laundry room, I noticed Misty's blood on my sleeve. I sprayed it with a stain remover, threw all my clothes in the washer, and stepped into a warm shower.

The past two weeks had been filled with traumas for my sister and the Winston families. I'd gone from one to the other to investigate, render aid, and offer professional and personal support. When we had answers to help them all move on, I hoped to do the same.

For one dilemma, Silas was in my office den confessing something big to Taylor. For the other, unidentified remains of two murder victims had been recovered from the Winston farmhouse. The discovery of the bodies helped fill in a blank left by Brett's curious and cryptic note.

He wrote it as he neared death. He was not in his right mind or he would have included details, like what happened and who the victims were. Had his thinking been clear, he'd realize someone would find them—a horrible thing for the unprepared—and authorities would have a mystery murder times two to solve.

I shut off the water, towel dried, and pulled clothes from the dryer: stretch pants, a sweatshirt, socks, and undergarments. I dressed, stepped into the kitchen, and listened for any shouting or banging noises from the office. The only sounds I heard were Queenie's sleeping puffs, the refrigerator humming, and furnace air blowing from the vents.

I glanced at the kitchen clock: 6:23. Smoke and the sheriff would be back in Oak Lea any time. I sent him a text, *To let you know, there are three vehicles in my driveway. Taylor and Silas are in the office talking. The suspect's SUV may be gone before you get here. Long story.*

He sent back, *No doubt, see you in about thirty-five.*

Roth phoned a short time later. "Hey, Leo."

"Corky, a couple things. A KT's tow truck will be headed your way to pick up Ms. Misty's vehicle. Weber and Zubinski, the crime scene team, will be at the garage to receive it and enter it into evidence. We'll get a search warrant written and signed later tonight."

"All righty. When Weber and Zubinski were here, they took photos, collected the guns, the bullet from the Kia, and a thumb drive with the video captured from my garage camera."

"The best supporting evidence to have," he said.

"I'll keep an eye out for the tow truck. How is Misty, has she settled down?"

"Somewhat, but she's still on the wild side. The doctor asked about her medical history, asked if she takes any prescribed medications. She delivered some choice words in place of an answer. I took the doc aside, told him we found a bottle in her purse, but the label had been removed.

"She wouldn't tell him what the med was for. We'll get it tested if we have to. One concern we share is, it might be a scheduled narcotic that she put in an old pill bottle. On the other hand, it could be a prescription she needs to take," he said.

"They can do a blood draw, look for illegal drugs in her system."

"You know it can take time to get the results. That said, we don't want her having some bad episode in jail because she's missed her meds."

"The cluster continues," I said.

"Tell me about it. The Renville County Sheriff's Office is contacting Jackpot Junction management, see what they can tell us about her, like her current address, family, and former employers."

"We know the Minnesota Gambling Control Board requires thorough background checks, along with drug and alcohol tests. I've heard some places are more thorough than others. But they wouldn't have hired her if she had a criminal record."

"Oops. Looks like she got herself a felony record now," he said.

"You gotta wonder if her unstable mental state is a recent thing, or if she's managed to keep it hidden a while. When I observed her behavior at the blackjack table, she acted a little too friendly, otherwise seemed fine. Not like today when she was totally *not* fine."

"You gotta wonder is right. The bullet wound is about an inch below her elbow. They did an MRI to check for internal damage on her arm and will repair any torn tendons and muscles. Could be hours before I clear from here. Sheriff gave me a call. He and Dawes are on their way back from Brainerd and should be here soon. It's Sheriff's call whether he wants me to stay or have someone else guard Misty so I can return to your place."

"Taylor and Silas are having family issues and have been in my den office since Weber and Zubinski left. Needless to say, we haven't written our statements yet."

"Sorry to hear about your sister and brother-in-law. Seems their day went from bad to worse."

"But it could've been even worse."

"Fatally worse."

"Yep."

The motion detection lights on my garage lit up as I heard the tow truck back into the driveway. I went outside and spotted Kyle, the K in KT's Towing, when he climbed from the vehicle.

"Hey, Sergeant. What the heck?"

"Just a not-at-all-boring, bordering on traumatic, afternoon at home."

"Sounds like it." He pointed at Misty's car. "Well, I'll get that puppy loaded up and delivered to the evidence garage for you guys. No offense, but you should get back in your house. No need for you to shiver in the cold another minute."

"You're right. Thanks, Kyle, and I'll see you next time."

I went back inside, and as I pulled off my boots, Taylor and Silas emerged from the office. They had both cried their eyes out, evidenced by red scleras and blotches on their faces. My muscles tightened, and my heart went out to them.

"I need to come clean and turn myself in." Silas sounded more matter-of-fact than he appeared.

What on earth? "Why don't we sit in the living room and talk about it?" I said.

After they settled on the couch, I sat in an armchair.

Silas sucked in a breath. "I've been stealing from Peter to pay Paul, and I'm at the end of my rope. I gambled my clients' money away. A ton of it. It started with a work party at the casino. I won a lot of money that night, and the addiction I overcame years ago overcame me instead."

"What do you mean by 'a ton?'"

"Half a million, a little more."

That meant he faced restitution, probation, and prison time. *Dear Lord. Calm yourself, Corky.* "Taylor, were you involved in any of Silas's financial dealings?" I knew the answer but had to ask.

Her mouth and eyes both opened wide. "Why, no. Corky—"

I cut her off before she mentioned our undercover operation in case she hadn't told Silas. "I believe you, Taylor. It's something authorities will need to ask you."

"I have inheritance money in a trust from my parents. We could use it, put the money back in the clients' accounts. But Silas doesn't want to dip into it," Taylor said.

Silas shook his head. "No. You'll need it for our children's educations. And chances are, my company or clients would figure out what I'd done. My company for sure when they do their audits."

Taylor had money in a trust. Could the authorities take that as his restitution?

"Silas, this is your sister-in-law—not a law enforcement officer—talking. I suggest you hire a good criminal attorney and work through it with him. He can go with you to the sheriff's office when you turn yourself in. The Brown County Sheriff will conduct an investigation, decide on the charges, and place you under arrest. Likely in that order."

He stared at the floor a moment. "I have no one to blame but myself. Total confession here: when Taylor found me gambling at Jackpot today, and I saw that look of horror on her face, it put the fear of God in me in an instant. It hit me how miserable I'd been the last couple months and hadn't recognized it.

"But most of all, I felt guilty and sad about how much I'd hurt Taylor and the kids. I had myself convinced I could win the money back I'd borrowed, but I kept losing more than I won. When Misty followed us, nearly killed us, it was the final straw."

I nodded. "Admitting to your crimes is the right thing to do, Silas. Smoke will be here soon, and he's been a cop a long time. He might give you different advice than I did."

"Okay."

"Silas, you didn't know Misty was following you?" I asked.

"No. I was focused on Taylor, where she was going. When she headed east, I thought it might be to your house. I felt compelled to tell her everything and how sorry I was. To answer your question, there were vehicles behind me, but it didn't feel like I was being followed.

"Once we got on County Road Thirty-five I noticed a small blue SUV a ways behind me, but I had no idea it was Misty, didn't know what she drove. Then when it got a little darker, I didn't see the vehicle again, not until she pulled in here with her lights off."

"All right. Sergeant Roth got tied up at the hospital, so I told him we'd each write an account of what we witnessed after Misty arrived. I'll grab legal pads from the office." I retrieved them, along with some pens, and we headed into the dining area by the kitchen. I set the supplies on the table, and they took seats. "Can I get you anything to drink, or snack on? I can check the fridge for something."

"Water is fine for me," Taylor said.

"Same here," Silas said.

I joined them at the table, and about halfway through my account, Smoke came in the front door. The Fransons' vehicles blocked the garage entrance.

"Excuse me," I said and went to meet him. He glanced at Taylor and Silas in the dining area. I pulled him into the office.

"Those two look mighty serious." He gave me a quick, sweet kiss. "In fact, so do you."

"It's been a serious couple of hours."

"Do tell. When Kenner got the call about an incident here, I about went crazy, couldn't wait to get back."

"That's all I wanted myself." I gave him a brief synopsis of how everyone had arrived, the drama with Misty, and that she was in the hospital. "The incident was captured on my garage camera. You can watch it after Taylor and Silas leave."

"Thank God for the video, and that you had the foresight to strap on your gun."

"It *was* a God thing, and I did thank Him for that. I'll let Silas fill you in on what he got himself involved in. FYI, I told him to get an attorney before he turns himself in."

"Turns himself in?" Smoke said.

"Let's go talk to Silas."

Smoke and I sat down at the table with Taylor and Silas. Both had filled one page and started another. When Smoke asked Silas to tell his story, tears formed in Taylor's cornflower blue eyes and rolled down her cheeks. I grabbed the box of tissues from the counter and set it in front of her. Silas held his back until he'd finished his story. Then he wiped away tears with the sleeve of his shirt. Taylor handed him a tissue.

Smoke had kept a poker face through the entire account, then said, "The bottom line is you intend to confess your crimes and accept the consequences."

"Yes."

"Corinne told me she recommended that you get an attorney before you turn yourself in, and that's sound advice. A lot of people ask cops questions we aren't legally able or equipped to answer."

Taylor looked at her watch. "I need to check in with the kids, see how they're doing. And tell them we might not be back before their bedtime."

27

Sheriff Kenner called Smoke at 7:21. Smoke listened for a moment then said, "I'll run them to the office when they've finished and put 'em in Roth's box. . . . Sure thing." Smoke pushed the end button. "Sheriff wants you to finish your accounts regarding the incident with Misty Bayner, so Roth can include them when he writes his report," he said.

Sergeant Leo Roth phoned me minutes later. "How are you all holding up?"

"Lots to process, to say the least."

'For sure. The good news on this end is, they got Misty stitched up, said she didn't lose much blood, and they'll prescribe a mild pain killer. The better news is, they're releasing her to my custody, and I'll transport her to the jail shortly," he said.

"What a relief to hear the patient will soon turn into an inmate."

"Agreed. I'll leave you to it then." Roth disconnected.

Taylor, Silas, and I finished our narratives. Smoke found a folder to put them in. "All right, I'll take off." He locked eyes with

Silas. "Oh, and if you need the name of a good attorney, I can ask a friend in your county for a recommendation."

Silas nodded. "Thanks, I appreciate that. A lot."

Smoke left, and Silas turned to Taylor. "We should get home. No idea what tomorrow will bring, and I want to spend a little time with the kids before bed."

She managed a small smile. "They've missed you. We all have."

"I want you both to know I've seen how a confession goes a long way in the justice system," I said.

Silas half-shrugged. "I did the crime, I'll do the time."

I walked them to the entry where they put on their coats and footwear. Taylor gave me a tight hug. "Thank you again for saving our lives. If I said it a million times, it wouldn't be too much. I love you, my brave sister."

"I love you too."

Silas hugged me next. "What Taylor said. And thanks for the attorney advice. She told me I need to forgive myself, but that'll take some doing. In my wildest dreams I could never have imagined how my bad decisions would lead to this bizarre episode that could've gotten us killed. We can't thank you enough."

With Queenie by my side, I watched their vehicles back out of the driveway. Taylor was the lead car with Silas behind. Their long drive home was nothing compared to what they faced given the crimes Silas had committed. He was right, it was a matter of time before he would've been caught. I prayed turning himself in would work in his favor.

Vincent Weber phoned me later that evening. "So we got the warrant to search that vehicle, and there was something interesting in the back."

"Like what?" I said.

"Like a gym bag with guy's clothes in it."

"Hmm, that is curious, seeing how she was after Silas. She did make a strange comment about the last one not getting away, and Silas wouldn't get away either."

"So what's that supposed to mean? There's no guy gagged and tied up next to the duffle bag, that much we know," Weber said.

His words made me chuckle. "Her brain was messed up. Maybe it was really the reverse of what she said. Maybe she was the one who had ended a relationship with the last guy, and she'd be the one to end the relationship with Silas. Instead of vice versa. Even though there was no relationship with him in the first place."

"This Misty sounds like a piece of work, all right."

"There was no odor of alcohol on her, so I'm waiting to hear if she was under the influence of some other chemical," I said.

"Or just plain looney tunes."

"Or that. Crazy is as crazy does. Thanks for the info, Vince. I wonder if Misty will tell us who the duffle bag belongs to and why it was in her vehicle."

"My guess? She's in so much trouble, either she won't care and will cooperate, or she'll refuse to say a thing so she can feel she has something over us," Weber said.

Smoke returned a short time later. When I told him about the duffle bag, he just shook his head. "Yeah, I stopped by the evidence garage, and the team told me about it. Another question for her to answer."

"Or lie about," I added.

"To let you know, a Renville County deputy paid a visit to Jackpot Junction to see what he could find out about Misty, but the human resources folks were gone for the day. He didn't want to question her co-workers at this point."

"Best to check with HR first. You'd be a good one to go talk to the people she worked with, get their take on her behavior. You do have a way with words. Too bad you can't interview Misty, given our personal relationship," I said.

"No. Sheriff said he called the Bureau of Criminal Apprehension. They'll handle the investigation since it's an officer involved shooting, off duty or not. We have the video and your statements to turn over to them. They'll likely want to interview the three of you. But most importantly, the assailant."

"If they send Roberts, Misty might be more willing to cooperate than if they send Meyer."

We had met the special agents on a previous case.

Smoke's eyebrows drew together. "Is that a sexist statement, Sergeant?"

"If you define it as some sources do: behavior toward someone based on the person's gender. She wanted Silas all to herself and called Taylor and me bitches."

"You do make a point. The fact that Roberts is movie star handsome doesn't hurt when he's interrogating certain people," Smoke said.

"Same with you. I've noticed how women swoon when you're near them."

"Hah!' He belly laughed. "Women old enough to be my grandmother you mean?" He took me in his arms. "I'm still in awe how you ever chose an old guy like me."

I nibbled on his neck. "Because you're perfect. Except for a rare, random flaw that pops up now and then."

Smoke gave me the sweetest kiss, stepped back, took my hand, and led me to the couch. "We haven't had much chance to talk about you. You've had a horseshit day off. Tell me about it, let it all hang out."

"It was actually a fine day until Taylor called me midafternoon." After I recounted some details, Smoke reached for my hand.

"It's downright distressful when we have to shoot another human being. Even when they're bad guys. Even when it's not fatal."

The quiet way he uttered those words, and the way his one eyebrow lifted and his eyes softened, turned me to mush. Tears filled my eyes too fast to blink away. Instead, they rolled down my cheeks like mini waterfalls. Smoke passed me a box of tissues from the end table.

I found my voice after a moment. "When Misty pulled out her gun, I was terrified she'd shoot someone before I could shoot her. I yelled at Taylor and Silas to get down, get behind the vehicle, but they just stood there like statues. I didn't have the heart to ask them about it later, not after Silas's confession."

"They probably didn't hear you, anyway. How many times have we seen someone scared witless and it takes an actual shake to rouse them?"

"Quite a few, I guess. It was a second before Silas noticed Misty's gun and pulled Taylor down."

"Speaking of those two, we got caught up in Silas's deal and didn't talk about the showdown with Misty. We should try to get on a Zoom or Facetime call, talk them through it."

"Another debrief?" I asked.

"Another debrief. How about you, do you feel a little better after you released some of your pent-up angst?"

I laid my head on his chest. "Exhausted, but in a good way. Thank you, Detective Dawes."

"My pleasure, Sergeant Aleckson. We need you to stay healthy, for both professional and personal reasons." He held me tight. "I'm guessing you're not ready to view the video of the incident."

I shook my head. "No."

"All right. I'll wait until tomorrow when I get to the office to watch it myself. Let's relax as best we can, appreciate that we're both safe and sound in a warm house on a cold winter's night."

"Yes."

The next morning, I was making a cup of coffee when Smoke phoned, a little after nine. "I just watched the video. With its wide pan, it did a good job of capturing the incident. All of it.

From the time Taylor drove in to when you and Zubinski and Weber went into the house to get the recorded tape."

The incident sped through my mind, as it had too many times to count. "Good to know. Plus the crime scene team can swear the tape was not tampered with," I said.

"Not that any of us would doubt that, but a good defense attorney would argue it might have been. Corinne, even though I knew how it turned out, my heart still pounded as I watched it. Dear God. You said it happened fast, and from the time Misty pulled out her gun to the time she was down was under two seconds."

My own heart hammered in my chest, and I started to pace. "Oh."

"I've witnessed how fast you respond but that was awesome." I'd been timed on a stop watch and knew it took about a second to draw my weapon.

After a little silence, he said, "Special Agent Elijah Roberts *and* Special Agent Tamra Meyer will be out at any time now to watch the recorded video, read the reports, and interview Misty Bayner. Before they talk to you."

I took in a cleansing breath to calm myself. "Wow, a special agent twofer, huh?"

"If Bayner won't talk, maybe they'll do a good cop bad cop deal," Smoke said.

I walked into the living room with my coffee. "Roberts will make Meyer the bad cop if his smooth coaxing demeanor doesn't make her tell all?"

"Something like that," he said.

"Let's hope her night in jail improved her attitude."

"I'm curious to hear what she has to say."

"I'm curiouser. I'd love to witness the interview, see how it goes, but I know I can't of course," I said.

"No, you need to stay clear. I'll be in the viewing room, however. The special agents want to talk to you after that, and may need to interview Silas, depending on what Misty has to say."

Smoke sent me a message about an hour later. *They interviewed MB. I'll fill you in.* I responded with a thumbs up.

Special Agent Tamra Meyer phoned a moment later. "Hi, Sergeant, it's good to hear your voice again. It's been a while."

"You too, even under the circumstances," I said.

"Understood. Detective Dawes told you we needed to talk to you, for the record."

"He did. I can be there whenever you're ready."

"We're ready. Interview room A," Meyer said.

That was fast. "I'll see you in about ten minutes."

I knocked on the interview room door to alert them before I opened it. "Hello, Special Agents Meyer and Roberts."

They smiled, and after we shook hands, their body language shifted from relaxed and casual to serious and professional. "Have a seat, Sergeant," Meyer said.

I sat opposite them, with the table between us. Roberts perched his pen above his notebook. "Let's get right down to business, Sergeant. We watched the video of the incident at your house. We also showed those first minutes to Ms. Bayner. It captured her arrival, her drawing and aiming her weapon at the couple identified as Silas and Taylor Franson, her getting struck by the bullet, then dropping down in an attempt to retrieve her weapon."

"Even without audio, the video provided the proof of what happened. However, the interview with Ms. Bayner was non-productive. She looked like a statue when she viewed the video. Then, instead of answering our questions, she started rambling on about men, how she didn't know if she could ever trust another one again, " Meyer said.

What she said about Misty Bayner did not surprise me.

Roberts pulled the witness accounts that Taylor, Silas, and I had written from a folder. "The three of you had very similar statements, all supported by the video. Did you discuss the incident with the others afterwards?"

I had to think a moment. "Not many specifics. We were all surprised—shocked—when Misty pulled into my driveway and started yelling at Silas and Taylor. Her behavior was irrational. It scared us half to death. Taylor did ask me later why I had my gun on when I wasn't working. I told her I often did.

"And in this case it prevented at least one fatality, possibly three," Roberts said.

I studied my hands as the scene replayed in my mind. They asked more questions: did I know Misty Bayner, what was my relationship to Taylor and Silas, what had initiated the incident, and so on.

I gave them the background, how Taylor was concerned about Silas's behavior, how Smoke and I had followed him to the casino and learned he had a gambling problem. Silas's embezzlement was a separate crime that had nothing to do with what happened with Misty.

"Sergeant Aleckson, I think we've got everything we need on our end. Your office made a copy of the video for us. The two weapons have been entered in evidence. Both will be checked, of course. Ms. Bayner's gun will remain there, and yours will be released when we've finished our part of the investigation," Roberts said.

"That video is key in the case against Bayner," Meyer added.

Misty Lee Bayner made her first court appearance before Judge Feiner Tuesday afternoon. Smoke sat in the back of the room as she was escorted in from the jail.

He phoned me soon after. "Sorry, I got caught up in another deal after Bayner's interview this morning."

"No problem. Roberts and Meyer highlighted it for me."

"She just made her court appearance and kept a blank look on her face, a flat affect, the whole time. She'd settled way down after how she acted in the interview with Roberts and Meyer. When Judge Feiner read the charges against her, she was quiet, seemed respectful. He appointed a public defender to represent her, and she entered a plea of not guilty. Judge Feiner took the recommendation the county attorney had made. Based on the serious charges, he set her bail at two million dollars."

"I hope she doesn't have connections among any gambler friends who'd be willing to get enough bond money together to bail her out," I said.

"Hope not. Special Agents Roberts and Meyer will dive into her background. We know Bayner cleared at least one background check, so we'll see what they turn up. I'm also waiting to hear what Renville County found out at the casino about Bayner."

"I'm interested in that too. I think Misty must be a darn good actress, knows how to act normal until her evil twin takes over. When we observed her at the casino, she seemed like Silas had described her: 'flirty.' I thought at the time she might act that way to garner bigger tips. Now we know what she really wanted, or rather who."

"Yep. Speaking of Silas, have you heard anything from them, if he's hired an attorney, turned himself in?" Smoke said.

"No, and I hoped to hear by now. Taylor knows we're waiting."

"Silas wouldn't do something stupid, like take off, would he?"

"Don't feed my fears, Smoke. I'm already stressed enough over the whole thing."

"No need to panic. We both need to remember it takes time to find, and vet, a good attorney."

"I'll hold on to that," I said.

I was on a run, headed down Brandt, when Taylor called me. At last. I caught my breath as I pushed the accept button. "Taylor."

"Corky, are you okay?" She sounded a little breathless herself.

"Yep. Out on a run, going a little faster than I realized. How is . . . everything?"

"So-so. We're figuring things out here. It was too late to talk to the kids when we got home last night, so we'll do that after school. They'll be home soon. Silas checked out some criminal attorneys and found one who has a great reputation."

"Good to hear."

"The down side is, he's really busy, and Silas couldn't get an appointment until Thursday. Silas doesn't feel it would be honest to go into the office. Or pretend like nothing's going on if he called in sick. It's a tricky situation because if he tells his boss what he did before he meets with the attorney, his boss might call the sheriff," Taylor said.

The tangled web. "So, what does Silas plan to do?"

"Ask the attorney who they should go see first: Silas's company, or the sheriff."

28

As I logged a few more miles, I tried not to obsess over what the future held for Taylor, Silas, and their precious children: Katie, Charles, and Isabelle. Like with George after he was caught, Silas's career as a financial planner had come to an abrupt end. Taylor was smart, had a bachelor's degree in psychology and planned to get her master's degree to pursue a career as a counselor or therapist at some point. That point may be on the horizon.

A bright spot in the whole mess was the trust fund she'd inherited. Taylor didn't name an amount, but I got the impression it was substantial, large enough to pay for their children's college educations. Silas's parents had lived in Arizona year-round for some time. His sister was a musician in New York, and they didn't see each other often.

What would Silas tell his family? What would Taylor tell ours? We could lend emotional support and advice and love. It wouldn't alter the charges against Silas, but should provide some comfort. When Silas said, "I did the crime, I'll do the time," my respect for him went up about hundred notches.

When I got home, I released Queenie and Rex from their kennel to let them outside to run around and explore while I got cleaned up. I called the dogs back into the house and settled on the couch with a bottle of water. They laid on the rug by the round coffee table. My thoughts settled on Kirby Sawyer. He'd been on my heart and mind since he told me about his son. I picked the phone from my sweatpants pocket and called him.

"Oh, Sergeant, what a nice surprise," he said.

"How are you? In the middle of something?" I asked.

"No, just playing solitaire."

Just. Solitaire. The way he said those words sounded sad. I liked solitaire on a rare occasion. "Ah. You play the classic version, or a different one?"

He chuckled. "I stick to the classic one. It suits me, and I like to say, 'pun intended.'"

I chuckled in return.

"I'm not one to watch much television. Since I retired, when I'm not puttering on something in the garage or around the house, I find solitaire relaxing."

"I agree with you. My gramps likes it too. Kirby, I wanted to check in, and also ask how everything went for you in court. We hadn't talked about it."

"No. I would've told you but figured you got the reports," he said.

"I haven't checked with court admin yet."

"Okay. Well, I was thinking I'd get the book thrown at me. Instead, the judge just ordered me to pay a fine. He asked me to promise to remain law abiding. I said I would. He made me raise my right hand and swear to it."

Judge Feiner had a kind heart. "The judge made the right decision, in my opinion."

"It surely turned out better than I figured it would. You know Sergeant, I try not to think of that mean woman in the café who provoked me. Then I start questioning things, like did I know her after all? Jay only brought two women home to meet my wife and me over the years. The two he was serious about. I think I would've remembered if she'd been one of 'em," Kirby said.

"Yes. Unless she looks different, maybe."

"It has been a lot of years, but I don't know."

"She may have confused you with someone else, like we'd said. We both know how insults can cut us deep inside. But as time goes on, I hope your hurt will lessen until it's just a bad memory you rarely bring to mind," I said.

"Thank you."

"I'll let you go. Feel free to call me anytime, all right?"

"I will. Always good to talk to you, Sergeant. It gives me a lift," he said.

Me too. "Thanks, Kirby."

I was in the middle of a solitaire game myself—thank you Kirby for reminding me about a good way to relax—when Smoke came home. The dogs were happy to see him. I was elated.

"You're playing solitaire? Don't tell me you're bored," he teased as he sat down on the couch and kissed my cheek.

"Oh how I long to be bored for one whole day sometime."

"Hah! That does have a nice ring to it. So you know, the media's been all over the Misty Bayner story. They checked the court calendar and saw her list of charges. Terroristic threats, three counts of attempted murder, assault, brandishing a weapon, and a few others. They even threw in trespassing." Smoke said.

I shook my head. "All valid charges. Think how riled up Misty must've gotten when Silas left with Taylor instead of staying with her. When Taylor called and said Silas was following her, it seemed like a crazy thing to do. But after his confessions, his reason made some sense at least.

"But Misty? She had her reasons all right. They were not reasonable, however. By the time she got here, she had worked herself into such an angry tizzy she was ready to shoot Taylor, or Silas, or both. And why would she have an unholstered gun in her pocket?"

"Scary deal. Because of that, a prosecutor might argue it was premeditated. However, it was a spur of the moment deal. The chain of events was triggered after Taylor's unexpected visit to the casino. You asked why the gun was in her pocket. Maybe she watched too many old cop shows where they did stuff like that," Smoke said.

"Did you ever hear back from Renville County about Misty?"

He tapped his forehead. "Slipped my mind." He pulled out his memo pad. "Yes. Deputy Sommers talked to HR first. They said Bayner began employment there last October. She'd been at Mystic Lake in Prior Lake for a few years before that.

"That's close to Chaska, at least."

"Yep. HR didn't have a change of address for her, didn't notice any red flags. One dealer told Sommers that Bayner said she had a boyfriend but never talked about him. No one seemed to know much about her. Bayner was friendly at work but didn't discuss her personal life."

Wednesday I spent the morning on chores, paid bills, ran errands, and picked up needed essentials at the grocery store. I searched for an idea for supper that night and took the easy way out. I bought a broasted chicken, fried potatoes, and coleslaw from the deli. The next best thing to one of Mother's homecooked meals.

I finished putting the groceries away a moment before Smoke phoned.

"I got called to the Winstons' place. There's been a development. You're not on duty, but you'll want to head out here," he said.

"What is it?"

"It's not an emergency, but by the time it took to explain, you could be here."

That reassured me somewhat. "All right, be there shortly."

I slipped on boots, jacket, hat, and gloves, told Queenie to be good, and was on the road. I pulled into the Winstons' driveway and parked behind Smoke's car. In addition to the cleaning crew's vehicles, the dumpster and portable storage unit, the Winnebago County Mobile Crime Unit was parked near the shed.

I rarely had my sheriff's radio on when I was off duty so I hadn't heard the team get called to the scene. Smoke stood next to Shane and his two sons by the open shed door. When I walked over to them, I spotted Deputies Weber and Zubinski inside, near the back of the shed. *Dear God, please not another body.*

Smoke pointed at a white SUV. "That's Deena Winston's vehicle parked back there. Keys are in the ignition, a woman's wallet—with her driver's license—and two cellphones were found in the center console."

Shane rubbed his forehead with the back of his hand. "Tricia flew home for a few days to take care of things. Leah went home for a while too. The boys decided to stay with me to check what was in the shed, the vehicles in particular. Tricia and I had decided we should figure out what to divide up, what our kids could use."

His sons gave short nods.

Shane waved his hand at a Ford pickup. "You can see Brett had a nice truck. We were interested in what other vehicles underneath tarps might be, and took off some to have a look. When we opened the doors to the Chevy, I noticed the wallet and cellphones. My first thought was: more stuff Brett found and put in there for some reason.

"Then I opened the wallet and saw who it belonged to. I really cannot describe how it made me feel. Just that it was the worst gut punch ever. I didn't know what vehicle Deena owned anymore. I laid the wallet back on the seat and called Detective Dawes."

His sons each put an arm around Shane's shoulder. "It's okay, Dad," one said.

Smoke said, "Sergeant, let's go talk to Weber and Zubinski."

We wove our way around a pickup, an aluminum trailer, wheelbarrow, dolly, a shelving unit filled with more flower pots, garden tools, hand and power tools, lawn mower, snowblower, garden tiller, and more. Brett—or someone else—had backed Deena's vehicle in.

Weber lifted a gloved hand. "A hoarder's paradise."

"One way to describe it," I said.

Smoke's eyebrows drew together. "We ran the plate, and the vehicle is registered to Deena Winston. The tabs are good until July of this year."

"That means she renewed it before the end of July last year," I said.

"Yes she did. We checked with the state, and it was July eighth to be exact."

"Deena's wallet and two cellphones? She was here with a man in Brett's house, someone shot them, then Brett hid her vehicle in his shed?" I said.

"Makes you wonder if Brett was the shooter after all," Smoke said.

"We'll have the vehicle towed to our evidence garage. When it warms up, it'll be easier to collect DNA from the phones. Along with the steering wheel and door handles," Mandy said.

"We got the phones and wallet in evidence bags," Weber said.

"I have her DL in a baggie in my pocket. Her address shows she lived in a Minneapolis apartment. We'll check with the landlord, see who knows what," Smoke said.

"As soon as we get signed warrants to search the vehicle, and interrogate the phones, we'll find out for sure who they belonged to. Just 'cause they were in her vehicle is not proof positive one belonged to her. Anyway, we can get their names, and their lists of contacts. See who they called and messaged, who called and messaged them," Mandy said.

"Depending on the carrier, some keep phone records for a year. I know one that keeps them for five years," Smoke said.

"We also need to ask Shane and Tricia the last time they were in contact with Deena. She told them she'd met someone and was moving away with him," I said.

"Yeah. If Deena turns out to be the one on the couch, and the guy next to her was the one she was moving away with, they met a bad, sad end instead," Weber said.

"Tragic, no doubt about it. It shouldn't take the forensic scientists at the crime lab long to find out if the DNA from items collected match the skeletal remains at the ME's office," Smoke said.

29

The earth rumbled when KT's Towing arrived. We stepped outside to meet them. Ted was the driver on that trip. While Kyle was on the beefy side and more laid back, Ted was wiry and serious. He climbed out and nodded at the group as he surveyed the scene.

Smoke greeted him. "Morning, Ted. We're going to tow the Chevy in the back there to our evidence garage. So we'll need to get that pickup out of the way first."

Ted nodded again. "Okay, okay."

The cleaning crew had removed some items earlier. They'd wheeled and carried out more and cleared the way to Brett's pickup. Ted backed up, and the smell of diesel drifted around in the shed. He hooked straps up to the pickup and pulled it into the yard to the other side of the shed.

Brett's pickup was packed with stuff and could easily have sheltered mice or rats or chipmunks. I looked around inside and listened for critters, but didn't spot or hear any scurrying about. The family and cleaners would figure out how to proceed with that cleanout project.

After the path was cleared to Deena's vehicle, Ted centered his flatbed with the Chevy's center and backed up to it. "Deputy Weber, you have gloves on. Will you shift the vehicle into neutral?" Ted asked.

"Sure." Weber slid into the driver's seat and moved the gear shift from park to neutral.

Ted pulled the ramps from the truck's rear, hooked straps to ports under the Chevy's front bumper, hopped on the flatbed, and used the hydraulic winches to bring the Chevy into position on the flatbed. He secured all four tires with cables and hooks.

As he climbed down from the truck, he said, "I'll grab the release form for you to sign." Ted returned with the form on a clipboard and a pen attached to it via a string. "Detective, you want to sign?"

"Will do. The crime scene team will be on their way to let you into the evidence garage," he said.

"Okay." Ted held the clipboard for Smoke as he scratched out his signature. I thought about Ted's nearly expressionless face. In serious situations it came across as respectful. He gave a single nod to each group: the family, the cleaners, and sheriff's deputies, climbed into his truck, shifted into gear, and rumbled back the way he came.

"Have you ever seen Ted smile?" Mandy asked me in a quiet voice.

"I don't think I have, come to think of it."

Smoke looked at Weber and Mandy. "Team, your biggest piece of evidence is on its way to the sheriff's office."

"Let's get rolling ourselves, Zubinski," Weber said.

As they drove away, Smoke asked Shane, "Do you have the date when you last spoke to Deena?"

"It was last summer. And we didn't actually talk. I told you how we'd fallen out of favor and hadn't communicated for some time. So it was out of the blue when Leah got the text message saying she was leaving her old life behind to start a new one with someone else. Something like that."

"Shane, could you ask your wife if she still has that text message? It should be on Deena's phone too, but we need to wait for clearance to check hers," I said.

He walked away and made the call. His sons headed to the house, maybe to warm up. Some minutes later, Shane joined us and held up his phone. My wife took a screen shot of Deena's text message. She sent it August nineteenth. It doesn't sound like the Deena we knew."

Shane handed the phone to me, and I read it out loud. "I need to leave my old life behind and start a new one with someone special. We're moving away and cutting all ties. I hope you understand. Bye for now and forever."

The creepy crawler sensation I'd felt since I arrived on the scene spread down my arms and up my spine. "Shane, you said it didn't sound like something she'd write, and maybe she didn't. Can you forward that to Detective Dawes's phone? Is that okay, Detective?"

"Of course. Please do that, Shane," Smoke said.

I handed Shane his phone, and he sent the message. Smoke's eyebrows lifted as he read it again.

Smoke went back to the office. I hung around the Winstons for a time and watched the cleaners carry out load after load. Shane acted like he had lost interest in what must have seemed like a never-ending battle.

"Sergeant, I called Tricia, told her about this latest . . . business. She said she'd try to get a flight out tonight. I told her there was nothing she could do at this point, given the investigation and all. She should stick to her plans and return here in a couple of days. I'd keep on top of things till then.

"Same with Leah. When this whole thing started, Brett dying was bad enough, and he had all this stuff we needed to take care of. Then come to find out two people were killed in his living room besides. It felt like everything else in our lives stopped, but they didn't. It would've been nice if we could've pushed a pause button. Leah said she'd drive back tomorrow, but I told her to wait until we get a confirmation about . . . Deena," Shane said.

"Any idea why Deena would've been here at Brett's?"

"Not a clue. The one thing that crossed my mind is maybe she wanted to say goodbye to Brett in person." Shane teared up. "If that was the case, I guess she did."

"What about your sons?" I asked.

"They want to hang with me a while."

"I'm glad to hear that."

Smoke tracked down the apartment landlord at Deena's address and phoned me with the report. "The landlord checked the records. They showed Deena asked for a short-term lease on a furnished apartment. She'd sold her home and was deciding on next steps. Deena was able to sublease an apartment for four months, from May until August. She turned in her keys on August 19th. The landlord said Deena didn't leave a forwarding address."

"Hmm. Well it's one piece of the Deena puzzle anyway. But why a furnished apartment? Brett had too much stuff, and she had no stuff?"

"You gotta wonder. I'm just happy she updated her address on her license, or we wouldn't have had that lead. We'll look up her old address, talk to the folks who bought it, ask if they have any information."

"Now to figure out who she was moving away with, that's the next question."

Taylor phoned me late Thursday afternoon with the news. "Silas and his attorney went to the sheriff's office, and he turned himself in." She started to cry, but managed to say, "They arrested him . . . took him into the jail." She sniffed. "He got fingerprinted and booked in. He'll get into court tomorrow."

"I'm so sorry, Taylor. Would you like me to come down there for the night?"

"Thanks, but two friends are here, and they're good supporters."

"Okay. But remember, whatever you need, call me anytime, day or night. Promise?"

"Promise, and thank you, Corky."

Shane called me late evening. "Tricia returned here, even though I said she didn't have to. Anyway, she told me I had to take tomorrow off, and she'd work with the cleaning crew."

"I think that's wise. You do need a day away."

By early Friday afternoon, much of the clutter had been cleared from Brett's room, and the family was able to gain access to the two dressers. He had one drawer filled with photos and personal records. On top of the pile was a letter Brett had written. It spelled out the details of what happened the day his wife and friend were shot in his living room.

Tricia found it and called Shane, who called Smoke, who called me. "It's a letter Brett wrote that will wrap up this case."

"What? Tell me."

"Too much to get into over the phone. Can you meet us in the sheriff's office in twenty?" Smoke said.

"Sure. Unless I get tied up on a call."

"I'll tell Communications to assign them to someone else for the next hour," Smoke said.

"Copy." *The next hour?* As I approached Whitetail Lake, I pulled onto the shoulder and glanced at its frozen surface and the handful of fish houses. The same spot I'd been when Communications dispatched me to Brett Winston's house. The call that led to a complex murder investigation. A letter from Brett with the information we'd sought had finally surfaced. *Thank you.*

I knocked on Sheriff Kenner's doorjamb, then stepped inside. Shane, Leah, Tricia, and Smoke all stood with Kenner around his desk. The sheriff held the letter in his hand and glanced my way. "Come in, Sergeant."

I felt like a kid at Christmas about to open a gift from Santa when Kenner offered the letter to me. My pulse raced as I took it and looked at the scrawled penmanship that matched—except was neater—the note we'd found in Brett's Bible.

"Will you read it out loud?" Kenner asked.

Me? "Okay." My voice sounded a bit shaky. "It's dated September fifteenth of last year."

I blinked and refocused my eyes when the words got a touch blurry, then began:

"'A terrible thing happened. I couldn't stop it and couldn't make myself do the right thing afterwards. My wife and best friend came to see me. They told me they were in love and planned to get married. They wanted to tell me before Deena moved into Jay's apartment. I noticed Deena was wearing the sapphire ring Jay's mother always wore.'"

My stomach did a flip flop. I stopped reading and looked at the others' faces. "*Sapphire ring*? *Jay*, as in Jay Sawyer, whose father was told he'd died in an apartment explosion?"

"Keep reading," Smoke said.

"Okay. 'I felt sad and happy at the same time. I was not the man Deena married. After Aiden died it made us sadder to be together. Deena knew Jay from when we hung out years back. She contacted him because she was worried about me. They both loved me and told me their love for each other got stronger.

"'They loved me still and hoped they could help me. I'm not sure how. We were in my living room when a woman burst in. She looked like a witch with a scary scowl on her face. Jay jumped up and yelled, 'What are you doing here, Misty?'"

Misty. I stopped again.

"'She screamed something like "he's mine, you can't have him, bitch." The next thing I knew she had a gun and shot Jay. He fell back on the couch about the same second I heard another shot and Deena jerked. I'd been frozen to my chair until then. I got up to try and do something and she shot me too. The bullet went through my shoulder. I went down and must have passed out for a while. When I woke up and saw Deena and Jay were dead I knew I should call the police but couldn't.

"'Deena's phone and keys were on the table. Jay's phone was there too. I took them out to Deena's car. I left the ring on her finger. Her wallet was on the car floor. I set it in the middle holder. I put the phones there too and pulled the car into the shed. I tried to call the police lots of times over the next weeks but couldn't. I didn't know the woman shot us, just that her nickname was Misty.'"

I paused and looked from Sheriff to Smoke. "Brett didn't know her real name was Misty." Smoke shook his head.

I continued, "'The next day I found a bullet on the floor and put it in my top dresser drawer. I'll give it to the police sometime. I built a burial vault around Deena and Jay and out to the doors to keep people out and to protect them. I stayed upstairs so they had the downstairs to themselves. I'm writing this so someday when you find us you'll know what happened on August 19th.'"

Tricia and Leah dabbed away tears.

Shane sniffed back his. "We can't grasp this whole thing at all. It's like Brett was in some weird kind of alternate reality. He had to be to justify not calling the authorities. And he wrote his account like he was a reporter, or something. Not like one who experienced the whole thing."

"We've talked about Brett's mental health issues. It seems that traumatic incident led to his further decline," I said.

"Misty killed Jay and made up the story he died in the apartment explosion that occurred two days later," Smoke said.

"And we got the text message from someone who claimed to be Deena. But not the number we had for Deena. Same thing. It was two days after she died," Shane said.

"After Misty killed Deena and Jay, and thought she'd killed Brett, she must've got to thinking she should notify family members so they wouldn't report their loved ones as missing. The apartment explosion provided one explanation, and a text message about moving away provided the other," Smoke said.

"I wonder why she didn't notify us about Brett?" Shane said.

"My guess? She didn't have his phone with his contacts. Didn't know who he was. Maybe she figured he was a hermit, given his living conditions," Smoke said.

"You're probably right," Shane said.

"I have to wonder why Misty didn't return, have Deena's car towed away," I said.

"Maybe she did and when she saw it was gone, she maybe thought someone stole it," Smoke said.

"Maybe. I hope someday Misty will confess everything," I said.

"Kirby needs to get his wife's ring back," Tricia said. "And this might not be the time to talk about this, but I think we should bury Deena's remains with Aiden and Brett's."

Shane put an arm around his sister. "I agree. About the ring and the burial. Their family had a lot of happy years together."

We all appeared lost in our own thoughts. Then, as if by mutual agreement, we bowed our heads for a moment of silence.

After the Winstons left, Smoke said, "I didn't want to get into the details of the case with the family, but we did recover the bullet from Brett's drawer. It appears to match the bullets our crime scene team ejected from Bayner's gun. Since no spent shells were found in the house, she must've collected them when Brett lay unconscious."

"I can't help but think it's by the hand of God we have Misty in our jail, on other serious charges. We believe beyond a reasonable doubt she's the same person Brett named in the letter," Kenner said.

"Kirby Sawyer, poor Kirby. Phone records will prove whether or not Misty is the one who called him. But who else would it be? She had to have known Deena was planning to move in with Jay. Maybe had gotten a hold of either her phone or Brett's to access their list of contacts. Same with Jay's to call his father.

"I can envision how it went down. Jay told her he was in love with Deena, like Silas told her he was in love with Taylor. She followed them, and murdered them in cold blood," I said.

"She was likely delusional enough to think it might be weeks, or months, before the three victims were found," Smoke said.

"That part turned out to be the sad truth for two of the victims."

30

I printed a copy of Brett's letter and Misty Lee Bayner's mug shot with her big scowl and wild blonde hair. I asked Smoke to meet me at Kirby Sawyer's house. He pulled in and parked a minute after me. Kirby opened the door before we could ring the doorbell. "Come in, come in," he said.

We stepped into the spacious rambler and exchanged greetings. Smoke and I slipped off our boots and coats.

Kirby pointed at a wall by the closet. "Hang 'em on the hooks there. We'll go sit at the kitchen table and have a cup of coffee." He glanced at the 8.5 X 11 envelope in my hand. "You said you had something to show me, Sergeant."

"Yes," I said. As we walked to the kitchen, I noted a family photo on a table behind a couch. I'd ask about it later.

Three cups sat on the counter by a full pot of coffee. "Have a seat," he said as he filled the cups. "Cream, sugar?" he asked.

"No, black for both of us," I said.

Kirby set the cups on the table and sat on the chair to my right. "You got me pretty curious after you called, Sergeant."

I still had the envelope in my hand and leaned a little closer to Kirby. "We had a development in the Brett Winston case. You know about the remains found in his living room?"

"Yes."

"I know this will be difficult to process all at once, but we have reason to believe one of the victims is your son."

He shook his head. "Jay? How could that be?"

I pulled the letter out and handed it to Kirby. "Brett wrote this about a month after the incident."

Kirby looked at it and handed it back to me. "Will you read it to me?"

I couldn't and passed it to Smoke. He pulled readers from his breast pocket, put them on, and read aloud. If not for the content, his baritone voice would have soothed me. Kirby made 'ah!' sounds here and there. Smoke paused after the line about Jay's mother's ring.

I reached into my pocket, pulled out the diamond-surrounded sapphire ring, and gave it to Kirby. Tears filled his eyes as he slid it partway down his pinkie. "My wife's mother passed it down to her, and my wife gave it to Jay before she died, said he should give it to a special someone someday. Well, I guess he did."

Smoke continued reading Brett's note. When he finished, Kirby began to weep.

I stood and wrapped my arms around the man who'd grieved his son for months, and now had tragic new information to digest and cope with. Kirby picked a napkin from its holder and patted his face. "Do you know who this Misty might be?"

I sat down again. "Yes. I'll tell you what we know." I shared the facts we had on Misty Bayner: the two places she'd worked, her last known address. I didn't get into the details, but told him how Misty had followed my sister and brother-in-law to my house and threatened them with a gun.

"When she wouldn't drop it, I was forced to shoot her."

"The whole thing was captured on Sergeant Aleckson's garage camera too," Smoke added.

Kirby's lips curled up a tad. "Good."

"Bayner's been in the Winnebago County Jail ever since. Detective Dawes is the lead on your son's case," I said.

"The BCA interviewed Bayner after the incident at Sergeant Aleckson's house. They're the lead on that investigation. I spoke to her today after we found your son's letter. She wouldn't say a word," Smoke said.

Kirby studied his folded hands a moment then looked at me. "Wait. You said she worked at Mystic Lake?" he asked.

"Yes," I said.

"My son liked to go there. He wasn't much of a gambler, but enjoyed blackjack once in a while."

Bingo. "You just provided us with another piece of the puzzle. Bayner won't talk, so we had no clue how she knew Jay. He never told you about a stalker type woman who was after him?" I said.

"No, but if that were true, I can see why he didn't. He was one of those 'look on the bright side of life' kind of guys," Kirby said.

I pulled Misty's mug shot photo from the envelope and slid it over to Kirby.

"It's *her!* Only with blonde hair. Same mean look," he said.

"Who?" Smoke said.

"That witch in the café who called Jay a loser," Kirby said.

I reached over and put my hand on his. "I wondered about that after we read Brett's letter. She's the only one who could've called you and lied about Jay's death. She knew who you were, either from Jay, or through his phone contacts." I gave his hand a squeeze. "You can be assured she will spend decades in prison and may never breathe free air again."

"Now that would be an answer to prayers," Kirby said.

"To confirm Jay's identity, we'd like to collect your DNA. I have a collection kit in my coat pocket," Smoke said.

"Now I'll be able to lay our son to rest next to his mother."

I blinked to hold in my tears. "Kirby, may I see Jay's senior yearbook, look at his photo?"

His shoulders lifted. "Sure." He left, returned with the book, and opened it to that page.

"Mind if I take a photo of it?" I asked.

"Go right ahead," he said.

I snapped a pic. "Also, I noticed your family photo in the living room. May I take a photo of that too?"

"I don't see why not," he said.

"The sergeant here likes to have photos of people she's worked for," Smoke said. I was glad he said "people" instead of "victims."

"I'll get that photo," Kirby said.

"And I'll get the DNA kit set up," Smoke said.

Smoke swabbed Kirby's mouth, as I took a photo of the family.

I gave Kirby a hug. "Thank you."

He hugged me back like he didn't want to let go.

Kirby Sawyer was calmer by the time we left. His sister was on her way over to spend the rest of the day with him and to discuss arrangements after the medical examiner released Jay's remains.

I called Mandy when I was back in my squad car. "The woman in the café who caused the ruckus with Kirby Sawyer, the one you said was Rose somebody?"

"Yeah. Rose Ebert."

"Turns out it was Misty Lee Bayner with dark hair," I said.

"Serious? Rose Ebert is the name she gave, but she didn't have her DL with her, and I had no reason to run her for warrants. I'll take another look at your video, zoom in on her face. I haven't seen her in person since her arrest."

Mandy got back to me about an hour later. "That was her, all right. Misty Lee Bayner."

"Okay, so she has a Chaska address, worked at Jackpot Junction in Morton, and we can confirm she was in Emerald Lake, not far from the Winstons' place in Emerald Lake Township on the Tuesday morning the crew started their cleanout project. Who knows how many times she's been in our county."

"Yeah, who knows? Vince and I read Brett's letter. We know who killed Deena and Jay, now it It'd be good if Bayner would fess up to the break-ins at the Winstons'."

"She is taking the right to remain silent to the nth degree."

Friday afternoon, Misty Lee Bayner made an appearance in court for the numerous new charges against her. Judge Feiner set her bail at $5 million. Kirby Sawyer told me, "I can't say I'm sorry she'll rot in jail, probably forever."

Taylor sent me a text Friday evening, *Silas appeared in court, and under the circumstances, the judge released him on his own recognizance (I had to look up the spelling). His next court date is in February. He's relieved and ready to face the consequences.*

I wrote back, *Tell him that he, and your whole family, are in my thoughts and prayers.*

The Midwest Regional Crime Lab matched the DNA from Deena's phone and steering wheel to her remains. Jay Sawyer's DNA, that included the gym bag clothes found in Misty's vehicle, matched Kirby's. Both families felt a sad sense of relief Deena and Jay had been identified. Their remains were released to the funeral homes for cremation or burial.

The Winstons planned a private graveside memorial service for Deena at Crystal Lake Cemetery in Minneapolis where Brett and Aiden were buried. They wanted to contact her friends to let them know what happened. Shane phoned me with the report.

"The sheriff's office provided us with Deena's contacts and numbers from her phone of people she'd talked to the month before she disappeared. Her brother was not one of them so we still can't reach him."

"That's a shame," I said.

"It is. Besides Jay, there was only one other—Patsy—who she called three times. Tricia called Patsy and she was beyond shocked about Deena. She said Deena was very private—which we knew—that she'd quit her job, sold her house with most of the furniture included, and planned to put the rest in a storage unit.

"She found a special guy but wouldn't say who. Then she disappeared. Patsy talked to the police but they told her Deena was an adult, and the steps she'd taken indicated she planned to move away. Patsy will be at the service, so we'll talk to her more about Deena," Shane said.

"Good. Maybe the sheriff's office can track down the storage unit. She must have personal items, things she treasured. Jay's father said they found things that belonged to a woman when they cleaned out his apartment. Must be Deena's," I said.

"It'd be good to figure that out. Even though we've had a lot to go through already."

"Progress continues on the house, I see."

"It's getting there. We'll take Brett's papers and photos home with us to go through them. We're looking at either having an auction house take the big things we don't want, or holding an auction there in the spring," Shane said.

Kirby Sawyer felt it was important to have a church funeral for Jay. It was a small gathering, mostly his church family and friends. Sadly, I was tied up on a burglary and couldn't attend. Kirby told me later that the priest's words had given him great assurance.

Word about Jay's murder reached the high school where Jay served as a counselor and dispelled the prior rumors he'd died in the apartment explosion. The school board planned a gathering in their gym to honor Jay. They invited Kirby Sawyer and he invited me. It was my day off work, and I offered to drive him. Kirby didn't like city traffic.

Hundreds of students and staff filled the bleachers. The principal, teachers, and students spoke about Jay and how he'd helped guide them. I thought Kirby's chest might burst with gratitude and pride because his son had been so popular and well loved.

Kirby was invited to say a few words, and he took my hand to accompany him. *As long as I don't have to talk,* I thought on the way. We moved behind the podium. When Kirby sucked in a breath it puffed out his chest.

"I'm not a public speaker, and all I can say is I can't thank you enough for this wonderful tribute to my son. He was a fine man who didn't deserve to die the way he did, as you all know. I can tell you that despite the reason we're here today, I will cherish your kind words for the rest of my life. Thank you."

People rose and clapped as I guided Kirby back to his seat.

Smoke and I cuddled on the couch later that night.

I shared things people at Jay's school said about him and that I thought Kirby had delivered the finest speech of all. "You know what Kirby told me on the way home?"

"What?" Smoke said.

"If he'd had a daughter, he would've wanted her to be just like me."

Smoke squeezed me tighter. "You won his heart all right. Maybe someday we'll have a daughter just like you."

We had never discussed children. I moved to look him square in the eyes. "Shouldn't we get married first?"

"Of course. We've been engaged a while now so I'm thinking when things settle down a bit, given Taylor and Silas's situation, we should settle on a date."

Be still my heart.

I hope you enjoyed this story, and perhaps learned something new. If you will, please post a review on your favorite site(s). Thank you!

I love hearing from readers and visiting book clubs. Feel free to contact me at: christinehusom@aol.com
www.christinehusom

Winnebago County Mysteries

Murder in Winnebago County follows an unlikely serial killer plaguing a rural Minnesota county. The clever murderer leaves a growing chain of apparent suicides among criminal justice professionals. As her intuition helps her draw the cases together, Winnebago County Sergeant Corinne Aleckson enlists help from Detective Elton Dawes. What Aleckson doesn't know is that the killer is keeping a close watch on her. Will she be the next target?

Buried in Wolf Lake When a family's golden retriever brings home the dismembered leg of a young woman, the Winnebago County Sheriff's Department launches an investigation unlike any other. Who does the leg belong to, and where is the rest of her body? Sergeant Corinne Aleckson and Detective Elton Dawes soon discover they are up against an unidentified psychopath who targets women with specific physical features. Are there other victims, and will they learn the killer's identity in time to prevent another brutal murder?

An Altar by the River A man phones the Winnebago County Sheriff's Department, frantically reporting his brother is armed with a large dagger and on his way to the county to sacrifice himself. Sergeant Corinne Aleckson takes the call, learning the alarming reasons behind the young man's death wish. When the department investigates, they plunge into the alleged criminal activities of a hidden cult and the disturbing cover-up of an old closed-case shooting death. The cult members have everything to lose and will do whatever it takes to prevent the truth coming to light. But will they find an altar by the river in time to save the young man's life?

The Nodding Field Mystery When a man's naked body is found staked out in a farmer's soybean field, Sergeant Corinne Aleckson and Detective Elton Dawes are called to the scene. The cause of death is not apparent, and the significance of why he'd been placed there is a mystery. As Aleckson, Dawes, and the rest of their Winnebago Sheriff's Department team gather evidence, and look for suspects and motive, they hit one dead end after another. Then an old nemesis escapes from jail and plays in the shocking end.

A Death In Lionel's Woods When a woman's emaciated body is found in a hunter's woods Sergeant Corinne Aleckson is coaxed back into the field to assist Detective Smoke Dawes on the case. It seems the only hope for identifying the woman lies in a photo that was buried with bags of money under her body. Aleckson and Dawes plunge into the investigation that takes them into the world of human smugglers and traffickers, unexpectedly close to home. All the while, they are working to uncover the identity of someone who is leaving Corky anonymous messages and pulling pranks at her house. An unpredictable roller coaster ride to the electrifying end.

Secret In Whitetail Lake The discovery of an old Dodge Charger on the bottom of a Winnebago County lake turns into a homicide investigation when human remains are found in the car. To make matters worse, Sheriff Twardy disappears that same day, leaving everyone to wonder where he went. Sergeant Corinne Aleckson and Detective Elton Dawes probe into both mysteries, searching for answers. Little do they know they're being closely watched by the keeper of the Secret in Whitetail Lake.

Firesetter In Blackwood Township Barns are burning in Blackwood Township, and the Winnebago County Sheriff's Office realizes they have a firesetter to flush out. The investigation ramps up when a body is found in one of the barns. Meanwhile, deputies are getting disturbing deliveries. Why are they being targeted? It leaves Sergeant Corinne Aleckson and Detective Elton Dawes to wonder, what is the firesetter's message and motive?

Remains In Coyote Bog Bodies marked with religious symbols are recovered from Coyote Bog and send Sergeant Corinne Aleckson and Detective Smoke Dawes on a quest. Who buried them in the bog? They pore through missing persons' files, consult an FBI profiler, and are soon in pursuit of an angel of death. Their investigation leads them into unchartered and dangerous territory, but they'll stop at nothing to end the death angel's reign.

Death To The Dealers When a man finds his deceased wife's secret phone, her list of contacts sends him on quest to uncover who caused her death. As he navigates his way into the dreary, drug-dealing world, danger holds a constant presence. The one bright spot in his life is his growing attraction for his canine patient's owner, Sergeant Corinne Aleckson. It's a relationship that will not blossom as he had imagined.

Deputy #714 Is Down When Deputy Vincent Weber is gunned down in a café, Detective Dawes and Sergeant Aleckson respond to the scene, and work to keep their friend alive till EMS arrives. Then it's all hands-on deck to find the shooter. When a deputy in another county is killed, the FBI takes over the investigation. They follow leads and paths, then set a trap for the shooter. No one could've predicted the stunning way it would end.